HONG KONG
REDUX

CHINA'S ULTRA SECRET PLAN FOR TAIWAN

A Novel By
STEPHEN PHARO

DEFIANCE PRESS
& PUBLISHING

HONG KONG REDUX

Copyright © 2024 Stephen Pharo

First Edition: 2024

ISBN-13: 978-1-963102-29-1 (Paperback)
ISBN-13: 978-1-963102-28-4 (eBook)

Published by Defiance Press & Publishing, LLC

Bulk orders of this book may be obtained by contacting Defiance Press & Publishing, LLC. www.defiancepress.com.

Public Relations Dept. – Defiance Press & Publishing, LLC
281-581-9300
pr@defiancepress.com

Defiance Press & Publishing, LLC
281-581-9300
info@defiancepress.com

CHAPTER 1

TWO PLANS

Vice President Han Zheng paced the floor in the Operations Center (National Defense Complex), a complex structure located several hundred feet below the side of a mountain, which was itself approximately sixty miles southwest of Beijing. President Xi Jinping was late due to the heavy wind and rain accompanying the latest typhoon. May 1, was early for the storm season to begin, but the tension in the Operations Center was so intense that no one noticed the weather. "The President has arrived," someone announced and all present snapped to attention. As the illustrious man entered the room, he paused and looked around before moving slowly toward the seat proffered to him. As he sat down, he moved his hand to motion that the rest be seated as well.

The Red folder resting on the table in front of him had a large white star in the center. Sighting the star, he paused briefly, reflecting on the significance of this meeting. Then he looked up, rose to his feet, and walked slowly to the one map board that would soon play a major part in the upcoming event that he had longed planned. He stared at the board for several seconds before turning to the group and asking only one question, directed at the PRC Chief Advisor, Leong, "Has anything changed from our last meeting with regard to proceeding with the plan?" The flustered CA Leong looked the President in the eye and slowly shook his head to indicate that it had not. Then after a long pause, President Xi looked at the senior staff group and said, "The souls of our ancestors cry out for their rightful place in the world. The wait was far too long, having to tolerate the Westerners as they forced their will upon us. Those days will be no more!" The President paused and shot a piercing glance at all assembled in the room. With this operation, we will take a big step forward to ensure China will once again take her rightful place in the heavens—as the 'Bright Star' that will outshine all others. As we rise, our memory is clear and focused on the long-term payback, our great vengeance, on all those who have sought to keep her down." He flipped open the thick red folder and with one slashing gesture of his pen, he set in motion something he had only dreamed of till then.

The final phase of a long-awaited effort was about to begin. The senior General of the People's Liberation Army scooped up the folder and moved to the door, signaling his aide to alert his staff so they could prepare for the important meetings he would need to attend once he arrived back on base. Meanwhile, President Xi made his way down the hall to his office, followed closely by Vice President Han and CA Leong. Upon entering his expansive office, the President immediately noticed a large array of flowers in a huge, royal-purple vase with the words "Victorious Together" etched on the side. The aide-de-camp looked at the note attached to the vase before turning and informing the President that it was a gift from the North Korean Premier, Kim Jong Un. The President sat down, turned to CA Leong, and said, "You know what to do, Leong. Commence operations immediately. And keep me updated." Xi knew he would have to lead his political opposites in competing nations down a path of deceit. To this end, he had already set things in motion years ago, to prepare the international political battlefield. Or as Sun Tzu's teachings had guided him—"to win the battle before it begins."

Vice President Han and CA Leong departed the President's office and left for their respective headquarters. Leong felt a sense of pride at the thought of exacting revenge on some of his previous associates. With tonight's approval of operation "Bright Star" and the previous approval of operation "Northern Star," Leong was intent on showing that he has what it took not just to survive, but become in his own words, indispensable.He had backed Xi early on during the latter's rise through the ranks, often at great personal risk. Short in stature, he was the best at seeing to it that Xi's competition often ended up dead or at least disgraced to the point where they ceased to be an obstacle. In turn, Xi did his best to guarantee that Leong survived the numerous purges that had plagued the party for many years. Leong was sworn to ensure that his protector would eventually rise to the top. Though he had a distaste for the West, he had become one of its best scholars. He had attended college in both Europe and the United States and had mastered the English language. He had a gift for building relationships and was as comfortable in the US as in China. That attribute had proven essential while he had set up his network in America.

June 1, saw the temperatures in South Philadelphia starting to creep in to the unseasonable 80's. That did not slow down the drug business; it only meant that more of the transactions were conducted in the very early hours of the day. That was the preferred time of day for Big Taylor or "BT," as he was usually known in his circles. His right-hand man was referred to as "Mountain Man": At a statuesque 6 foot 6 inches and 320 pounds, he made for quite an imposing figure. No Chevy or Cadillac for BT and Mountain Man—Range Rovers were their preferred vehicle. BT had grown up in South Philly and knew the area like the back of his hand. So if there was to be trouble with the Feds, local cops, or other drug dealers trying to cut into his sales, he could use his territory to his advantage. He was infamous for ambushing trespassers with a ruthless hail of bullets from the M-60 machine gun he had somehow acquired from one of his numerous contacts. Though Mountain Man had barely made it through high school, BT was a very different animal, having completed graduate courses in Chemical Engineering after his B.S. in Chemistry. But he ultimately found drug dealing more to his temperament and had made a hell of a lot more money without having to put up with the "corporate crap." He remained in the area where he had grown up, in part to ensure that his grandparents were taken care of. He was one of the more fortunate children that had relatives to take him in after a very rough home life due to the crippling effects of drug addiction affecting both his parents. That kind of exposure fit with his questionable moral code, "no drugs to adults with young children." There was trouble brewing in his hood with the arrival of "King Leon" from Baltimore.

King Leon (whose given name was Leon Rodrigo Ortiz) did not have BT's educational background. What he did have was a nose for detecting when there were extra dollars to be made selling drugs and chopping cars. He also had a sense of who he needed by his side—from a business stand point—to confirm his hunch that there was more money to be extracted from a given area. His band of CPAs had looked at what was coming out of South Philly and concluded that this was a fertile area for further growth. King Leon was as a direct communicator as anyone could be. He was moving into South Philly and promised he would leave BT's operation alone for a small percentage of BT's earnings.

BT started to put heavy pressure on his "ladies" and "drug reps" (as he liked to call them), making them aware of the need to ramp up the money stream or risk starting a war with King Leon and his band of professional thugs. BT was sure that a couple of collectors had been skimming the profits. BT spread the word that those who might be holding out would soon discover what the bottom of the nearby Delaware River looked like.

Ultimately, it all came down to a collector who went by the name "Cue," short for "Cue Ball," due to his early-onset baldness. Cue had made it a point to stay out of BT's sight until he could figure out how to cough up the money he had spent gambling. On June 3, while having a burger and beer at Max's 24-hour Eatery, he noticed a Range Rover heading down the street and made a quick move to the back exit, which to his disbelief was already blocked by Mountain Man —who promptly proceeded to lay out Cue with one punch.

By the time Cue came to, it was three in the morning, fog rose off the river and he could hear the tugboats in the distance. Chains were wound around his ankles and he heard Mountain Man chuckling as he added more weight to the chains. BT didn't say a word, just casually waved as Mountain Man started to drag Cue down the pier. Cue started to struggle, but all of his efforts only succeeded in kicking up some dust. As Cue was dragged closer to the water's edge he grabbed on to a piling and desperately tried to hold on. He held on with all his strength, but with one quick jerk, he was back on his way to a watery grave. Just as Mountain Man was ready to drop Cue into the river, he cried out!

"I know of a major score that I intended to cut you in on to make things right."

Cue pleaded with BT to hear him out!"Come on man! You gotta trust me on this, I'm being straight, there is big money waiting to be picked up and I can put you into it! Cue's voice 'cracked,' man, do you think I would lie to you at a time like this? Please give me one more chance to make things right, you can trust me!"

Mountain Man held Cue out over the water. There wasn't much light, but Cue could hear the waves lapping up against the pier as he starred down at the cold river water below. Then what must have seemed like an eternity to Cue, BT motioned to Mountain Man to hold off while he gave Cue just sixty seconds to save himself.

"It's an electronics heist, top of the line stuff, I'll show you, then you'll see for yourself!" Though the night air was chilly, Cue was sweating profusely as he waited to hear BT's response. BT was not one to change his mind once he had a decision, but the extra dollars would help offset what King Leon would be taking.Cue sensed an opening, "look man, no bullshit, you'll see that I'm being straight with you on this, big money!" BT motioned to Mountain Man to bring Cue back to the car. BT grabbed Cue by the collar and looked directly in his eyes and through clinched teeth, "what and where is this 'big' money!"Cue explained that they would need to go to an abandoned house further down in South Philly, next to some government warehouses. It was an area that had been earmarked for demolition of old houses to make way for a larger riverfront commercial project.

As they drove down the mostly unlit streets, they could see that some of houses were still occupied, mostly by seniors in their 80's and 90's who had little or no money, even if they had someplace to go. The houses were poorly lit, signifying that the total death of the once-proud neighborhood was not far off.

But one house at the end of the street was well lit and seemed to brim over with an unusual amount of activity. As they neared that house, Cue cautioned that they should turn into a dark street two blocks before the targeted house. He motioned to turn into the backyard of one of the abandoned houses just up the street. His chains were removed and grabbing a flashlight from the trunk, he started to lead them into the house, all the way up to the bedroom facing the street where they could clearly observe the other house bustling with activity. "If you try anything funny, Mountain Man's gonna torture you well and good before your swim in the river. Got it?" BT hissed at Cue. "Please man!" Cue gasped. "This could be a potential jackpot if we handle it right."

BT looked at Cue and with some doubt before wryly muttering, "Since when did you know what a jackpot looks like?" As they approached the second-floor bedroom, they could see the outline of another person. Sensing an ambush, BT grabbed Cue by his throat and put his 9 mm Smith & Wesson pistol to the trembling man's temple and cocked the hammer back into the firing position. Sweat pouring off his face, Cue motioned to his nephew, Martin to make himself more visible. A young boy, no more than ten years old, came out of the shadows. Seeing the boy more clearly and noting that he had nothing more than a flashlight, binoculars, a can of coke and a sandwich, the pistol to Cue's head went back into BT's belt.

BT pushed Cue headfirst into the dark room. "BT, over here!" Cue whispered urgently, beckoning the men toward him. "I think this is the best location, especially to see inside the back of the truck." As they took turns peering through the binoculars it was clear that the contents of the house were of little note, but the electronic equipment that filled the back of the truck could be a major score that would resolve both BT's and Cue's money issues. At BT's order, Mountain Man retrieved a notebook from their Range Rover and gave it to Cue's little nephew, so the boy could record any comings and goings as well as when the truck was opened up for shift change.

"Look kid, keep a sharp eye out, and for God's sake, don't fuck up and let them see you!" BT snapped at him. He had reasoned that if they planned it right, they could steal the truck and have it stripped in less than three hours. They had plenty of pawn shops and "fences" that could move the electronics for a nice payday and not have to sweat the Feds or local police because who is going to pay any heed to the foreigners. Both BT and Cue started think that this scheme was a godsend: easy, profitable, and with little to no danger to them.

CA Leong was elated that the time was fast approaching when all those in the CCP who had doubted his capability would soon real-ize that he was someone who had to be taken seriously and given the respect that was long overdue. He directed his driver to not take him back to his quarters but to another government building where several individuals were waiting to meet with him. Leong had long cultivated a knack for getting individuals into situations where they were beholden to him in one way or another...and he used this skill to perfection!

It was now almost two in the morning as Leong's ride ended at a shabby, old government building. Outside, the rain and the wind intensified. As the guards waved him through the gate, he could see that several cars were already in the parking lot and the lights were on in a second-floor office space. This was to be the first and only meeting of his handpicked experts, as a group.

As Leong entered the room, he was greeted with a barrage of questions about why all the other personnel in the room had to be present, as each of them had been previously assured by Leong that their identity and role in this undertaking would remain confidential. Leong merely had to put his finger to his mouth to silence them. Then he took a moment to remind each of them about the consequences should he chose to expose their sins. Each of the participants had been assigned a task that required their specific talents and expertise. While previously, he had kept each of them in the dark about the others involved in the plan, it was now time to bring them together for the confluence of their different parts of "the project" as Leong often described it. In other words, it was now time to formally set up the "chess board." Leong had informed every participant present in the room about what the penalty would be if any of them were to divulge what or for whom they were working. Leong collected papers and digital copies after each presentation. He had recently sent them instructions on what he wanted to accomplish during this meeting. All the attendees were prepared to give a final briefing on their particular assignment related to the "project."

First up was Le Wo, who had been sprung from a long prison term by Leong for misuse of government computer facilities for attempting to fatten his own bank account. He was a brilliant computer specialist who was really skilled at uncovering gaps in the computer systems of other countries' commercial and governmental facilities. He had been singled out by the state to head their "cyber spook" division, but promises of national glory proved inferior to the idea of a luxurious lifestyle somewhere other than China. He had contacts and knew system specialists that would prove necessary for Leong's plan to succeed. The other participants in the room were trying to understand how they fit into the picture, given what they had heard so far.

Next up was Dr. Won Liu, noted surgeon and head of pathology at the Center for Research on Lung Disease and Respiratory Infections. He had developed a taste for certain drugs while on loan to France's National Center for Disease Control. Once back in China, his reoccurring drug habit had exposed him to various criminal groups that had bargained off information about Dr. Won's drug addiction to Leong in exchange for the freedom of one of their own. Dr. Won's influence and contacts, along with his research, would prove to be the linchpin of Leong's plan and the key to a successful outcome of the "project."

One by one, the rest of the participants made their presentations and handed over papers and relevant information. This gathering included the likes of Dr. Kin Lee, noted political scientist on the West, and Dr. Chin Hse, psychiatrist and author of many research papers on group dynamics during a crisis. Dr. Chin was followed by a small frail-looking woman who stood at less than five feet, Dr. Lily Lee. She had just spent the last ten years at Stanford University, working in the field of gene splicing. Similarly, Col. Le Shu, who had been the liaison to the Chinese ambassador in Washington D.C., was a noted expert on foreign weapons systems. The last to present was Li Chang, Leong's longtime friend and a government banker who had been funneling funds toward this plan without CCP's knowledge or approval.

At the end of the presentations, one could see in the participant's faces the realization that they were part of something big and that seemed to add some pride to their assigned tasks. A few saw themselves as unwilling participants in something very risky, something that could prove their undoing in the long run. Leong reassured each of them that they were safe and he would not, under any circumstances, reveal their participation.

As each of them left the room, Leong thanked them and wished them well. But he was no fool and could not risk basing this large of an operation on individuals who, either willingly or under pressure, could reveal what they had witnessed tonight. Leong gazed out the window as the cars left the parking lot with the full knowledge that none of the passengers would make it home tonight, nor would they be heard from again…even his longtime friend.

When Leong got into his own car, he instructed the driver to step on it. He would need to finish packing and get at least some rest before his flight in the morning. Leong had made it a point to stay in China whenever possible since the "problem" in Singapore and the ensuing nasty business in Australia. But the complexity of this operation and the need for a strong hand required this visit out of the country. His North American "manager" was reliable, through and, when necessary, lethal. It was a long flight to Vancouver, Canada, and he looked forward to catching up on sleep as the aircraft reached cruising altitude.

At the same time, 7000 miles further east, US Marine Corps Major Stephen V. North (Res) was boarding Delta flight 524 from Washington, D.C. to Los Angeles, setting off for Camp Pendleton, a Marine Corps Base in California. He was looking forward to a welcome change of scenery and conversation that was direct and logical, unlike the steady stream of political double-speak that he encountered in his day-to-day position at the NSA. Starting out at the CIA (Central Intelligence Agency) after the end of his active duty had been a real disappointment since they had only wanted him to focus on the Middle East—to the exclusion of China. So when he heard that the NSA (National Security Agency) wanted to expand its "China Watch" section, he decided to take the position, Deputy Director China Intel Unit. His time on active duty had provided an opportunity to work with the Australian Royal Marines and develop some lasting friendships. He had met Australian Royal Marine Captain William "Will" Knowles, the Regimental Intel Officer. At that time, "Captain" North was his battalion's Intel Officer, both men had Top Secret security clearances and could speak freely about what they were each involved. North was astonished to find that the Aussies were not looking so much at the Middle East or Afghanistan as they were focusing in China. Will Knowles had come out of the University of Sydney with a degree in Civil Engineering and a fascination with China. The two interests had merged when Knowles had visited China when some of the country's largest engineering projects were being implemented.

In addition to his involvement in the engineering projects, Knowles had also met some Chinese citizens who were not pleased with the Chinese leadership. The ruling CCP had kept a tight grip on power and many of his Chinese acquaintances had conveyed a sense of foreboding. In fact, some were sure that at the national level, the Chinese political scene was looking more like that in the time of the dictatorial Imperial Emperors of the past. That extreme fascination with nationalism, coupled with the continued rule of one party, was cause for great concern. Knowles had made it a point to stay in touch with those individuals. When he departed China, he enlisted in the ARM (Australian Royal Marines) and was assigned to its Intel Branch—that is how he first met North. As part of his current active duty training, North was to fly to Australia in two weeks to brief their Intel section on the US Marine Corps plan: "Engaging Chinese Expansion of their Maritime Boundaries." Major North was ready to re-engage with others who saw China as a major threat to America, quite unlike many of the politicos in Washington, the ones who were so sure that China was just going to be a lap dog that they could control, a great trading partner with no other ambitions.

In South Philly, based on what he had seen the other night, BT was ready to allocate the electronics to some of his more reliable "material movers," to minimize the hang time of the stolen goods. While he was appreciative of Cue for informing him about the opportunity to acquire a truckload of expensive electronics, he had no intentions of including Cue in the operation. Why? Because Cue had a way of leaking information to all the wrong sources, including undercover federal agents. BT was a perfectionist when it came to "unloading" stolen goods. Over time, he had refined his crew of fences based on their performance and knew they could be counted on to move items quickly and with maximum return.

When Cue heard that BT was planning the heist, he feared he would be cut out of the whole deal, so he made a hasty move to BT's location. As Cue burst through the door he let out a string of expletives that stunned even Mountain Man. "Listen you motherfucker, you're not cutting me out of this action, don't forget I am the guy who—"

He had stopped midsentence because BT had pulled out his pistol and laid it on the table. He motioned for Cue to take a seat. BT listened to Cue's plan for acquiring the electronics. BT thought the plan was missing some parts, but he reasoned that if he let Cue do the dirty work, he would still profit while incurring minimal risks.

What BT didn't know was that Cue was already in the process of selling him out to King Leon.

Cue thought if he could get King Leon to back him, he would be off the hook with BT and his standing with King Leon would finally get him the recognition—along with the money and the women—he deserved. Cue had already confirmed the heist's date and timing. In reality, it was scheduled to take place two days *before* the date he had proposed to BT. Cue's planning process was not as detailed and thorough as BT's. And this would prove to be his undoing.

As Leong's flight approached the Vancouver Airport, he was gathering his thoughts on how he would clarify and expand on what his "North American Chief" already knew. Leong had been very careful never to reveal the "Bright Star" plan in its entirety to anyone except a select few in President Xi's inner circle. Much like a chess match, all the pieces were finally moving to their assigned locations, but no piece would have any idea about how it fit into the overall plan—until the proper signal was given.

As Leong left the terminal, he saw a very large man wearing a bright, floral Hawaiian shirt waving him over. As Leong moved closer, he recognized the man as the "Chief's" main bodyguard/muscle man, Mr. Ling. As Leong approached the man, they acknowledged each other with a slight nod. Ling opened the car's door and Leong stepped inside, happy that the long flight was over and he could get down to business. Ever since the nasty business in Singapore and Australia, traveling out of China had become riskier then he cared to acknowledge. As the car sped along the highway Leong remembered how much he enjoyed Vancouver, for its cosmopolitan atmosphere, climate and transportation access, which was why he had selected it for the import/export business that served as a front for his chief North American operative, Mr. Wei. He also realized that Wei could blend in well with the large Chinese-Canadian population here, and as a businessman he could come and go as he wished, generally without arousing any suspicion.

As they arrived at their destination, Leong noticed that Wei had upgraded the building and added a manicured lawn to the front. He thought that was a nice touch, something that would endear a respected business owner such as Wei to the business community. They greeted each other with a firm handshake, closed the door to the office and got down to business. Wei sat across from Leong in a chair that had been designed to make him appear taller than visitors in other chairs in his room. Wei was very conscious of his short height. Leong always noted the difference between Wei and his co-worker, Ling who towered at six feet five inches. Their personalities were polar opposites too: Wei was more talkative, more aggressive and "in your face" type of guy. In contrast, Ling was quiet, unassuming and laid back. But, the pair worked well together and that team was critical to accomplishing the North American portion of Bright Star.

Leong was carrying the North American contact list in his bag, and now for the first time Wei had a glimpse of what was to unfold in the near future. Over the next six hours, the two men went over the plans and the timetable for their execution in great detail. Wei was quite disturbed that he had been kept out of the operation for this long. "It's inexcusable that you have withheld the contacts and list of operatives list for this long!" he fumed, pacing the room. "I could have been keeping an eye on their activities. You know what I think of operations that fail to ensure that the teams, if that is how we want to refer to them, stay in line, so to speak." Wei did not like leaving what he referred to as "loose operators" unsupervised for long periods. He would insert himself into the varied operations around the US as soon as Leong departed for China.

Leong was well aware of Wei's style of getting the "job" done but cautioned him not to over react because it might draw too much attention. Wei uncharacteristically snapped back at Leong that he had taken care of the "business" in Singapore and Australia for Leong when it seemed that no one else could or would handle it without the "Central Committee's" knowledge and approval. After several more tense minutes, Leong suggested they break for dinner to cool down and talk later that evening.

After dinner the two met again. The meeting lasted until well after two in the morning. Leong went over what and how he expected Wei to carry out his duties to ensure that the operation was a success. Wei grew tired of Leong's repeated instructions on how he should execute the tasks assigned to him. He got up from his chair and started to pace around the room, then leaned back over his chair and with a clinched jaw, "I've heard enough of your lecturing for the night, let us have a drink and toast to the success of our operation." Leong was due to fly out to China that morning. At seven, the men shook hands for the last time and parted, each giving the other a weak smile and a nod. Clearly, neither man fully trusted the other. But Leong knew it was too late in the game to bring in a new player. And so did Wei.

As Wei watched Leong's car disappear into the morning traffic, he wondered to himself how a man so morally weak and lacking in physical courage could have risen so high in the ranks. Wei had decided that the operation was his to make successful, which would finally get him the recognition he deserved. Then he could return to China with great honor. And he knew that if what he had done for Leong ever came out, Leong would just permanently disappear. So Wei reasoned that he would get credit for the success of the North American part of the plan and then Leong would have to support whatever Wei would want. Lost in such thoughts, Wei leaned back in his big chair and envisioned a fancy office with all the furnishings success would bring. The daydream did not last long; soon, they would start the journey of inspecting the other elements of the NA operation.

Cue arrived at King Leon's new outpost in and wondered why it was so far out of Philly. Cue had never been to Hulmeville, Pennsylvania before, even though it was a short 20 miles north. In fact about the only places he had been was Philadelphia and parts of the Jersey shore. But to him this was way too "country" and he wanted to leave the minute he arrived. King Leon had set himself up in a new warehouse complex a short distance out of town. The King's instruction to all of his "employees" was keep a low profile and cause no problems for the locals. That philosophy had worked well for the past five years that the King had operated one of the biggest "chop" shops in the tri-state area.

To the locals he was just a visiting owner of a respectable auto repair and parts facility. It was one of his most profitable operations and he intended to keep it that way. Cue wondered why the King wanted to see him, because he was busy planning the "move," as he was now referring to the electronics heist. When he entered the room, he saw the King sitting behind a rather large desk and quickly set himself down in front of it. As he sat down he threw down a stack of papers and started talking about his plan for the "Move."

"Man, I got this motherfucker figured out so tight it will go down as smooth as 50-year-old Hennessy Cognac," he bragged before jabbering on about the plan and the fences he would use to move the "products." Just then, the King motioned for him to stop talking, which Cue did immediately. The King looked through the papers briefly before tossing them into the trash can and then slowly turned to look at the little man sitting before him. "Hey, you didn't even give a good look at my plans," Cue yelled out, leaning forward in his chair. "I mean, hell, this is my 'move,' I got this thing figured out!"

Leaning back into his big leather chair, the King drew a deep breath and said, "This is how the whole operation is going down."

As Major North's plane approached the LA Airport he realized he had slept through most of the flight. His driver from Camp Pendleton was waiting outside the arrivals gate. The driver, GySgt. Thomas Parker, had grown up in Manahawkin, New Jersey, just minutes from where

Major North used to vacation as a boy. Major North's grandfather had been wealthy enough to own a large Victorian home on the Jersey shore, in Beach Haven, just a short drive down Long Beach Island. His grandfather also owned a large fishing boat, "Eleanor," on which GySgt. Parker used to work during his summer breaks in high school. This was how the two men had initially met. Major North had worked extensively with GySgt. Parker on Black Ops and Intel briefings. So there was always much to talk about.

On this day GySgt. Parker was very quiet and seemed reluctant to initiate any conversation. Finally, he said, in a hesitant voice, "Did you hear that there was some trouble with the Intel folks in Australia?"

That caught Major North by surprise! He had been sequestered in highly classified "war gaming" scenarios at the Army War College for the past ten days. Once that had ended, he had hurried back to his apartment in DC, thrown his uniforms into his overseas travel bags and headed for the airport. "What happened?" he asked Parker.

"Above my pay grade, Major," Parker replied, continuing that the only thing he knew was "it wasn't good." That reminded North that he was expecting a letter from his Australian Royal Marine buddy, Will Knowles. When his Intel briefings at Camp Pendleton were done by the end of the week, Major North was to fly out to Australia to brief some of the senior General Staff of the Australian Armed Forces on US Op Plans covering Chinese Maritime Expansion.

Truth be told, he had been expecting a letter from Will and his family. It was likely in the stack of mail that North had gathered up as he ran out the door to catch his flight to the West Coast. He always looked forward to visiting Will and his family, who always welcomed him like he was one of their own. Their letters were usually signed by all members of the family—Will, his wife Peggy, six-year-old Will Jr., and in Will's words, the light of his life, four-year-old Mary Claire. Next to all these signatures, North would find the paw prints from Stanley and Livingston, their two German Shepherds. So the first thing North planned on doing after checking with the Base Commander was look for the letter. *Not so long now,* North thought as the Base Guard gate appeared in the distance. Coming back to Camp Pendleton was, for North, like coming home. He was always most comfortable in the company of other Marines. For him, it was the no-nonsense, unvarnished relationships between men and women who believed deeply in the promise and future of America and their willingness to, if necessary give their lives to ensure that those ideals and freedoms were protected. As they drove through the front gate, GySgt. Parker commented, "Just seems like the rest of the world is never sure what direction to go, but once you come through that gate, it's like the North Star has appeared in a dark sky!"

Wei did not want to waste a moment before starting on his inspection tour of those who would now be considered under his control. But he also knew he must not be so impatient that he ends up alerting Canadian or US authorities. Wei called Ling into his office and said, "Start packing. I have reservations for a rail trip for two days from now. I have spoken with the warehouse manager and he will keep an eye on things in our absence. My gut tells me that Leong has left his deep operatives alone and on their own for too long. I'm going to see that they get a sense of what CCP and I expect them to accomplish."

Even though he and Ling had diplomatic passports he had decided that they would travel through Canada on the Great Canadian Railway Trans-Canadian Special as members of a Chinese business group on tour. He had traveled on the same train years earlier and had noticed that by rail, Canadian officials did not seem to inspect passports and IDs as closely as they did when one flew or crossed the border in private vehicles. Once they were well inside the US border, they would leave the tour group and rent a car in upstate New York and travel independently.

Relaxing in one of the domed railroad cars, Wei continued to reflect on what he considered to be weak points in the plan. In his mind the only way to ensure success was for him to be on scene as the timetable was set. Wei did not know or understand the complexity of the entire plan, just that of the North American operation. Ling was a hit with the younger crowd on the train as they marveled at his many colorful Hawaiian shirts. For at least a limited period, time moved more slowly for the both of them. Their contacts in the US were aware that the "handler" would soon be in touch with them. For years, they had built their lives in the US and were part of their local communities. But all this was meaningless compared to their dedication to the mission and to "modern" Imperial China. Soon they would be heading back to what they considered to be the only country fit to follow. The deep cover personnel's anticipation of meeting their handler was building; they had heard that "the man's" instructions should be followed to the letter. But, until he arrived, they were to carry on with their daily routine.

After crossing the border, Wei and Ling rented a car in Plattsburg, New York and set off south to their final destination—Philadelphia.

Cue sat there dumbfounded as the King tossed Cue's "plans" into the trash can. The King sipped on his cup of tea and then explained how the operation was actually going to unfold. With his extensive connections with entities that moved car parts and even whole cars, the King had all the bases covered. He would move not only the electronics but also the truck and/or its parts. Obviously, he did not want to leave a trace of the vehicle or its contents behind. Cue sat there and did not say a word the whole time the King was speaking. Through the entire twenty-two minutes, Cue heard his own name mentioned only twice: The first time was when the King was talking about the opening night of the "operation" and Cue's role of acquiring the "target" vehicle at the precise hour and minute that the King had set forth, and the second time was when the King announced that he would the drive the target vehicle to the Hulmeville location.

"You damn well better follow all the traffic laws, keeping under the posted speed limits," the King said solemnly, looking Cue in the eyes. "The last thing we want is you getting pulled over because you have a heavy foot. The warehouse complex is on the way into town so you can't miss it. You pull into the parking lot, drive around to the back of the building, and park the truck in front of the fourth door on the backside of the main building.

"Then turn the engine off, leave the keys in, get out, and walk away—oh and don't forget to turn the lights off!"

At this point, Cue was getting a little pissed. "What the hell!" he protested. "Do you think I'm stupid? Are you going to draw me pictures next? Look, why don't you give me the keys to the warehouse door, and I will pull the truck in and help take out the equipment?"

The King looked at Cue and said, "Okay smart guy, how many stereo systems have you installed? Or maybe you can tell me the number of times you have helped put in computer systems. Would you be able to figure out which switch it takes to turn the system on? Or how about I gave you an electronics diagram and you could tell me what all those fancy symbols mean?" Here, the King paused, but Cue didn't say a word, just stared at the floor.

Then the King stood up behind his desk and leaned forward. The next instant, he had sent his tea cup and saucer flying across the room with one swipe of his hand. "That's right, you moron," he snarled, eyes glinting with outright contempt, "stare at the floor! If I let stupid son-of-a-bitches like you do what they fancied, I would have gone broke a long time ago. I can just imagine the scene: You'd have ripped out the gear with no thought about how you can put it back together and the value would have fallen by more than half. So, don't you ever presume to tell me—wait, let me rephrase that—*help* me in conducting my business again…or it might be the last bit of advice you ever give, got it?"

Cue was still looking at the floor and said in a low voice, "Got it."

"Now get out," the King spat out. "Oh and by the way, get your own ride out of town. I do not want to risk having any of my local employees associated with an unknown man walking the streets of Hulmeville in the early morning hours." Then the King went on to detail that if Cue or anyone of his associates brought attention to his Hulmeville operation in any way, or if they violated or failed to follow King's plan to the letter, they would be in for a "one-way journey" in the King's new fishing boat, and unless they could breathe under water, it would be the last ocean cruise they would ever take.

Cue was taken aback by King's thorough approach, but this time words just jumped out of his mouth before he could stop them. "I was the one that found the truck and started the plan to make some real green from it! It sounds to me like I'm the one taking the biggest risk and you're not even looking at my plans or ideas. Maybe it should be me who walks away from this whole deal!"

The King took just a second to clear his throat before he set forward in his chair and said, "First off, you would not make it ten feet out the door before one of my men takes you out. Secondly, you do not have the sophisticated contacts to deal with the type of electronics we will likely find in the truck. Consequentially, you would not even know the loots true value and would be quickly arrested due to the, let's say *unreliable* nature of the folks you deal with. So, just put your pride to bed right now and agree that you will perform the tasks I outlined for you."

Cue knew immediately he had over played his hand and agreed to follow the King's plan to the letter. What the King did not realize was that Cue had already betrayed BT, thinking he could get a better deal from the King. With expectations of a greater cash return by working with the King, Cue had already acquired sizable cash advances from the other fences he promised would be given the first cut of the loot. Now Cue found himself in a terrible situation, facing a rather risky decision: Who was he going to short change to cover his many bets? As he departed the warehouse, he thought of all that he had now put at risk. Soon, he started to wonder if there was a way to play BT against the King. Then a smile came back to his face and he rolled down the window of his car and thought to himself that this country air was really clean and maybe when this is all over, he would move out there.

As Major North departed the Base Commander's office he rushed back to the BOQ, flipped open his travel bag, and started going through the mail that had accumulated while he was at the Army War College. Half-way through the pile he noticed an Australian stamp; the envelope was different from all of the other letters he had received in the past. The handwriting on the front was clearly not that of Will's wife, Peggy. North stopped and just stood there for a few seconds and then drifted slowly back on to the bed. He just sat there with the envelope, not really wanting to open it. After a few minutes of staring at it, he finally flipped open the letter. It was not the usual correspondence. To the average person it read like a forecast of bad weather approaching, but North knew what he was reading was something even more chillingly frightful....

Dear Yank,

I'm afraid that the weather forecast is so alarming that we need to put off our get-together until we can be sure the dark clouds, violent storms, and lightning have passed and will not put my family at risk. The storm seems to be coming from the North via an easterly track around the Singapore area.

It seems to be following the same path as my return from my conference on June 5. I am in the process of moving my family to a safer location where we can ride out the storm. I am truly sorry for the delay! Give me a call asap and I will give you an update on our situation and the status of the storm. Please keep in mind, if something were to happen and you cannot reach me, Henrietta can assist you with more information. Take care, old friend and hope to see you soon!

Will

North sat there, stunned! Of course it was not a real weather report. Will had come upon some information so important that it posed a very real—and potentially lethal—threat to him and his entire family. North decided to go down to the special ops communications center and get a message off to Will to see how he could help, and also to remind him that he had to be in Sydney in a few days to brief some senior generals and would be at his disposal for as long as it takes to secure his family. And to ask, "Who the hell is Henrietta?"

By the time North made it to the SOOCC (Special Operations Overseas Communications Center), it was almost midnight by West Coast time, which would make it a little before five in the evening (the next day) in Sydney time. He was hoping to speak with Col. W.B. Sutherland, Commanding Officer of the Special Intel Group (C.O.S.I.G.). W.B. stood for Wilson Bennet, but most often he went by Col. W.B. or—to those that really knew him—Col. "Wild Bill" because he often found it necessary to ignore the laws and rules and just get the job done!

Major Knowles was under his command, so if he could speak with Col. W.B., North was sure he could get in contact with Will in short order. The sergeant at W.B.'s headquarters said that he was in a meeting for at least another two hours and if North would like to call back tomorrow.

"This is an urgent matter," North insisted. "I need to speak with him about Will Knowles and I will stay at the Comm center until Col. Sutherland calls me back." North had barely finished with his sentence when the sergeant said in a rather strained voice, "Did you say Knowles, Major Will Knowles?"

"Yes, Major Will Knowles," North repeated. "I'm a very good friend of his and I need to speak with him." There was a long silence during which the sergeant made a call and even though he had cupped his hand over the phone, North could still hear him tell someone in the office to get Col. Sutherland on the phone. North realized that if they were going to interrupt a high-level meeting to pull Col. Sutherland out, something was amiss.

Within two minutes, Col. Sutherland was on the phone. "Major North, I know that you're a very close friend of Major Knowles, so I will tell you that we are very concerned and the circumstances are not at all in line with how he normally conducts himself. It is one thing to have an undercover agent like Will go offline, as it were, but it has been several days since we have heard from him.

"When we questioned the neighbors, they mentioned that they had seen Peggy literally throwing clothing, toys, and other kids' stuff into the car before speeding off with the kids and the dogs loaded—and that is the last time the neighbors saw the family. So we have started a formal investigation and listed Will and his family as missing."

He explained that this was all he could say at this time, but once in Australia, North could receive more information. "All I want to do is speak with him, if you locate him!" North said again. After a pause, the Col. Said, "Stop by my office as soon as you arrive." Then he hung up.

The part where the colonel had listed Will and his family as missing didn't bother North too much. If Will wanted to hide his family in order to protect them, not even God would be able to find them! North had two major Intel briefs to present in the morning and had to prep, which would leave him little time to sleep. So as he went over his presentations, he couldn't help but wonder, "What's up in Australia?"

As they made their way south, Wei decided that their first order of business was to have their main contact for the East Coast Unit (ECU) assemble his contacts for a meeting, as soon as possible.

"Professor Lo, I'm visiting from out of state, and I'm hoping that you can help me. I would like to view a raven, or even better, a flock of smaller ravens as soon as possible," Wei spoke on the phone. The word "raven" was code word for the operations handler for North America.

"I don't think that is a wise thing to do. You see, the flock has become part of the everyday scenery and forcing the flock to expose their location would create an unnecessary risk to the flock's long term survival."

The request invoked a strong protest from Professor Lo, a senior climatologist at Rutgers University. Ever since his arrival in the US almost twenty years ago, he had been warned never to bring more than one or two contacts together at once. Wei's order to bring all eight together was beyond belief! Lo implied that this idea was such a major violation of his standing instructions that a call to his mainland contact was warranted. Wei calmly insisted that his experience meant that his decision was sound! Then he continued to say, in a calm but stern voice, that if Lo failed to follow his orders, he and his family, both in the US and China, would disappear! Lo knew exactly what Wei meant and could instantly tell that Wei was someone you did not mess with.

Wei had made prior connections to be included on the list of Chinese businessmen visiting Philly to promote investments in the area. Soon after arriving at the hotel, the group went down to the reception put on by the Mayor's office. Wei immediately introduced himself to the Mayor and Police Chief, who were very impressed with Wei's offer of investing upwards of 50 million dollars in factories and jobs around the area. "Mr. Wei," the Mayor said cordially, putting his hand on his shoulder, "I can't tell you what a pleasure it is to have someone like you visit our fair city."

"Mr. Mayor, thank you for your gracious hospitality," Wei responded with a polished smile. "I can see now that under your leadership the city will indeed blossom!"

"Mr. Wei, feel free to call me any time, day or night." In fact, Wei had made it a point to get all their private numbers, so they could be reached at any time. For such a little man, he left a very big impression on the two, which would work out in his favor later on.

With this task accomplished, he headed back up to his room to get some needed rest. But, before resting he needed to make a follow-up phone call to the local contact whom he had directed to co-ordinate a group meeting. He also phoned the "distributor" of the "goods" to redirect the shipment to a singular location, so that he might have greater control over the final steps of the operation. The local contact informed Wei that he had located the needed rental houses in a small town called Beach Haven located on the Jersey shore. He mentioned, he had vacationed there before and knew that with all the other summer tourists, the ECU members and their families would just be another face in the crowd.

As such, one of the many Chinese "plants" had owned and operated a "Teepee" (number 36) mini mart for a number of years in Spray Beach, just minutes from Beach Haven. When the contact finished his report, Wei complimented him on his efforts. Then he made another phone call to the distributor to redirect the shipment to Teepee number 36 and to facilitate appropriate packaging of the "goods." Then Wei called his contact back and informed him that the goods should be available at Teepee number 36 on the prescribed date and time.

After all this back and forth, Wei was tired and needed to get some rest.

CHAPTER 2

A VERY DEAR FRIEND

North was in a plane, cruising at 32,000 feet over the South Pacific Ocean as the flight made its way to Sydney, Australia. Though exhausted, North could not get Will and his family out of his mind! Throughout the week's many Intel presentations on threats in the Pacific region, China's aggressive expansion and provocative actions had become the main topic. Will was one of Australia's military experts on Chinese influence in the South Pacific. North wondered if he had stumbled upon something so alarming that his knowledge had proven to be a threat. Did Will learn something about China's clandestine operations that it had made him and even his family targets?

At this point North could only guess at the answers to those questions, but soon the apparent knowledge possessed by Will would prove to be even more dangerous than even Will could have imagined.

Upon arrival, North was met by the designated ARM driver who would take him to meet with Col. Sutherland. When, at about eleven in the night, the vehicle pulled up in front of not the ARM headquarters but a plain-looking concrete warehouse on the outskirts of the city, North was more than a bit surprised. In the distance against the moonlight, the building looked plain enough but as the vehicle approached the compound it became clear…that it was anything but a plain warehouse.

From the distance, North couldn't have seen the guard dog patrols, the 14-ft barbed-wire fences, and the communication antennae and laser weapons systems neatly tucked away in the structure's many crevices and in the surrounding foliage. The car pulled inside the building. They then took an elevator down four floors below ground level.

Even though North had an ultra-high-level Intel clearance, he had never been to this location before in his many trips to Australia. He was quickly escorted to a conference room where the Colonel had a couple of his ultra-secret "China squad" members, Captains Finley and Roth.

Col. Sutherland remarked that the new National Security Center was a recent addition to their roster of secret meeting locations, all due to a subtle and uncharacteristic change in China's interactions with her trading partners. The Chinese had always taken the long, slow approach of nudging their neighbors to see things their way. But, in recent years an "air of arrogance" had started to make its way into the negotiations. This fortified location had been built in direct response to the aggressive nature that China had been showing toward its neighbors to the south.

North sensed that this wasn't good news and his intuition was correct!

Col. Sutherland started the conversation with what North had hoped not to hear: Will and his entire family were dead.

One of his best friends in the world…was gone. Col. Sutherland put up a photo of the house where they had thought no one would find them. But someone had. And the countryside farmhouse had been turned into a slaughterhouse.

North could not believe what he was looking at. He had been part of many battles where many a Marine and enemy soldier had been so badly mangled you couldn't tell which end was up. But that damage had been inflicted either by machine or explosive.

But Will and his family must have been put through hell, a bit at a time. Worst of all, they had not died at the same time, which meant that at some point some of them would have witnessed the death of a beloved family member.

"This very day, this very hour and this very minute," begun North in a trembling, seething voice cracked with despair and anger, "I swear I will not rest till I avenge their deaths. I swear this will be the most important mission of my life." At the last word, his voice threatened to break down, but he held it together. Col. Sutherland mentioned that North was welcome to ride along with the investigation team in the morning. It seems that Will had done such a good job hiding himself and his family that even the Intel teams could not locate them…but someone else had.

"The…bodies were discovered by a postal office clerk who had noticed that the new occupants had been there for eight days, but they had yet to send or receive mail," Col. Sutherland mentioned in a pained voice. He noted that there were vehicles parked by the house so the clerk had thought he would welcome them to the neighborhood and ask if they would be using mail service or if they were just staying for a bit before moving on.

As the postal worker drove up to the house, the front door was wide open. He got out of his van and as he approached the house he detected a strange odor and what appeared to be bullet holes in the glass windows. Looking in through the open door he saw what can best be described as a "butchering." At that point, he had dropped the welcome packet from his hands and lost his lunch. After regaining his composure, he called the local constable, Bradford Richmond.

"When Richmond and his deputy arrived, they taped off the area as an active crime scene. When the constable found Will's ID and security clearance documents, he shut down the location and called us in," Col. Sutherland continued. "Realizing that this could be related to the national security, we informed the postal service employee that he was now subject to the National Secrecy Act and could not say a word about what he had discovered to anyone else. Of course, the bodies were removed and taken to a local funeral home.

"Upon arrival at the funeral home the mortuary director noted that they were in part, dismembered. The agent in charge informed him that they had been in a terrible plane crash, which was why the bodies were in such bad shape. But when the director pressed for more information, the agent in charge flipped open his ID card. The director looked closely at it, then turned and walked away without another word." Here, the colonel paused and glanced at North to gauge whether he should go on. North gave him a nod.

"The best crime scene investigators and forensic specialists were called; we had to quickly determine whether or not this was, for lack of a better term, a typical home robbery gone very bad or something that had a direct relationship to Will's job."

Additional Intel personnel were due to depart the headquarters at six in the morning and go to the crime scene. Col. Sutherland offered to let North accompany them if he so desired. He quickly accepted the colonel's offer. After the long flight he was very tired and was in desperate need of some sleep, but by the time North would get to his hotel, it would be time to return to the headquarters for transport to the crime scene, so he got approval to sleep on the sofa in the Commanding General's conference room.

At six the next morning, North departed with the investigative personnel. The crime scene was about 120 miles northwest of Sydney, on the outskirts of Bathurst. Looking at the surroundings, the renovated farmhouse that Will used seemed like an ideal location— a place very difficult to track indeed. For someone to determine a connection between this place and Will, a detailed inspection of tax records would have been necessary. That would have yielded the fact that Will's great-great-grandfather had owned a small farm at that same address. Will must have thought that the district's tax records were in such bad shape that the probability of anyone tracing the location to his family would be very remote.

Regrettably, such was not the case.

The long drive gave North the time to reflect on how much he had been looking forward to this visit. Will had felt more like a brother than a co-worker and he had often turned to Will for advice. Washington's political landscape was so different than the environment Will worked in. North always looked for reasons that would take him to Australia, not the least of which were the unmarried girlfriends of Will's wife, Peggy!

Presently, there was a chill in the air as they pulled into the drive leading up to the farmhouse. North felt both a sense of loss and regret that he somehow could have prevented their deaths. Before he entered the house he was warned to be prepared for a horrific sight. He saw that along with the blood stains, the photos taken at the beginning of the investigation were taped on the wall. North commented that he had endured heavy combat and had seen it all. Upon entering the main room, he saw that the blood stains were everywhere, but when he viewed the photos of what was left of the children, he lost it and had to go back outside to catch his breath.

"Whoever did this clearly loved to make their victims suffer for as long as possible before death," one of the forensic experts commented to him. North asked if this could have been work of a local psycho or a trained professional. The investigator's reply was definitive. "This guy was trained, but he had a sadistic temperament. That much is obvious."

North followed up with a question on the technique used by this "butcher," as he now referred to this monster. The expert said that he used to work for the Brits in Hong Kong before they had turned the territory back to Chinese control. This was clearly the work of the, as he referred to them, "the Commies from Beijing!"

Two days later they were all assembled in the headquarters conference room to review what had happened at the farmhouse. Before any of the investigators had a chance to speak, Col. Sutherland announced that perhaps there had been a break: They had two suspects.

A local photographer had been requested to take some photos of an overpass that needed to be repaired. As he was finishing the session, he told the local constable that he had almost been run down by a black sedan that was clearly exceeding the posted speed limit. As he turned around just in time to avoid being hit, he snapped a photo of the vehicle and its occupants. "While it was not the best photo we could have asked for, it is something," the colonel said in a grave voice. Then he put the photo up on the screen. It clearly showed a person sitting in the right rear seat and another on the left side. "This second person's face is partially blocked, but as you can see, he has a preference for brightly colored shirts. We also have a side view of the driver. The photographer also got a photo of the car's plate number. We've traced the car to a rental agency.

The car was rented by a man from the Chinese Embassy in Sydney. So, we may not have a smoking gun so to speak, but we know where to start looking," Col. Sutherland finished with a determined expression on his face.

As the meeting ended, North asked for a copy of the photo showing the man's face. The next week, North spent his time preparing and giving Intel briefs to the general staff. He had a couple of days left before heading back to the States and something was still nagging at him. He had yet to figure out who Henrietta was, the woman Will had mentioned in his last letter to North. He felt like he needed to visit the farmhouse one more time. He was not sure why…but had to go, painful as it would be.

He rented a car and retraced the previous week's drive. When he arrived at the scene, the same deputy was on duty and agreed to let North have one more look around. Then as North stated to drive through the gate, the deputy muttered, "What kind of guy would name his chickens' Beatrice, Constance, or even Henrietta?"

North slammed on his brakes so hard that the deputy thought something was wrong. "What did you say?" North demanded. The deputy quickly offered an apology. "I'm really sorry sir, I didn't mean your friend was strange or something like that, but very few people that I know give their chickens such formal names!"

"No, no…you did not offend me, but what did you say about the chickens?" The deputy recounted the names of the chickens. North stepped on the gas and headed straight for the chicken coop. Sure enough, the deputy was right. On a board attached to a wall of the coop was a list of names painted in white. The third name on the list was "Henrietta." North stared at the word with wide eyes and a beating heart. Was this what Will was referring to?

But as North headed for the open gate of the chicken coop, he thought "What is even the point of going into the hen house? I'm too late! They're gone…" But another surprise awaited him in the chicken coop. Whom ever had murdered Will and his family had gone on a rampage and killed every animal on the farm. When the team of investigators had concluded their initial investigation, they called in the personnel that handled site cleanup. North realized that the dead animals would have been cremated by now. There was a note in the investigators' report that all the chickens had leg bands. Thereafter, it was concluded that keeping the remains would serve no further purpose and they had been destroyed.

For a moment, North thought how easy it would be even for a seasoned investigator to overlook a tiny attachment to one of the chicken's leg bands. Will could have concealed a significant amount of information in a microchip. That information might have proved critical to identifying both his killer and the secret whose keeping had led to the gruesome murder of the whole family. North murmured to himself that perhaps he should have told Col. Sutherland about the Henrietta comment in Will's letter. Will would have certainly told Col. Sutherland if he had thought it important and the opportunity.

The stench of death still lingered in the air as North entered the hen house. Even though it was late fall in Australia, the bright sunlight made the small structure very hot and uncomfortable, but North felt he owed it to his friend to check out any leads. Looking around, he noted there were bullet holes everywhere, even in the roof. With a quick glance around, he concluded that the Henrietta lead was going nowhere. As he started to leave he abruptly stopped and turned his head around for one long, last look. His mind was telling him that there was something in plain sight that was nevertheless out of place or inconsistent with the rest of scene. His mind was still processing what he was looking at when noticed that all the egg-laying boxes were scattered all over the hen house. Some were upside down, while some were on the floor or on their side. There were some whose names were still recognizable. The nesting straw was all over everything.

Between the bullets and the frightened chickens, everything had been dislodged, turned over or broken apart. Then he focused on a large pile of nesting straw on the far edge of the second tier of laying boxes. The straw had piled up against the only laying box that had not been dislodged. As he brushed away the straw, the name on the box became clearer…Henrietta.

The corner of the box had been nicked by one of the bullets, but otherwise it was intact. What struck North was that all of the other boxes had been dislodged or moved to some degree, except for Henrietta's. He pushed lightly on the box, it did not move. The he pushed harder, and the box moved only a bit. As he cleared away the remaining straw, he noticed the box was attached to one of the shelf boards. Taking a coin from his pocket he slowly removed the screw that was holding the board in place. Soon the board was loose enough and the laying box tilted over to reveal a folder wrapped in plastic. North said to himself, "Henrietta was still able to communicate with me after all."

Cue's meeting with the King had provided zero assurances that things were going to work out in his favor. *I just know that motherfucker is going to trim my take to line his pockets*, Cue thought venomously. *But I'll figure out a way to ensure that I can pay off my debts and have cash leftover!* Cue was feverishly thinking how he needed to piece together his plan soon, so he could meet all of his obligations—without getting himself killed in the process. King Leon had given him a rather exacting timeframe that he had to stick to, if he was going to get his cut of the payout. He knew that he had to deliver the truck to the Hulmeville warehouse at just the right moment: Too early or too late would raise doubt in King Leon's mind and he most certainly did not want him to start questioning his motives. Cue figured his payout would cover all of his outstanding debt, except for what he owed to Junior.

Junior's given name was Angelo Vincent Carletti II, but his parents always called him Junior, as did the rest of his extended family. After a while everybody just called him Junior, which he hated. He worked (if you could call it that) in his father's pawn shop. His father had three successful pawn shops, but Junior's passion was gambling. He would bet on just about anything and always seemed to have a large roll of cash in his pocket. Cue had hit him up several times for cash to cover what he had to give BT. Make no mistake about it, Junior was pleasant enough when things were going well, but if you tried to stiff him, he was meaner than BT and King Leon combined! Cue was pretty sure he could cover what he owed Junior, but Junior was shrewd enough to demand that Cue explain just how he was going to cover what he owed. By the time Cue explained his operation, Junior was content to believe that his money would be paid back.

However, being in the pawn shop business, Junior felt he could get a better return if he handled some of the loot himself. Cue was now caught between three dangerous men (BT, King Leon, and Junior), none of whom he could control. Needless to say, he agreed to provide Junior with some of the stolen electronics. Since the pawn shop that Junior ran was on the same route that Cue would take to get to Hulmeville, he figured a few minutes' delay at the pawn shop would hardly be noticed.

After returning to his apartment, Cue called his brother, Albert and his nephew, Martin to go over the plan. "Look trust me, I've got this move down to the last detail," he snapped at them. "You two are looking at the man...I mean after this gig, there's going to be only bigger and better action ahead. I am going to show both BT and King Leon they can't push me around nor my main brothers. Once we pull this off, we're gonna get respect, you hear me?"

He then explained in detail that if they followed his plan and kept their mouths shut, in the end they would have several thousand dollars in their pockets. His next move was to speak with BT. When he arrived at BT's, he was immediately grabbed by the collar and taken to BT's office. "Get that little shit in here," BT was yelling to Mountain Man. "Where the fuck have you been?" he snarled when Cue was shoved into the room by one of his goons. "I sure hope you haven't been trying to pull off the job without me knowing about it. Well, speak up!"

Cue said that he was making some improvements to the plan and if BT would let him finish he would be happy with those changes, as they would greatly improve their chances of success. Cue explained, he had run into an old friend who worked for the local power department. "I asked him if it was possible to turn the power off to that part of the neighborhood for, say, about thirty minutes? He asked why? I told him, 'Is $500 a good reason?'" Cue stopped and let out a nervous laugh, but BT looked impassive as ever so he continued, in a more subdued tone, "He said that is all he needed to know." "So, those Chinese or Japs or whoever they are will be in the dark when we relieve them of their truck! Is that cool enough for you?"

After several tense moments, BT smiled and said, "Yeah, very cool." He leaned back in his chair, cracked a smile, and for once seemed pleased with Cue's thinking and said, "I'm impressed. Even I did not think of that option." Of course, what BT could not know was Cue had done nothing of the sort with regard to the power department and the date had been changed to comply with King Leon's plan.

Cue was so pleased with himself that he called his brother and nephew to join him at Max's 24-hour Diner for some Southern Style ribs. As they waited for their orders to arrive, Cue went over the plan again. "Remember brother, you slowly drive down the street making a lot of noise, after removing the muffler and adjusting the timing so that the engine would be misfiring. Then a little further down the street, you make more noise by shouting at the car, 'is a piece of shit.' Then, you set the car on fire by throwing a couple of lit road flares into the backseat. Given the additional can of gasoline in the backseat, an explosion would soon take place. And since the vehicle would have been stolen just the day before, there would be nothing to trace it back to the three of us. Got it?" Cue looked at his brother and nephew, they nodded fervently.

"While the flaming car has everybody's attention, Martin, you'll sneak up to the other two vehicles on the near side of the house and slash their tires. I will be hiding in the bushes directly across the street," Cue continued. "With the foreigners' attention focused on the burning car, I will rush out of the bushes, grab the keys from the side door, where the little man always leaves them, start the truck, and drive away. Then I will stop at Junior's pawn shop to drop off some of the loot and then back on the road to King Leon's warehouse."

"Remember, brother, you should leave the scene as quickly as possible, return to your car that would be parked a couple streets over, pick up Martin and then drive to Hulmeville. Once you pick up me at the warehouse, we drive back to Philly. All this should take place in less than ninety minutes. Once back in Philly I will call and tell BT that King Leon's men hijacked the truck and dumped me off. So I can shift the blame to King Leon and BT would have to battle it out with him."

Cue was sure that BT could not match King Leon's fire power and would just walk away. That would leave Cue just where he wanted to be— out from under BT's thumb, all debts paid off, and on good terms with King Leon. As he started on his ribs, he thought to himself, *It won't be long now…money, women, and respect. I'll have all three.*

Wei was now in full command of all the moving parts of the North American portion of Bright Star, and he promised himself that when the operation was over he would be recognized as a critical player and someone who could be trusted with greater responsibility. The meeting of all the principal players of the East Coast Unit ECU was set to take place on Long Beach Island at the State Park located next to Barnegat Lighthouse. Wei's main contact had reserved an area in the park for conducting a BBQ meeting. In the summer, the island was packed with tourists and the group would be just one of many extended family groups celebrating with a get-together.

Wei's principal logistician for the East Coast portion of Bright Star was Professor Nelson Lo. He had been in the States for more than twenty years but had never lost the desire to return to China. Lo had always been a dedicated Communist. He had gotten to know Leong during his college days. When Leong had approached Lo about being a deep-cover agent, he had wholeheartedly jumped at the chance. He felt Leong's plan to keep every member of the ECU secret was the best way to ensure that the whole unit would never be completely exposed.

But, Lo knew how to follow orders and had reserved short-term rentals for each of the previously unidentified ECU members. Under the previous plan they would have received a package by courier and it would have detailed instructions on how it was to be used. That way if one of the ECU was uncovered, the others could still keep functioning as intended. Wei had changed that portion of the plan so they could all pick up the "item" at the same location, Teepee #36, in Spray Beach. Lo thought that this change was dangerous, but Wei would hear none of his concerns.

When the other members of the ECU contacted Lo about housing, he was surprised at some of the locations they were coming from. As ECU members called in to confirm that they were coming, Lo finally got a sense of how large a geographical footprint the unit had. Members that had already called in were from Boston, Winston-Salem, Washington DC, New York City, Savannah, Virginia Beach, and Cherry Hill. Based on Wei's instructions, he had made rental reservations for eleven (including himself, Wei, and Ling), so he was expecting one more to call in at any time. Most of the unit members had families, with children, some of whom were in high school and some in the grade school. Those ECU members had been handpicked by Leong as long as twenty-five years ago. Their objective was to blend into and become productive and respected members of their communities. Even their families were not permitted to know their true background or identities. In this way, ECU members were placed in deep-cover positions and were left to live their lives until everything that Leong had envisioned was in place.

At that point, they would receive an "item" and employ that item as per the accompanying instructions. Following the activation of that "item" they were to leave the country as soon as possible, meeting in El Paso and then moving on to Mexico, where they would meet up with Chinese contacts for transport to China. Leong was planning on a big homecoming celebration to celebrate the sacrifice of these heroes. What neither Leong nor any of the ECU knew was that Wei had already changed instructions for the contacts that the ECU members and their families would meet. A sizeable payment had been made to one of the Mexican cartels and there were to be no loose ends. All were to be executed and buried in unmarked graves—men, women, and children. Wei was to be the only hero the Chinese people would meet. Wei was concerned that the items would not make it in time for the group meeting and that all ECU members had not confirmed that they would be at the meeting. About an hour later, Lo informed him that he had heard from the "distributor" of the items: They just arrived via Canada and would be at the Teepee Mini Mart #36 not later than July 22. He also informed Wei that the last ECU member, the one from Portland, Maine, had confirmed their travel plans and would be at the BBQ scheduled for July 25.

Leong was on the final leg of his flight to Caracas, Venezuela, for a meeting with the President Maduro and his Chief of Internal Security, Rodriguez. At the meeting, Leong would hand over the keys to a heavily guarded shipping container currently sitting behind the Chinese Embassy. The container's contents, approximately 10 million in gold bullion, was payment for "hosting" a secret operation that would involve very well-paid participants from all over the world. At the meeting the President demanded to know who they were and what they would be doing. Leong replied that their identities, what they would be doing, and why, were not part of the agreement and if he persisted with this line of questioning or made any effort to uncover who they were, what they were doing, or interfere in even the smallest of ways, the 10 million would be withdrawn and in all likelihood, he would be assassinated.

Maduro and the Rodriguez were stunned!

"Oh, and if this hosting is successful," Leong continued with a fierce glint in his eyes, "there will be an extra $10,000,000 in a Swiss account for each of you." Here, Leong leaned forward in his chair and reminded them that an additional $10,000,000 had been used specifically to pay for the Mexican cartel's illegal immigration enablers. Then, Leong stood up and started for the door. Just then, he stopped, turned around, and said, "I assume we have a deal?"

The President said that his country would do everything in its power to ensure that the hosting event will be a great success and that other events could be hosted in the future as well. Leong handed them a list of requirements before stating that someone from the Embassy would contact them in the future. As Leong departed the Presidential Office, video footage of him was captured by a CIA agent doing routine surveillance. The agent had previously been stationed in Hong Kong, and he thought that something seemed very familiar about this guy. He decided to check him out more thoroughly and sent the video to the CIA headquarters in Langley.

Within twenty-hour hours, the Langley, CIA, HQ had dispatched two more agents to Caracas. As Leong's flight took off for Mexico City, he knew that neither the President nor his Chief of Internal Security would ever see one cent of that money they had been promised. Once the operation was over, they were both scheduled to meet with an unfortunate accident. Leong was now settled in first class on his flight to Hong Kong. In his head, he was constantly reviewing what had taken place and what was yet to come. Considering how complex the plan was he thought the operation was going smoothly. The few members of the Central Committee that knew of the plan thought it was rather soft on America...*but what do they know*, Leong thought sarcastically.

He knew that few, if any, could understand the depth and genius of his plan. He still remembered the long conversations that had taken place between him and his grandfather as they fished in the lake near the farm where he had grown up. That was of course before the People's Army had taken everything and beaten him and his wife. Then came the "Great Leap Forward" driven by the "little red book." Then, driven by politicized fools, arrived the great famine that killed millions—numbers driven by idiots who were only trying to impress Mao.

It's a wonder that China functions at all, except for the drive of its everyday citizens, Leong thought to himself. *What I often come back to is my grandfather's strange fascination with the Americans who had fought with the Chinese against the Japanese, during World War II.* His grandfather had said, on several occasions, "How does such a young country amass such wealth and power in such a short time, compared to how long China has existed?"

Leong's grandfather had once remarked that he heard some of the Americans refer to their leaders as fools and idiots. He was sure that they would be taken away and punished, but they were not. "So you should get to know these Americans," Leong's grandfather had concluded. "Maybe there's something we can learn from them." No wonder, Leong struggled with the instinct to damage the US in order to promote his country.

I love China, her people, and her desire to grow and improve the lives of her citizens, Leong had often told himself. *But time and again she has produced leadership that can only be called self-serving and power hungry.* Driven by power and greed, he knew that such politicians would always lead the country to war and destruction. So the only way to elevate China was to reduce America's standing in the world. The only way that could be achieved was to reduce its belief in itself and to increase guilt and self-doubt. To have the Americans lose trust in the future and make them feel guilt and shame for their outsized achievements and wealth. Few of China's leadership, old or new, realize the great changes Leong and his kind had been able to effect in the American media and college curriculum. For almost twenty-five years, Leong was able to convince wealthy socialists, communists and self-described revolutionaries, and the progressive elite to fund efforts to undermine American values that had served the country and the world so well. Most of all he searched for "weak links" in the current and future political,elected and appointed officials who, over time could be programed via cash, sex trade or other means to accommodate China's future interests in a favorable light.

Those who donated, saw it was an opportunity to further their own blind ambition and to obtain more power for themselves. Moreover, the current leadership in Washington was perceived as weak and lacking substance. It seemed to thrive on creating distrust and fear that all will be lost unless the people placed their faith that only government seems fit to "control" and not the people. By having so many elected officials leaning left, they would always hesitate to confront China head-on, and Leong saw that as a chink in America's armor.

However, lately the American people appeared to be getting tired of their preaching and may well vote them out soon. Leong felt that they were perhaps three to four years ahead of when they should be before attempting to execute Bright Star. He concluded, if they delayed any longer, the Americans would likely regain their confidence and the outcome would not be in China's favor. *My grandfather admired the Americans for their can-do attitude, sense of justice, and desire to always keep improving,* Leong kept thinking. *But I must try to save China from destroying itself. And for that, America must step down and China must rise.*

Leong knew he had many moving parts to this plan that needed his attention; soon, he would have one more trip to take. As he settled back in his seat, he smiled to himself and considered the real genius of his plan: America will focus on its own, internal divisions and not even consider that it was a foreign nation, along with the unwitting support of coddled and misguided citizens, had created the troubles it must deal with. The subtle hum of the plane's engine was all he could focus on; no more work for now! He realized sleep was something he badly needed.

Wei was now confident that the ECU's performance would live up to his expectations. "I knew that I needed to shape up the ECU," he remarked to Ling. "Once I can visit the other two units, there will absolutely no chance of failure. I spoke with the Embassy travel coordinator; she'll have our flights to Chicago and San Francisco booked by tomorrow afternoon." Wei had heard from one of the embassy security specialists that there was an observation and tracking unit (O/T) in Philadelphia. Wei was familiar with their classified mission, to locate and monitor facilities that store US advanced weapons systems. He was informed that staff had been on-site at the station for over nine months. That news convinced Wei that they probably have gotten sloppy with their security measures; he felt he was just the person to snap them back in line!

Wei also notified the Midwest Unit (MWU) and the West Coast Unit (WCU) to anticipate operational changes and that he would review those changes upon his arrival at their locations. Later that day, he received an encrypted email stating, "What operational changes?" Wei sent a reply to all, that he would discuss the changes at the all-member meeting.

That response drew a howl from the main contact for the WCU. He stated that Leong had made it clear that they should never get together as a group. Wei responded to both the MWU and the WCU that he was in charge of all units in North America and "if you complain about this to anyone else or fail to follow my instructions to the letter, you and your entire family will find how ruthless I can be. Do I make myself clear?" Given the tone of his response, the only feedback he received was a phone call from the most senior member of the WCU, someone who sought to reason with Wei.

The phone call lasted less than a minute. Over the course of that one minute, Wei's voice became increasingly intense and then only silence at the other end of the line. After a long pause came the reply, "Yes sir!"

Wei threw the phone down and shouted at Ling, "They have been on their own for too long and have picked up bad habits from the Americans." Now, more than ever, Wei was convinced that if he did not intervene, these idiots will screw up the operation. His worst fears were coming true: Leong may have chosen good men in terms of being smart enough to know what they needed to do, but they lacked the will to execute the mission with the degree of discipline that would amount to the difference between ultimate success or failure.

"We have got our work cut out for us," Wei said to Ling. "failure is not an option." Wei looked at the calendar and realized there was scant time to waste. "I will work out the schedule and you can work with the embassy on the specific flight and hotel reservations," Wei rattled off, without giving Ling a chance to say a word. "I have a meeting with the Mayor of Philadelphia this afternoon, perhaps later we will visit the observation and tracking unit, down by the waterfront. The Mayor is lacking, but we must play the game to keep them in our pockets for as long as it suits us." As Wei opened the door on route to his meeting, he looked back at Ling and said, "They must be fools if they think we would give them more money. I mean, just look at this city and the crime." With those words, he shook his head and stepped out of the door.

North arrived back at Col. Sutherland's headquarters at eleven in the evening. He did not expect to see such a crowded conference room; it was that packed. He handed the unopened folder to Col. Sutherland, who in turn handed it to the chief investigator for the case. Since Will had an ultra-top security clearance, many were concerned that perhaps under torture he may have given up some important state secrets. When North heard a couple of the senior leaders make those comments, he did not hold back and abruptly interrupted their conversation. As courteously as possible, North said, "Will gave up nothing!" The two senior colonels glanced at each other, and one of them said, "Major North, we know you were close friends with Major Knowles, but our concerns are valid."

North cleared his throat and said, in a much calmer tone, "With all due respect, if Will was being tortured while his family was still alive or if they were being tortured while he was still alive, I am sure we would not have had this folder in our possession. He would have given them the folder on the sheer chance that they might spare his family. The initial report supports the theory that the family members were killed a few hours before Major Knowles died."

"The investigators have pieced it together, and they believe that this is the most likely scenario: Someone in Singapore acquired Major Knowles' address and alerted their contacts in Australia to stake out his home. Upon his return, Major Knowles went straight to the farmhouse. He dropped off his luggage and secured the file in the hen house. Then he departed to Mr. Gordon's farm to discuss them providing security for Will's family so he could come back to headquarters. Shortly after he departed for the Gordons' farm, Peggy and the kids arrived, closely followed by the men who were in pursuit of this file. During the four hours—from the time he left to the time he arrived back at his farm—Peggy, the children, the two dogs, and all of the chickens were killed."

"When Major Knowles arrived, he walked in on a scene that's too horrific for any of us to comprehend. As far as we can tell, he was beaten to death. We conclude that all said and done, Will arrived too late to save his family—in which case, he must have basically told the attackers to 'fuck off' and given them nothing. Which is why we have this folder before us now."

"Point well taken," Col. Sutherland commented. "Let's open this bugger up and see what we've got." The folder only contained a total of four sheets of paper. Two of the pages had been received by fax and the other two contained notes in Will's handwriting. Once fed into the digital video recording system, the pages could be viewed on their laptops or the screen at the end of the conference room.

The first page displayed was in Chinese, and it appeared to be the opening of a presentation on an operation referred to as "Bright Star." Some of Will's hand-written translations were difficult to read so the language expert read the first page out loud. In addition to the printed Chinese text, there were some handwritten notes that were clearly not Will's.

Underneath the Bright Star logo was printed the date: September 1. Then in Chinese characters was an individual's title and name; the English translation that Will had left said "CA, Leong." At that point, Col. Sutherland motioned to one of his Intel team members to leave the meeting, quickly gather up what they have on CA Leong and be prepared to brief the meeting's attendees in the next twenty minutes. Other handwritten notes in Chinese included a recommendation to spare no expense to obtain the highest-quality personnel who would enable lengthy delays in response times. Then there was a rather cryptic note that said the "pawn" should not know how the "king" is willing to use his "pawn." One attendee commented that there was not much to go on and questioned the authenticity of the documents. But the general consensus was that this was an operation of such magnitude that it could not be ignored.

Also on the page was what they presumed to be the date of the meeting: March 5. And under the date in large letters were the words "Final Briefing and Review." The second page also appeared to be from the same briefing. But, it appeared that much of page had been disrupted in transmission. What could be made out was a reference to "civil disruption timelines and expected outcomes" in conjunction with operation "Northern Star"—dated August 27. To those familiar with Chinese Intel, this was troubling new language. Will had placed a large question mark at the end of that line.

The last two pages consisted of notes of a conversation that Will must have had with his long-time contact in China and of the day immediately following the receipt of the fax. Will had made a point to maintain relationships with Chinese nationals he had met when he had worked on engineering projects there in the past.

Will's notes also included a reference to "contact number 6" who had in his possession "top-secret" documents that his grandson had inadvertently secured while trying to hack the website of a university that had rejected his application. How the grandson had ended up with the documents he was not sure, since he had lost contact with him shortly after the young man had dropped the documents off. Will had spoken with some Chinese engineering contacts who were very uncomfortable with what they saw in Xi: a dictator who would do anything to achieve his so-called "destiny." At the time, Will had been at a conference in Singapore, along with their country's Intel Chief and his senior staff. His stay at the Singapore Grand Palace was uneventful until the phone call and fax on the day he was due to depart. At approximately six in the morning, Will had received that phone call and it had abruptly ended. Shortly afterwards, the hotel manager had personally come up to Will's room to deliver the two-page fax, because the pages had been marked "top secret" on the top.

Additional notes read, while checking out, he noticed two men go into the hotel manager's office: one was a well-dressed small man and the other was a very large man wearing a brightly colored shirt. A few seconds later, he had noticed the two men exit through the side door. Less than a minute passed, and then there were screams. Within seconds, hotel security had reached the spot. Within the next few minutes, the police arrived at a gory scene: The manager was lying in a pool of blood, his throat cut. Had the two assailants been pursuing whoever had seen the fax? Will was pretty sure the manager would have told them about him. His last note said, "Call Peggy, get to the old farm as soon as possible, and do not tell anyone!"

North now assumed that Will had realized that those men would do anything to acquire those documents in an effort to ensure that the top-secret information remained secret. Will had obviously sensed great danger to his family. His first thought had been to secure a safe location for Peggy and the kids while he would figure out a way to get the fax and notes to the Intel unit. He had most likely penned the "storm danger" letter to North as he was on the first leg of his flight back to Australia. On the back of the second handwritten page, Will had made some additional notes and written down some questions he felt needed to be answered:

1. Leong, big or little player as far as influencing Xi?
2. Go much deeper into his background and recent travel.
3. Go to FACE AI, identify two men in Singapore.
4. Is contact number 6 still alive? If yes, get him out of China!
5. Do we have any intel on the March 5th meeting?
6. Ask Col. Sutherland to assign an intel team to this immediately!

Finally at the bottom of the page and underlined were these lines: "Call Peggy from plane change in Kuala Lumpur and tell her that I will most likely arrive at the farm before she does, and I will send the caretaker on 'holiday.' Then I will go to see Mr. Gordon, and check if he and his five sons will act as security for her and the kids while I contact Col. Sutherland and we work out the details of what we need to do next."

Just as they finished viewing the last page from the folder, the man Col. Sutherland had assigned to research CA Leong came back into the conference room and started handing out printed sheets to the assembled personnel. The handout did not have much information on it. The Intel team member launched into a very short briefing session. The data and verified research appeared to indicate Leong was no one of any importance. The information available indicated he was only an academic who had attended graduate schools in the US and the UK. He was an assistant professor of political history and regularly held graduate seminars on the subject of "Internal dissent and political dynamics as a lead up to war."

One of the new investigators murmured, "What the hell is that?" North, who had actually read one of Leong's papers on the subject, spoke up. "Essentially, it is building on an updated variation of Sun Tzu's ideas in the *Art of War*—about preparing for battle by forcing your opponent to use his limited resources to resolve internal issues triggered by the aggressor in such a fashion that they would never be seen as the instigator. In layman's terms, you cause unrest or problems in some form that causes your opponent to misjudge or take his eyes off the upcoming battle long enough to give you an edge. Then capitalize on the mistakes to a point where your opponent chooses not to engage and looks for a way out, politically or physically."

One senior officer at the table commented that all this was not really new information! North spoke up again. "What's new is the way Leong approaches the idea. From what I can tell, he takes it to a whole new level— by way of mathematical models, computer simulations, detailed studies, and actual events that they have triggered and measured the response by country, race, time of day, time of year, and so on. And the key, as I read in his way of approaching the meat of the subject, is you do just enough to trigger a required response without being detected."

"If you can't be pegged as the perpetrator, the opponent would be reluctant to go to war with you. If you can provide your opponent with a benefit of some type, your adversary will unknowingly help you achieve your objective without a battle being fought."

"We will put this Leong at the top of our watch list," Col. Sutherland remarked. "And we will start digging to identify the two men who likely murdered Will and his family." As the meeting broke up, Col. Sutherland put his hand on Major North's shoulder and said, "I know we are sending you home with just one photograph of the suspects and little else to deal with the loss of a dear friend. But I assure you we will continue the hunt with vigor. We will see if we can get a better photo of the two from the Singapore police."

It was a little after two in the morning when North started his drive back to the hotel. On the way back, his mind kept moving between two lines of thought: Plans to exact revenge for the murder of a dear friend and his family and questions and vague ideas about if Leong was the primary author of Bright Star. If that was the case, then he might be up to no good at this very moment and no one would even see it coming? As North's flight reached cruising altitude his mind kept on playing out different scenarios regarding what the target of Bright Star may be. His immediate plan upon arriving back in Washington was to update Homeland Security, the CIA, and the FBI about everything he had discovered in Australia.

Wei and Ling were on their way to inspect the observation and tracking (O/T) unit in south Philly near the docks. They drove right by the house used by the O/T unit and further down the street that passed by a huge warehouse fitted out with both high- and low-tech security features. They noticed no markings or signs that would identify it— other than the assigned street address.

The warehouse had fourteen-foot-tall reinforced concrete walls with an additional six feet of barbed wire on top. Numerous video cameras and dog patrols had been deployed strategically. The O/T scouts had found the correct location and had positioned the O/T unit in such a way that they could clearly monitor all the comings and goings at the targeted warehouse. After giving the warehouse a good once over, they headed back to the O/T location up the street.

As they drove back to the O/T location Wei remarked about how rundown the neighborhood was. He was surprised some of the houses were still occupied. Once Wei arrived at the house, he remarked to unit leader, Chin that he had expected the US Government to have chosen a better location. The O/T unit leader pointed that their proximity to water, land and air movement was pretty good. To accommodate the transportation by air, commercial there was Philadelphia International Airport. Military access was available at McGuire Air Force Base, nearby in New Jersey. The warehouse had its own docks and loading equipment for shipment by water and it was close to several Interstate Highway interchanges. Wei listened intently as the Unit leader went over his operational guidelines. Wei thought that this O/T unit leader, Chin seemed very well prepared and knowledgeable of how the operation should be run. Wei then asked if they had experienced any trouble from the neighbors or the local Police. He replied everything has been quiet, with very little contact from the neighborhood residents. He pointed out that the local food was not to their liking. Also, the house they were staying in was falling apart and only one of the bathrooms worked. Wei looked him in the eye and said "what do I look like, your Mother" take your complaint up with the Embassy? Wei then stressed that there would be dire consequences for any of the unit that failed to do their job or jeopardized the mission. Then Chin made it clear that they would not fail to perform their tasks. Wei and Ling left and headed back to their hotel to check with the embassy on their travel arrangements. The time was fast approaching when they would leave for the Jersey shore and the BBQ meeting with the members of the ECU, closely followed by meetings with MW and WC units.

Upon arriving back in DC, North went straight to the NSA head-quarters and filed a report of what he had encountered in Australia. He also persuaded the clerk handling the input for the new AI Face Matching and Image Reconstruction System to put in the photo he had received from Col. Sutherland and see if it could come up with a match. It did not. He made a copy of the photo with the intent of giving it to FBI Agent Tim Cole, with whom he was scheduled to have dinner that evening.

North and Cole had been friends for many years and had first met in the US Marine Corps Basic School (for officers) after which they had stayed in touch for many years. Over dinner, North gave Cole a copy of the photo that showed the one man clearly and only the colorful shirt of the man seated next to him. Tim said that he was now assigned to the Philadelphia field office, but he would see what he could find out. Agent Cole was aware of how things had not worked out for North at the CIA.

"How's it going at the NSA?" Cole asked. North's blank stare told him all he needed to know.

"Sucks, eh?" Cole replied, to which North responded with another blank stare.

"The director thinks I'm a loose cannon," said North in a matter-of-fact tone, "and that I think I'm the only one who can really figure out what is going on and take charge of the situation without any senior approval."

Cole looked at North and said, "Well it's nice to know that some things don't change. That's good old Steve North for you!" That statement brought on a good laugh, and they continued trading stories till they finished dinner and then headed their separate ways. North thought that he would put in a couple more hours at his work desk in an attempt to catch up with all the information and in-house memos that had piled up. As he drove back to the office he kept going over one question: How had all the agencies missed Leong as a key player? Was he the primary author of both the "Bright Star" and "Northern Star" plans?

The two hours he had planned to spend at the office soon turned into four. He kept saying to himself, *One more folder to review, and then I'm outta here. I need to get some sleep!* But as he flipped open a yellow folder, he could not believe what he found! It was a DVD labeled "CA Leong's meeting with the President and Chief of Internal Security of Venezuela, dated July 10."

The video on the DVD did not show much, just Leong entering and leaving the main government complex and the time elapsed, which was forty-two minutes. There were some additional notes from the CIA agent about how their operative on the inside had confirmed that they did meet and that the operative saw Leong give each of the men a letter-sized envelope that they each promptly put inside their suitcoats. He had also given the President a large, brown, manila envelope. The President had opened it briefly, looked at the papers inside, and then placed it on his desk.

Once Leong left, the two men had gone back inside the office and closed the door. The memo went on to say that the operative would try to get a look at the memo. North wondered how a man who was assumed to be a bit player in Chinese politics and military activities had flown under the radar of so many intelligence agencies? What could he want in Venezuela and why? North knew he needed to contact the chief of the South American section of the CIA and see if he could get the information that Leong had given to the President of Venezuela. North shot off a quick email to W. Allen, CIA, Chief, South America, requesting any info on activities and contacts of Leong. Though North was in fact the chief of the Chinese section of the NSA, this matter appeared to overlap with other national security interests, meaning he would need to take it up with the NSA Director.

He started to put together a comprehensive file in an attempt to get additional resources assigned to his unit, to include the CIA and the FBI. He would also be asking for clearance to access records that were strictly outside his Chinese Intel Unit. North left a message with the NSA Director's assistant that he needed to speak with her as soon she arrived back from her morning meeting.

North did not look at his relationship with the NSA Director Case as a normal professional relationship. It was more like a test of wills between two individuals who viewed their jobs very differently. The path to the Agency Director's job was through various congressional staffing positions with a short stint at the CIA. North did recognize that she was very smart and could handle the White House and congressional challenges, but in his opinion, she was too damn bureaucratic. He also realized that the Agency Director position was very different than his. To North, paperwork was left for those who couldn't personally take up the challenge of a war that never ends. You had to be on your game 100% of the time, with little margin for error. Otherwise the bad guys win!

North had a very confrontational style when it came to getting the things he felt he needed to protect the country. To him, if he needed something that would give him or his team any edge in the battle, he was ready to fight for it. That passion was often the key ingredient that helped him achieve his objectives, but few, including NSA Director Case, had the stomach for an outright battle with North. However, in a big bureaucracy, passion was usually not rewarded, but stifled.

Director Case arrived at her office at ten in the morning, fresh from the daily White House briefing. When North entered the office, she motioned for him to take a seat. As North started to speak, she raised her hand for him to stop. She had her assistant call in Robert Harris, the Chief of the African section of the NSA and the man who acted as her eyes and ears in the operations divisions.

Actually, he acted more as a snitch and you had to be careful what you said because everyone knew he would report anything he heard to her. He was an attorney from the congressional staff, just like the Director. From North's point of view, their actions reflected more of an interest in not upsetting anyone than ensuring national security. As Harris took his seat, they smiled at each other, which was a signal to North that this encounter, as it were, was a preplanned ambush.

"I know we are going to discuss some events that pertain to China," the Director began. "However, no matter what the circumstances may be, you are *directed* at this time to report your concerns to me directly, or in my absence, to Mr. Harris. Under no circumstances will you initiate any operations toward China that extend beyond the West Coast." Here she paused and gave North a steely glare before continuing, "The Chief (President of the United States) does not want anyone rocking the boat with China. Also, he now requires that a White House approved operation designator be assigned to any operation that takes place beyond the West Coast that might impact US and Chinese relations. So the White House National Security Advisor will review the ops request and then schedule a follow-up meeting with the President, if he feels it is necessary. If anyone violates this process, they could be facing up to five years in prison. Just to make sure you understand what I said, please sign this paper, and there is a copy for you."

North now realized that the two attorneys had tied his hands and taking the reviews to the White House would slow down the process of getting any approvals to a snail's pace. His authority to take steps to detect, deal with, and stop certain actions where China was concerned had now been effectively removed. The current administration was so afraid of offending China that they were willing to turn a blind eye to whatever the Chinese leadership might try.

North was stunned, but he was ready to pitch his idea. "Director, I have obtained information that a Chinese professor may be directly involved in—" The Director stopped him mid-sentence and said,

"We'll continue this discussion at a later time." And just like that, the meeting was over!

North decided to put together a memo for the Director detailing what he had learned from his time in Australia. Once the memo was complete, North would turn his attention back to his top priority—Leong.

CHAPTER 3

THE SOUTH AMERICAN CONNECTION

North was dead on his feet and ready to finally head home when a call came through from the CIA Chief of Operations for South America, Walt Allen. He had just arrived from Bogota and needed to stop by the Pentagon. However, he could meet North before leaving for his home in Virginia Beach. Deputy Allen was an old hand when it came to knowing his way around DC. He, like North, was a Marine and had been G-2, Intel as well as serving as a staff attorney at HQMC. A short stint at the Department of Justice was enough to sour him on any permanent position in DC.

Allen was fluent in both Spanish and Portuguese, so he had jumped at the chance of being posted in South America. Allen asked North if he knew where Ted's BBQ and Catfish House was located. "I do, but that kinda restaurant's never open this early," North responded. "Don't worry about that. I'll meet you there, okay?" Allen replied before hanging up.

Allen was just getting out of his car at the restaurant when North arrived. The place was dark and the front door locked, but Allen started to pound on the door. Just as North was mouthing "I told you so," he stopped mid-sentence as a rather large man with an angry look on his face came to the door. North could tell he was getting ready to unleash a tirade of "Who in the hell are you and can't you read that we're not open yet?" on to him when the man recognized Allen. As the big man opened the door, he barked out, "Allen are you still a worthless lawyer? Cause you know all lawyers are worthless!"

To this, Allen replied "If we didn't have to spend our time defending crusty old warrant officers from allegations such as misappropriation of replacement parts, forgery, knowingly entering an off-limits strip club, having multiple intoxicated women in various state of undress at the base officer's wives' club facility, and numerous other violations of demeanor and good taste, we might have actually accomplished something for the Marine Corps!"

That said, the big man gave Allen a hug and asked how his family was doing. Allen turned to North and said, "This is warrant officer Clayton Sealy. Look alive my boy; it isn't often you get to meet a legend!" Allen had known Sealy for many years, mostly from his time on active duty. Sealy had also done time in the CIA and was still a consultant. In fact, he was responsible for most of the CIA contacts working undercover in South American governmental positions.

As they chatted, Sealy called out to the chef in the back, asking him to put together some eggs, bacon, and breakfast corn muffins. While Sealy poured the coffee, Allen said, "The CIA has been monitoring the bank accounts of senior governmental officials in various South American countries due to the presence of Chinese efforts to gain a foothold for their operations on the continent. We discovered that the bank accounts of the President of Venezuela and his Chief of Internal Security had grown considerably over a very short period. So, I assigned a team to record the visitors as they came and went. That is when we recorded a meeting between Leong and those two. Shortly after the meeting, we discovered another spike in their bank accounts. So of course we asked our inside contact if the records show Leong had been there before.

"She came up with the date of November 18, of last year. We went back through the bank records and just as we suspected—a large influx of cash into their accounts on that date. So then we looked into the bank records of anyone who met with both of them at the same time. What we found was only one person who fit that profile: a real estate developer by the name of Carlos Ruiz. He's a very big player in the construction of hotels and office buildings. The pattern we found was that each time Leong came to meet with Maduro and Rodriguez, their bank accounts went up; then those two met with Ruiz, then his bank account went up. So our next objective was to see if we could confirm that Leong was in fact was trying to acquire some specific real estate."

"This is where we continue to benefit from WO Sealy's hard work. He had once gotten a builder out of hot water with the local drug cartel. The cartel had pegged him for the person who had informed the local police about their operation. Sealy told them that someone else was responsible and had gotten the builder off the hook. We have used him from time to time to gather information for us. He came to us with some interesting information from some subcontractors that have been working on new high-rises, seventeen-story luxury offices, condos, and penthouse buildings. They had heard from a reliable source that all the office space had been sold or leased and that the condos and the penthouses still had no takers. So it would make sense to finish the office spaces first!"

"But Ruiz had demanded that they stop all other efforts in order to finish the seventeenth floor, the penthouse first, then the fifteenth and sixteenth floors on the condos. The work on the remaining offices would be totally suspended until October 1. And furthermore, he gave the electrical subcontractor a comprehensive new set of drawings and requirements that in no way mirror the building's original plans. To one of the senior electrical engineers on the project, it looked like the owners of the building had decided to convert those top three floors into a technology center. So the order was to get the top three floors finished with the associated electrical improvements and then suspend all other work until October 1."

Here, Allen paused and looked around to ensure that North and Sealy were following his narrative. When they nodded back at him, he continued, "Then we got some more interesting info. Apparently our inside contact had an opportunity to briefly look at the letter that Leong had given the President. Our inside contact informed us the envelope was light gray with a big white star embossed on the first page. It mentioned that operations would commence on August 24 and continue through September 18. The location on Maria Drive was acceptable, that there must a special police or National Guard unit posted and no one is to know who's in operation at that location and why."

"And wouldn't you know it—Ruiz has work on a new seventeen-story building going on in Maria Drive. And we checked and confirmed there were no other large construction projects in that area. So, we know this much? Leong has purchased the co-operation and direct support of the Venezuelan government! We are relatively confident where the "activity" is going to take place and the dates of operation. What we need to find out is what that "activity" and who will set it in motion. We need appropriate resources to deal with what might be a major international event."

"We have also determined that something's in the works with the Mexican drug cartels, especially in relation to illegal entry into the US across the southern border, especially through Texas." Allen and North noticed Sealy shaking his head.

"Gunner, you've got some concerns or suggestions?" Allen asked.

Sealy took a deep breath and said, "You need to get your local hired guns ready for this stuff. I can tell you that the Venezuelan President, Chief of Internal Security, and Carlos Ruiz are three of the most ruthless sons of bitches I have ever run into, and I've met quite a few! They will stop at nothing to line their pockets and remain in power."

Sealy continued, "I've never had the occasion to go up against or deal with Leong, but Major North, Leong impresses me as one of those zealots who considers himself so smart that he thinks he can actually control those monsters he helps with his big-time plans for saving his country or whatever. I will tell you this: Once guys like these get a taste of power, they will stop at nothing to acquire more of it. Then they lament what they have done but they are too caught up in what they are doing, so then they try justifying their actions as noble or right. In turn, a man like that becomes the mastermind of everyone's destruction, never fully understanding what he has done."

Noticing the ashen expression on the faces of North and Allen, Sealy stopped and chuckled, muttering, "Damn, I guess that's enough philosophy for one day." Then he turned to Allen with a very straight face and said, "This restaurant stuff is really boring. Let me know if you need me to come back and rough up some folks for you!"

"It sounds to me like we need to keep a close eye for potential operations at the Maria Drive location," Allen cut in. "And to avoid giving the impression that we are focusing on the Maria Drive building, we need to target all of Ruiz's buildings at the same time."

"He has a total of four operational hotels/office buildings and two under construction, of which one is the Maria Drive building. If we target all of his locations at the same time we will not draw special attention to the real target, Maria Drive."

"I have connections with a group of businessmen who had been targeted by Ruiz and with intervention from the Maduro and Rodriguez, they were subjected to violent riots that literally torched all their businesses and they lost everything," Sealy responded. "They would be more than happy to raise a small army, with our support, and attack those locations we have identified. By having the locals attack those locations, we can make the whole thing look like a strictly Venezuelan dispute and the US and CIA would not be suspected."

North turned to Allen for his take on Sealy's solution. Allen smiled and said, "Gunner it looks like you'll have to take a break from your boring restaurant days! You've got a small army to raise and not much time."

Gunner smiled and said, "Man, it's good to be back in the game! I'll need between $500,000 and $750,000 to properly arm them!"

Allen said that should not be a problem, and North added, "If you need more, call me! And remember, gentlemen, we do not want to spook them; we need to let this thing play out, whatever it is."

Sealy said he would start work on the plan immediately. Once the initial draft was done, he would submit it to Allen and North for their review and comments. Sealy said he realized that whatever was taking place at Maria Drive could quite possibly have major international implications and that North's guidance would be followed. While Sealy and Allen stayed to discuss further arrangements, North left for his apartment to get some much-needed rest. On his drive back, he called into work with instructions for his team to contact other intelligence agencies for photographs of Chinese personnel who have recently appeared to be involved in new operations or were new players on the international stage.

For Cue, the big day had finally arrived. *Tonight*, he thought, *I will prove to everyone that I have what it takes!* He leaned back in his chair and started to daydream about all the women and benefits that would come his way. He was confident that he had taken care of everything and his plan was going to work. Now he could just sit back and relax.

Just then, his brother burst through the door, Cue almost fell over because of the loud noise as the door slammed against the wall. Cue was clearly pissed as he yelled, "What the hell are you doing kicking in the door like that?" After catching his breath, his brother said, "We may have a problem with our timing for tonight!"

That made Cue even more upset. "Man what could be wrong with my plan?" he shouted in a whiny voice. "The hurricane!" his brother cried back, but Cue had a blank expression on his face, so his brother repeated, "Brother, I'm talking about Hurricane Claire; have you not seen the news?"

"The last report I saw said it was heading out further out into the Atlantic," Cue replied.

"It was," his brother replied, "but it turned back toward the coast. It's not going to make landfall, but the weather report said to expect extremely heavy rainfall starting tonight around one. They also said that the heavy rainfall could last up to three days."

When Cue continued to look confused, his brother reminded him that because it was so hot and muggy at night, the protocol was to keep the truck door open with the keys in the lock—which is what Cue had counted on for the successful hijacking of the truck. "And when it rains, they shut and lock the door with the keys inside because they can't risk the moisture damaging the electronics," his brother continued urgently. "Which also means we can't get at the keys to start the truck, which means, no truck, no electronics, no big payday, and lots of angry, pissed off people who have lots of guns and are not afraid to use them!"

Cue spoke up, "Look, no matter how logical it would be to postpone the hijacking, the folks I'm dealing with do not operate that way. Besides, King Leon has called in several players from out of state to bid on the electronics and the truck. We'll just have to move the timeline up to two hours earlier."

Cue's brother seemed very nervous, "don't you remember that the shift change seemed to be their best time to hit them, don't you think midnight timing could prove troublesome." Cue responded, "I'm in charge and midnight is the new target time, understood! Now go get Martin and we will go over the plan with the new timeline." Cue felt a little uneasy with the change, but if he did not successfully get the electronics and the truck tonight, there would be hell to pay from both BT and King Leon, something he did not even want to think about. While he was pacing around his apartment, Cue heard what sounded like a low-flying aircraft with a bad engine. He was still trying to figure out what was making such a racket when there was a knock on the door. His brother and nephew were standing there, and they were dressed in dark clothing just like the plan required.

"How do you like the car I just stole? It was the loudest one I could find," his brother remarked. "Man, you did great, those foreigners will wonder what kind of lame dude would drive such a piece of shit! Let's go over the plan one more time: at a quarter to midnight, you'll start driving slowly down the street, gunning the engine, causing it to backfire, especially when you are close to the house." Cue turned to his nephew and asked, "Did you manage to knock out a couple more street lamps near the house with that BB gun I got you?" His nephew nodded. "Remember to not approach the cars parked in the driveway until the men at the house have turned their full attention to the exploding car."

"Once you see everyone's eyes on the car going by, creep up be-hind them and slash at least one tire, but hopefully two, on each of the cars parked in the driveway. That will surely hamper their efforts to follow us—this is very important! Make sure you use the knife I gave you; it should be sturdy enough to do the job. Once you're done, quickly move to the corner of Delaware and Sunset, the pickup location."

Then he turned to his brother and asked, "Did you get the can of gasoline and the box of fireworks?"

"Of course, I know what my job is. I drive slowly down the street, making as much noise as possible to get their attention. Then I stop the car, douse the fireworks—which will be spread out on the back-seat—with the gasoline, throw a lit road flare onto the gas-soaked seat, and run like hell!"

"Right," Cue said, "but remember you must go at least 200 feet down the road before stopping…the diversion has to draw the guards far enough from the truck so I have a good chance to get the keys, start the truck, and have it going down the street before they even realize what's going down."

"Do you think they have any guns?" Cue's nephew asked, and Cue replied, "I haven't seen any. Besides, they're not from this country, so they aren't allowed to have guns." Cue's plan was that as soon as he put sufficient distance between him and the hijacking location, he would go to meet Junior at the pawn shop to pay him off with some of the electronics.

"Once finished with Junior, I will depart for Hulmeville to deliver the truck and its contents to the warehouse location that the King had finalized. I will back the truck in front of the fourth loading door, turn off the engine, leave the keys in the ignition, close the door, and leave the area. You guys will be waiting across the street from the parking lot to pick me up. Then we will come back to the apartment and wait for a call from King Leon about where I can pick up our share of the take." Cue was sure it would work out just as he planned.It was 11:30 pm, and Cue and his nephew were in their positions, just waiting for Cue's brother to come driving down the street.

The observation and tracking crew had been on station now for almost nine months. It was hot and muggy, and the food was bad. Their routine and daily procedures had slowly deteriorated, which often resulted sleeping on shift or just listening to their radio. They had recently been assured that they would soon find themselves on their way back to China. At 11:34 pm, they had finally located a soccer game on their international radio and were listening for the score when they heard a car with a very loud engine slowly coming down the street.

They turned up the volume on the radio. Soon the noise was so great they couldn't hear the game. They were more distracted than suspicious. There was never any traffic at that time of night in that neighborhood, so rather than getting out their weapons, they just casually walked out onto the porch to see what crappy American car was keeping them from listening to the game. As the car drove slowly by, the exhaust smoke billowed up and obscured the driver's face. A few seconds later the car's engine stopped. There was dead silence, and even the crickets could be heard, along with the river traffic a short distance away.

Although the car was out of view, they noticed what appeared to be flickering flames. What happened next woke up everyone in the house and half the neighborhood. The explosion from the gasoline and fireworks had also ignited the fuel tank under the car, which led to a rather large fireball. Every one of the on-duty personnel left their assigned posts and ran toward the burning vehicle. The only person who remained at his post was Chang, the little guy who stayed inside the back of the truck, with all the electronic gear. The fire and the resulting explosion peaked his interest, he pushed the truck door open a little further and appeared to have stepped out.

That's when Cue made his move.

He sprinted across the street and grabbed the keys that were still in the door. But just at that moment, a hand reached out and took hold of his wrist. The little guy was still in the back of the truck! Cue was shocked and quickly reacted by pulling his hand holding the keys, in turn yanking the little guy out of the truck. As Chang was falling to the ground, he managed to grab ahold of the mask Cue was wearing and tore it off, getting a really good look at Cue's face. Momentarily stunned by the little guy's actions, Cue snapped to attention, and with the keys now in his hand, he ran to the front of the truck. He quickly put the key in the ignition, and the truck's engine started right up.

All this time, the little guy had yelling for assistance and pointing to the truck. As other members of the crew ran back, one grabbed the door handle to open it, but Cue was one step ahead of him. Locking the door was the first thing he had done. Another guard jumped on the front bumper and started to pound on the windshield. Cue ignored him and pressed the accelerator pedal to the floor. The truck literally jumped forward as the gears engaged, knocking the man on the front bumper on to the street; he had to quickly roll to the side to avoid being run over by the accelerating vehicle.

Due to all the excitement, Cue was hyperventilating and driving erratically, swerving from one side of the street to the other. Though unintended, the swerving proved beneficial as a couple of the guards pulled two fully loaded AK-47s from the trunk of the first car parked in the driveway. The guards were breathing heavily from running back from the burning car as they struggled to get the escaping truck in their rifle sights! Between Cue's swerving and the two guards breathing heavily while trying to aim, not one bullet found its mark.

However, down the street, the surrounding windows, porches, and street lights suffered badly, as the high-velocity bullets penetrated walls and broke dishes, mirrors, and other household objects. Now, the few residents who had remained in the neighborhood all had their lights on, and a few even ventured outside to find out what was going on. Police sirens could already be heard in the distance.

At the exact moment that the truck hijacking was taking place, the O/T unit leader, Chin was speaking with Wei on the phone. The unit leader had dropped the phone and ran outside to see what was going on. The shots could clearly be heard over the phone, so Wei yelled at Ling to get dressed and bring the car around. After no more than a minute, Chin got back on the phone and informed Wei about what had just happened. Wei told the man that he would be on scene in a few minutes. He further instructed Chin to put the weapons back in the trunk, pick up *all* the spent brass cartridges, get everyone inside, and to not answer any questions from anyone. He also said he would have the Chinese Embassy's on-site attorney there as quickly as possible and he himself would be there within minutes. As Chin was hanging up the phone he could already see the reflections of flashing lights on the wall.

Chin walked onto the porch as a patrol car pulled up in front of the house. As the officer exited the patrol car, the little man who had been in the back of the truck ran to the officer, waving his arms and shouting in broken English that someone had stolen their truck! Chin moved quickly and began shouting at the little man in Chinese, asking him to be quiet and get back onto the porch! The little guy looked dumbfounded and turning to Chin, said (in Chinese) that he had seen the thief before and could provide a description to the officer. The officer, not understanding a single word the two were saying, asked the little guy, "Did you have a truck and was it stolen?" The little guy started nodding. But Chin again ordered him to shut up and move back to the porch! This time Chang complied and moved back toward the house without another word.

The officer, seeing that Chin appeared to be the man in charge, directed two questions toward him, "Sir you have a truck which was stolen and were the shots fired a result of the thieves stealing the truck?" In very clear English, Chin said that they had a truck, and it was missing, but he was not sure that it was stolen. And as to the shots the officer had inquired about, "Well I didn't heard a thing." The officer was now getting a little ticked at what he sensed was something way more serious than what the Chinese guy was willing to tell him.

At this point, the other officer in the car came up and asked the senior patrolman what he needed him to do. The senior patrolman told him to call in for back up and then check the area to see if he could find any evidence of a crime, especially spent cartridges. He also asked the other officer to check if someone had called for the firetrucks to attend to the burning car. The officer also noticed that the cars in the driveway were oddly tilted and upon closer inspection, he saw that the tires had been slashed. He turned and looked at the unit leader, now nose to nose, and said, "I'm asking you again, sir. What happened here?"

Chin simply told the officer that someone from the Chinese embassy would be there shortly to answer his questions before he turned and walked back toward the house. As the team leader walked away, the senior officer walked over to the cars in the driveway to get a closer look. He noticed that the dirt on the trunk handle had recently been disturbed. He called to the unit leader and said, "Would you be so kind as to open the trunk of the first car?" The unit leader just stood there on the porch and did not say a word. The other patrolman asked the senior officer if he wanted him to open the trunk, but the senior patrolman sensed something else was going on, something he couldn't quite put his finger on.

By this time the entire Chinese unit had assembled onto the porch. The senior patrolman backed up and said, "We'll wait in the car for higher-ups to arrive." He then called the other two cars up the street and told the patrolmen inside them to block off the street and put out the yellow tape over the areas impacted by the bullets. Then he called dispatch to hurry them up and get the precinct's senior investigator to their location.

The fire department had now arrived on scene! The fire Captain rushed over to one of the police officers, "did one of you check to see if there were any occupants in the car who escaped, that may need medical attention? Is the driver and passengers available so we can speak with them?" Another fireman walked up to the fire Captain, "I picked up several pieces of unexploded fireworks, we may need more time to investigate what now appears to be arson! "As the first police officer to arrive, I checked for passengers, there was none at the scene. I asked some of the bystanders if they had seen anyone exit the vehicle and got a negative response." While the police waited for backup, they inspected and marked the impact points of the bullets that had been fired.

At that point, dispatch called the senior patrolman to report that the lead investigator had gone home sick from a lingering battle with Covid. But there were two other officers who were just finishing up an investigation and would try to get on scene ASAP! A few minutes later, a black sedan ignored an officer's signal to stop and proceeded to pull up in front of the house where the truck had been parked. The senior patrolman had been sitting in his car and writing up a detailed report of what he had gathered so far. He jumped out of the car and pulling his .357 Smith & Wesson from its holster, slowly approached the vehicle, yelling at its occupants to get out and lie down on the ground. Chin, who had been quietly standing on the porch, started to run toward the black sedan, yelling that those men in the vehicle were from the embassy. "Don't shoot!" he kept shouting. Hearing this, the officer holstered his weapon and proceeded to very loudly advise the two men in the car that disobeying an officer of the law was a good way to get themselves shot!

Both Wei and Ling exited the vehicle very slowly. Wei immediately assumed an apologetic expression and said that his driver was new to the States. He proceeded to profusely reassure the officer that something like this would never happen again. At that point, the officer asked them both to produce their IDs and passports, which they did. If the senior patrolman thought he was going to get more information from the new arrivals, he was sorely mistaken. Wei did inform the patrolman that the embassy lawyer was on his way and would be there shortly, which he followed with some more stern words. "Until then, neither I nor anyone else will answer any more questions you may want to ask and by the way, please remove yourself from Chinese Embassy's property!"

To this, the senior patrolman turned and said quietly to his partner, "This is way above our paygrade. Let's leave this asshole for the higher-ups." The two officers returned to their patrol car to await the senior inspectors' arrival on the scene.

Cue was driving very carefully and staying well within the speed limit as he made his way to Junior's pawn shop. For someone who had never driven a large vehicle like the truck, he felt he was doing pretty well. Having caught his breath and calmed down, he was proud of himself. It was all going to work out, just like he had planned. Soon, Cue pulled up to the back door of the pawn shop, got out, and pressed the doorbell at 11:52 pm.

Junior answered the door promptly and gave Cue a high-five for pulling off the heist, as planned. "Man, I had planned things out so well it was as smooth as a fifty-year-old cognac!" Cue started to brag. "You should have been there; those guys were so afraid of this brother, they actually were begging me not to hurt them!"

"Yeah, yeah, tell me another fairytale you bullshit con artist! Tell me you got the goods!" Junior was eager to see what he could score and then resell to impress his father. As they climbed up into the back of the truck, rain started to fall, and the wind was shifting to the south as the squall line of thunderstorms approached. The showers of hail pelting the truck would mark the beginning of a stormy night.

As Cue and Junior entered the back section of the truck, Junior's eyes grew big. He had immediately focused on two heavy magnet speakers on top of the electronics panels. He examined how they were attached to the panels and said, "If we take out a few screws and pull these two cables, they will come right off the wall and no one will be the wiser." Cue agreed and it took less than ten minutes to complete the removal. Then, Junior noticed a small bright yellow case in the back. It opened up to reveal what looked like a portable karaoke machine. He held it up for Cue to see, saying, "Throw this in and we're square." *This is getting easier than I had assumed*, Cue thought happily as he pulled out of the pawn shop unloading door. He was smiling to himself as he drove off toward the drop-off location in Hulmeville.

Junior took the three items into the storage area of the pawn shop. As protocol required, he photographed each piece and entered the information into the pawn shop register. Upon closer inspection of the heavy magnet speakers, he felt certain he could sell them at a great profit, to some people who were looking to start a new music recording studio.

The other item would be a bit more challenging to offload. He opened the yellow case and took out what he thought was one of those portable karaoke players. But since the instructions for operating the machine, as well as the markings on it, were in either Chinese or Japanese, he would have to take the item to some friends to translate. He did not want to forget to take the machine when he left to go home, so he sat it by the back door and then placed his raincoat on top of it. Because of the heavy rain, he would need his raincoat and therefore would remember to take the machine. He stacked the two speakers and the empty yellow outer case in the "new" inventory section, then continued the inventory review.

At 11:54 pm, the Central Police dispatch got a call to dispatch detective unit 557.

Just as inspectors Lt. Kent and Lt. Howe had finished with case M1-34 and were heading in for the night, they heard someone from dispatch say, "Not so fast. The Captain wants you two to call unit 767 and proceed to their location to check out an incident involving multiple shots fired. The senior patrolman said he needs some seasoned investigators to deal with what is going on."

Kent and Howe looked at each other, and then Howe got on the radio, saying, "Does the Captain realize we have been working for the last fourteen hours without a break? Also, we think that this would violate the spirit and text of our latest contract."

The dispatcher replied, "Look guys, I'm just repeating exactly what precinct Captain Simpson said: 'You guys are very near the location, so stop your whining and crying. The sooner you get there, the sooner you guys can clear up the issues and go home.' The Captain also said that if you guys want to fill out a grievance sheet, feel free to take it into his office and put in to the file next to his desk, labeled "*trash*."

With that response Kent turned the car around while Howe called unit 767. It only took them eight minutes to get to the scene. Kent and Howe were two of the best investigators in all of Philly. Lt. Kent had a great reputation for being able connect with the various elements of the criminal underworld. While most other police officers worked hard to get out of the VICE division, he had worked very hard to get into it. Lt. Howe worked in Homicide and was considered the one person to see if you were trying to solve a difficult case. Captain Simpson had paired the two together hoping that Howe would keep Kent from "going off the reservation" and Kent in turn would train Howe in ways of using some of those underworld connections to solve certain homicide cases. Needless to say they were both tired and their tempers were getting shorter by the minute.

Upon arrival at the scene Howe instructed the homicide photographer who was accompanying them to start taking photos of all personnel housed at the location from where the supposed truck was stolen. At that moment another black sedan arrived in front of the house. The embassy attorney had arrived. Kent recognized him immediately and muttered, "Another fucking attorney. The bullshit will get even thicker now." As the attorney approached Kent and Howe they noticed some movement out of the corner of their eyes.

Ling had been standing on the porch when he noticed the officer taking photos of the O/T personnel. Almost instinctively, he ran off the porch and onto the street and grabbed the officer taking the photos. As if that wasn't enough, he had tried to wrestle the camera from the photographer. Howe quickly pulled out his pistol and put it to Ling's temple. Ling stopped mid-movement and just stood there. Wei and the embassy attorney rushed toward Ling, shouting for him to back off. Kent moved to stand between the two men fighting over the camera and the approaching two men, Wei and the attorney. Kent also noticed that other men were starting to move off the porch.

At this point, Kent pulled out his Colt .38 revolver and pointed it in their direction and yelled, "Stop!" The two patrolmen sitting in their car saw what was happening, got out of the car, and drew their pistols as well. Wei knew he had to stop what was happening or the whole mission would be a failure. Immediately, Wei yelled in Chinese for all his men to put their hands in the air and kneel on the ground, and they immediately compiled. Ling did the same. Howe called for the patrolmen to come over and arrest Ling for assault and interfering with a police officer. Wei and the attorney begged for them not to arrest Ling on the basis that where he had grown up, the police often took photos of innocent civilians to use them in their negative propaganda against the state. The detectives looked at each other and estimated that if they arrested Ling, it would mean another hour of paperwork before they could go home. In the end, Howe instructed the patrolmen to holster their weapons and move back into their unit. Then he told Wei to have all his men move slowly back onto the porch and not to come off it again.

Then Kent chimed in, "Tell Mr. Aloha [referring to Ling's shirt] that if he so much as touches another police officer, I'll have him arrested and jailed for at least six months!" Wei said he understood and was very sorry for the confrontation. Howe holstered his pistol and walked over to Wei and the attorney. Wei was just finishing a phone call when Howe said, "You seem to be the one in charge so let us hear what the hell is going on. Do you have a truck and was it stolen and further more did you have anything to do with the exploding car and the gun shots that neighbors claimed they heard?"

Wei smiled; he knew the cover story. "You see officer, we in

China are very concerned about climate change and how it may affect some countries more than others. At great expense, China has established many of these monitoring stations in many cities around the world—all to collect data that can be used to fight climate change. As you can imagine, the equipment is very expensive. My job is to monitor the equipment's use, ensuring it is properly protected and secure. I go from country to country and test the unit's security plan. In the present case, I set things up to have a burning car distract the security team's attention while my hired personnel drove the truck away to make it look like a real-life hijacking. And with regard to the supposed shots fired, I'm sorry, but I know nothing about that."

The two detectives looked at each other, both rolling their eyes at that story. Howe looked at the attorney and said, "Do we look that stupid? I've heard better stories than that from my son when he was five years old and was telling me how the goldfish we had just bought had escaped down the toilet without any help from him! Now let's try that again, shall we?"

Wei looked confused, sure he had been that law enforcement would believe him. The attorney assured the two that the story was true. Kent replied, "You know how you can tell an attorney is lying? His lips are moving. Or have you heard the one about how an attorney is there to help you? No? Well, neither have their clients!" They both laughed at that one. Howe asked Kent how that tale scored on his "bullshitometer."

"A solid 6.5 out of 10," Kent replied, "and the next piece of information you give us needs to score a hell of a lot higher than that!" Wei and the embassy attorney just looked at each other; then Howe said, "We're going to get to the bottom of what happened here tonight— with or without your help!"

At that moment Howe's cell phone rang. It was Captain Simpson and he wanted to know when the two would be back at the station. Kent took the phone and said, "It's going to be a long night; we've got a lot of witnesses to question and we are going to need a translator because most of them do not speak English."

Captain Simpson asked, "Is there evidence of a crime?"

Howe took the phone back and answered, "Well, not so far."

The Captain then asked, "Was anyone hurt?" and Howe said, "Not to our knowledge." "Just what do you have?" the Captain continued wearily. Howe replied, "A bullshit story from Wei, the Chinese guy in charge." The Captain said, "Then call it a night and we will discuss it tomorrow." Howe and Kent looked at each other; that was unlike the Captain they normally dealt with. Then the Captain explained that the Mayor had called the Chief who had then called the Captain. "It seems that the Chinaman in charge is discussing a million-dollar investment in Philadelphia real estate and he doesn't want you guys mucking it up."

"Captain, this guy is running a con on the Mayor," said Howe. "After 18 years of working the street, I can tell you that this guy is ready to sell the Mayor a 'buildable house lot, mid-stream in the Delaware River directly under the Walt Whitman Bridge.' If you catch my drift." The Captain replied, "So you want me to call the Mayor at 12:35 am in the morning and basically tell him that you guys are going to put the screws to this Chinaman till you get the info that makes you confident that he's telling the truth? In that case, I will also be implying to the Mayor that he has shit for brains if he thinks any sane person would invest more than a dollar in this crime-ridden city that he grew up in? Does that sound like something I'm going to do?"

There was a long pause, and then Kent replied, "All right sir, we will write up a preliminary investigation report in the next 10 minutes and shut down the onsite investigation." There was another long pause, and the Captain told Howe to have the patrol units go back to the station so that all law enforcement will have cleared out of the area. Howe hooked the cell phone back onto his belt and looked in the direction of Wei and the attorney, only to see that Wei had a thin smile on his face. *So that little son-of-a-bitch was calling the Mayor to get us off his back*, Kent observed to himself. *Well, it worked this time, but I swear that little bastard is going to make a mistake and I want to be there when the handcuffs go on and see if he is smiling then.*

As they were walking back to the car they looked around and saw that all of the folks in the neighborhood had gone back into their homes and turned their lights off. The car fire was quickly put out and the car was already on a flatbed truck, ready to be hauled away. The only noise being made was some of the Chinese crew changing out the tires on the cars in the driveway. Howe glanced down at a bright brass-like reflection under some leaves in the gutter. He kicked at the leaves to reveal a shell casing. He kneeled down as if to tie his shoelace and using his pen, lifted the shell casing and put it into a small evidence bag before slipping the bag into his pocket. Kent told the photographer to get those photos of the Chinese over to the Philadelphia office of the FBI right away. There was some taunting, laughing, and obscene gestures from the men on the porch toward the police car as it departed and at the last second before it would go out of sight, Kent stuck his arm out the window and gave them the middle finger. It would take about twenty minutes to get back to the station and not a word was said on the drive back.

It was 12:44 am when Cue turned on to Hulmeville's main street. Just a few blocks more and he would have pulled off the greatest gamble of his life. As he approached the drop-off location, he saw his brother and nephew in a car across from the parking lot. The rain had stopped. He turned into the warehouse parking lot and then around the corner to the fourth loading bay. Carefully backing into the space, he turned off the engine, left the keys in the ignition, switched off the lights, shut the door, and then walked briskly across the parking lot to the waiting car that would take them all back to Philly. No one said a word for the entire drive back to the city. As they pulled to a stop in front of Cue's apartment, they all started to laugh. Cue told them to come in and celebrate. He had a cheap bottle of champagne with which they could toast to their success!

CHAPTER 4

THINGS GET MESSY

It was 1:05 am in the morning when the O/T personnel finished changing the last tires to get one of the sedans operational. Wei was just finishing his briefing from Chin when Chang, approached both of them. The two men looked up at him as he stood there scratching his head. "Now I remember, I saw him at the 24hr diner not far from here; he was there talking with a man who drove a SUV," he blurted out. "And it was about this time of the early morning when I saw them."

Chang said that he was sure he could identify the men if he saw them again! Wei ordered the men to take out the AK-47s equipped with silencers and subsonic rounds. Soon, the two black sedans were loaded up and on their way; the little man was directing them to the diner. As they turned the corner, there sat BT's Range Rover right in front of the diner's entrance. Wei signaled one of the cars to the back of the diner. After a couple of minutes, Wei, Ling, the unit leader Chin, and Chang entered through the main entrance. The patrons noticed but paid little attention to them and carried on with their conversations. Right behind them walked in two men with AK-47s and the conversations ceased immediately!

BT made a subtle move for his pistol but abruptly stopped when one of the men raised the muzzle of his machine gun in BT's direction.

Mountain Man made a slight movement toward his handgun. BT looked him in the eyes and softly said, "No way, don't even try it. You haven't got a chance." The little guy pointed at BT, instantly identifying him as the man he had seen talking with the bald guy who had stolen the truck. About that time, a parade of the diner's staff came out of the kitchen area, followed by one of Wei's men with his machine gun stuck into the cook's back. Wei approached BT and said, "No games, I have little time for them, and if you cooperate, you all can get back to what you were doing before we so rudely interrupted you. I want the name and address of the little bald thief who just stole my truck." Wei stared directly into BT's eyes and said all this without flinching. BT was not one to be easily intimidated and looked directly back at Wei and said, "Can you give me a better description?"

"Let me help jog your memory!" Wei said and looked at Mountain Man and asked BT if he was his friend. But before BT could answer, Wei moved his hand ever so slightly and the first gunman pressed the trigger of his machine gun.

Just as Mountain Man's eyes were growing wide, a three-round burst from the AK-47 struck him so violently in the chest that it almost lifted his huge frame over the back of the booth where they were seated! Blood splattered all over the nearby seating, and one bullet exited through the front window. One lady screamed, one man threw up, another shouted "You'll never get away with this!" and the owner said, "Please! There's no need for anyone else to die!"

Wei looked at the owner and said, "I agree, but only if this gentleman will give me the information I have requested." The owner looked at BT and said, "For God's sake give him the information he wants, or we're all going to die!" Wei fixed his eyes back on BT. Making a point to move as slowly as he could, BT took a pen from his pocket and wrote down Cue's address on the back of an order receipt before sliding it across the table to Wei. Wei glanced at the address and looked back at BT and said, "This better be correct or we'll be back." BT looked Wei in the eye and said, "That's where you will find him."

Wei smiled and said, "See, that wasn't so hard, was it?" Then he turned to one of his men who had come in through the back door. Wei asked him in Chinese if he had gotten the surveillance footage from the surrounding CCTV cameras. The man answered back in Chinese that he had. Wei adjusted his collar, turned, and walked toward the exit. Just as he reached the door, Wei stopped and turned to look back before briefly nodding his head.

In the next instant, all four of the guns opened fire. There wasn't enough time to even scream! When the clips were all exhausted, there was just silence. Blood was everywhere along with broken glass, shattered china, and spilled coffee and food all over the floor and seating. BT's reign over that part of South Philly had come to a tragic ending. The last gunman to exit the diner turned off the master switch for all lighting in the diner, including the neon sign on the roof. Then he flipped over the sign on the door that said "Closed." As Wei's men left the diner and walked to the cars, Wei had them remove their bloodied shoes and place them in a black garbage bag for disposal before putting on a fresh pair of shoes. It was 1:37 am in the morning when they pulled out of the diner's parking lot in route to Cue's apartment.

It was 1:40 am and King Leon was still waiting for the last of the out-of-state attendees to arrive at the Hulmeville warehouse location to view the truck and its contents. The heavy rains had delayed both flight and ground transportation. The latest information stated that some could be as late as 4:45 am. King Leon was not happy with the delay!In the meantime he was having one of his bodyguards who was fluent in Mandarin translate the labeling on the electronics for the prospective buyers. One of the attendees approached King Leon and said that he would need to call his boss and that they might be interested in purchasing the truck and its entire contents. King Leon said if they wanted to do that, he would work out a special price and delivery at no cost to them! A number of the buyers were checking with their own experts via text and video regarding the potential value and use of the electronics. King Leon had several offers presented to him, but he was a shrewd businessman and knew they would soon be pressing each other, driving the offers up.

The King signaled one of his staff and they brought out some champagne and little sandwiches for the group. Everyone was in good spirits and complemented King on his good fortune. A couple of the buyers had brought experts with them and were constantly looking over the latest industry information to gauge the use and resale value of what they were viewing. One expert had a doctorate from MIT and looked a bit chagrined as he looked over the equipment. He was shaking his head and waving his hands as if to dismiss what the buyer was saying. Both men approached King Leon and asked in a low voice where and how he had acquired such advanced detection gear. The expert pressed King Leon for answers, which he refused to answer. "It's not that we are not interested," the buyer chimed in at this point. "But we're nervous that the Chinese are ruthless about protecting their tech stuff!"

"It's just that this stuff is like, well… most of us have never seen gear like this!" the expert went on to say. "If the CIA knew you had this gear, your life won't be worth a plug nickel…people get killed over this kind of gear and I don't want to be around when the big boys find out you have this stuff!" Then the expert walked back to the table to get another drink. The buyer told King Leon not to be concerned and that the expert had always been a bit "out there," that he was nervous by nature. As the buyer walked away, King Leon motioned to his head of security to double check the guards and lookouts. King Leon looked at his watch and decided to start the bidding at 4:30 am in the morning— regardless if everyone was there or not. Till then, King Leon would mingle with the group looking over the gear to see what other experts were saying.

The two black sedans pulled up just out of sight of Cue's apartment at 1:45 am. Wei told Ling to take one man and head for the rear entrance. For himself, Wei took one man along with Chang to confirm that the man inside was the thief who stole the truck. As Wei walked down the alley he kept an eye out for security cameras.

He knocked on the apartment front door.

Cue, his brother, and nephew were still celebrating! Cue was certainly not expecting to hear a knock at his front door at that late hour. Cue put his finger to his mouth for the other two to stop talking. Walking over to the window nearest to the door, Cue ever so slightly moved the curtain just enough to see who was at the door. The first face he recognized was that of the little guy from the back of the truck, the one who had pulled his mask off. Panic shot through his body and without a word to his brother or nephew, he sprinted toward the back door.

Just as he swung the back door open, Ling's large fist met with Cue's jaw and sent him across the room into a pile of boxes, where he lay...out cold.

When Cue came to, he saw his brother and nephew each seated in a chair with gags in their mouths and hands and ankles bound with fine copper wire that was attached to the chairs with cable ties. Cue could tell that they were both in great pain from the look on their faces. The color of their hands and feet was deep purple, the copper wire was cutting off blood flow. Cue was in full-scale panic by then and yelled, "Please don't hurt us! I'll do whatever you want!"

Wei stood directly in front of Cue and asked, "What did you do with my truck"? Cue was stuck: If he told the intruders where the truck is, King Leon would most certainly kill him, but on the other hand, it was clear that these guys meant business as well. He hesitated for just a moment. Thinking on his feet, he reasoned that these guys might do him the favor of taking out King Leon, so his best bet was to give up the current location of the truck. He looked at Wei who was clearly pissed that Cue had not answered his question yet.

But before Cue could say anything, Wei turned and motioned to the man standing behind his nephew. He turned back to Cue and said, "You waste my time and you will regret it!" Wei turned back to the man standing behind Cue's nephew and gave him the briefest of nods. Immediately, the man lowered a small, clear, plastic bag over his nephew's head. Cue could see the panic in his nephew's eyes and could not believe all this was really happening.

Instantly, Cue blurted out that the truck was in a warehouse in Hulmeville, just twenty minutes up the road. The man continued to lower the bag onto his nephew's head and tied it tight at the bottom. The nephew's chair was shaking violently as he tried to breathe. "Please! Please take the bag off!" Cue started to scream. "Look, I'll personally lead you to the truck. Come on man, take the bag off of his head! He's just a kid, oh God, no, no it was my idea, oh no, fuck man, I can't believe you would do this!" But Wei was unmoved, and his face was like stone; he showed no emotion as the wild movements of the nephew's chair started to decrease before finally coming to a dreadful stop. Cue and his brother had tears streaming down their face, and sobbing uncontrollably.

"Your hesitation caused that boy's death. If, for any reason, you further delay the retrieval of the truck you stole from me, the other man will meet the same fate," Wei said calmly. "The only way you can both survive is by giving me exactly what I want *when* I want it!"

By now, Cue wanted to attack Wei but knew he was outmanned and needed to go along with what he was told in order to save himself and his brother.

"All right man, I'll take you to the truck, but we need to make one stop first." Wei's head snapped around and focused on Cue. "Little man, you try my patience! I want my truck back now and you play games. Shall I have the other man meet the same fate as the boy?" Cue responded in a very subdued voice. "For God's sake no, no games! I dropped of a couple pieces of gear from the truck with a friend and I'm sure you will want them back. You gotta believe me, I'm being straight with you. I don't want anyone else to get hurt! Trust me, it will not take very long, its right on the way. I should probably call Junior, that's what he is called, to make sure he still working and hasn't left for home."

Wei smiled, "little man do you take me for a fool, there will be no phone call to warn your friend! I grow tired of your effort to delay the return of my truck. We leave now!"

Wei agreed to leave a man with Cue's brother at the apartment. The plan was that Wei would call and have the man release Cue's brother when the truck and gear retrieval was completed. Cue's last words to his brother were, "Don't worry, I will be back to get you!" Then Cue turned to Wei and said, "A deal is a deal, right?"

"Of course!" Wei replied with the same impassive expression on his face. They all left the apartment except for his brother and the man assigned to watch him. As they were getting in the car, Cue took a long look down the alley to his apartment. It was 2:28 am in the morning when one sedan pulled away from the curb and set off toward the pawn shop. On the way, Cue remembered how his father had once told him that one day, he was bound to get into trouble so deep that he could not find his way out. Cue now reflected that his father may have been right after all.

A few minutes later, they pulled into the back of the pawn shop.

Back at the apartment, Cue's brother's lifeless body was slumped in the chair, with a plastic bag over his head. As Wei's man was getting in the last sedan to depart, he glanced down the alley and could see the reflection of the flames from the fire he had started in the apartment. Of course Wei had lied, as he had done so many times before, but his principle was to never leave anyone alive who might be able to identify him.

At 2:38 am, the doorbell over the pawn shop's back entrance rang. Junior was just finishing the inventory verifications. Naturally, he was very suspicious of anyone who might be out and about at that time of the night. Just as a precaution he tucked his pistol into the back of his trousers. As he made his way over to the back door, he glanced at the security screen to see who might be outside. To his surprise, he saw that it was Cue. As he moved to open the door he removed the pistol from his trousers and placed it on a nearby table.

Disengaging the two heavy-duty locks, he swung the door open only to reveal a man with a machine gun standing next to Cue. Junior could tell by the look on Cue's face that this situation was not going to go down well. He knew his pistol lay just a few feet away and he thought that once he grabbed it, he could turn the table on its side to give him cover. He remembered that the table was topped with a layer of very heavy, gauge stainless steel. Another thought also raced through his mind that he would not even have to stick his head back up above the table to fire at the man holding the machine gun. He could just stick his gunhand up and fire in their direction. Furthermore, he remembered the time when he had been cleaning behind the table and was able to see his father coming through the back door due to the reflection off a nearby shiny stainless steel cabinet. All that went through his mind in a split second.

Junior put his hands up in the air and said loudly, "Don't shoot; I'm not armed!" As Cue and the gunman stepped inside, Cue momentarily stood between Junior and the gunman, blocking his line of sight. In a split second, Junior pivoted and made a leap for the pistol and got it on the first try. Seeing what was happening, Cue moved in the opposite direction to keep from getting caught in the crossfire.

Junior now had the gun firmly in his grasp and had a clear view of the gunman's position reflecting off the shiny stainless steel cabinet. From behind the table, Junior was getting ready to fire his first shot while yelling, "Eat lead motherfuck—" but just then, the yelling stopped mid-sentence and was followed by a dull thud, as Junior's lifeless body slowly slid from behind the table.

As it turned out, Junior's timing was bang on, but his luck was not. He was right to think that the table would shield him and that he could fire from a relatively safe position. However, it did not quite work out the way he had figured it would. The group entered the back room as his lifeless body lay bleeding all over some boxes of papers that had fallen over from the impact of the bullets. "See, you stupid little man," Wei hissed at Cue. "You have killed another due to your greed and incompetence."

It was clear to see where the bullets had ripped through the stainless steel table like a hot poker through butter. As Junior's luck would have it, the man operating the gun had used up his last clip of soft-nosed sub-sonic rounds at the diner. So when he got back to the sedan, he had opened the trunk and grabbed the first two full clips he found. One of those clips contained green-tipped, steel, armor–piercing bullets, which he had inserted into his machine gun. The table top did not even slow down or deform the bullets as they passed through the table top. The good news for Junior was that he didn't suffer. When the first bullets hit the table top, they did not mushroom as ordinary rounds would, but did deflect slightly in their path. After penetrating the table top one continued on and struck Junior in the right cheek, exiting through the back of his neck. In the end, Junior never knew what hit him.

Wei turned to Cue and pointed to his watch. Cue got the message and pointed out the two speakers and the yellow case that were from the truck. Wei's men loaded the three items into the trunk of the car. The man who handled the yellow case had never carried it before, so the reduced weight of the case, due to the removal of its contents, didn't cause him any concern. Junior's raincoat still covered the item that he had removed from the case. Cue mentioned that they should probably remove the pages from the receipt book that listed what Junior had received and put into the inventory. Wei promptly ripped out the pages that Cue pointed to and stuffed them into his pocket. Then he asked the unit leader to retrieve any security camera footage and to disable all surveillance systems.

Wei turned to Cue and said, "Now, where is my truck?" Cue said it was just a short drive up the road, and he would tell the driver where to go. Wei told the last man to make sure the lights were out and the door firmly closed. The sedan with Wei and Cue departed for Hulmeville at 2:55 am. The rain had started to intensify once again. The last man out the door had turned off the lights and pulled the door to shut it but the lock would not fully engage. The unit leader who was driving the second sedan was yelling at the man trying to shut the door, but it would not fully engage, so he pushed the door as far as it would go and then jammed a brick to hold it in place. Once he was sure the brick was going to hold the door in place, he ran to the car and they sped off, trying to catch up with the first sedan.

It was 2:57 am when the dispatch assistant came running down the hall to the offices of homicide and the vice squad. Howe and Kent were just finishing the night's report when he stuck his head into Lt. Kent's office and said, "You and the guy that runs the 24-hr diner down by the docks were good buddies?" Kent looked up and asked, "What do you mean *were*?"

"It's not pretty, preliminary report says ten dead, but it was such a mess that the patrol officer did not go in further then the doorway. I know you guys are beat, dead tired, and all that, but you two are the only ranking officers on duty." Kent and Howe looked at each other for an instant before hurriedly retrieving their weapons from the lockup, calling the photographer, and heading for their transport.

They arrived at the scene at 3:16 am. There were two patrol units already on station and they had taped off the place, so no one could affect the crime scene. Before they even entered the taped-off area they wanted to speak with the first patrolman to have arrived at the diner. After a couple of minutes, an officer came up to the detectives and said, "Officer Barr reporting, sir! I was the first officer on scene." Then he handed the two his report, saying, "You both might want to speak with that truck driver who first called 911. That's the guy," he pointed at a man sitting in the driver seat of a truck parked nearby. Howe waved the driver to come to their location, and when he did, they could see the man was still visibly shaken. He recounted that he had been running late because of the heavy rain and was due to deliver cases of Tastykake and Taylor's pork roll. "As I turned the corner I was surprised to see the diner dark with no lights at all. I thought there may have been a power surge and it overloaded the circuits to the point it burned them out. But as I drove further down the street, I noticed none of the other buildings appeared to be affected. So I backed up to the unloading ramp and got out of the truck, grabbed my clipboard, and walked up the ramp to ring the delivery bell. Then I noticed something very unusual: The back door was partially open. I opened it half-way and looked inside. Although no lights were on inside the diner, the street lights fell on a terrible scene. I could make out someone was slumped over the back of one of the booths, another person lay on the floor, and it appeared that half of his head was missing."

"I yelled 'anyone hear me?' There was no response and as the door opened wider, a slight breeze carried an unusual smell from inside the diner. After a while, I figured out that the smell was a mixture of burning grease from the grill that was still on and the blood that was... everywhere. I backed out of the doorway and quickly pulled the truck and trailer out of the unloading area. I stopped at the end of the street to call 911 and besides I was shaking so much, it was not safe for me to drive."

"I mean I've seen bad accidents before, but this is burned into my mind. I doubt that I will stay with the delivery company if they require me to stay on this delivery route. What is strange is that I was cursing the rain because I had to reduce my speed and it was making me late for my deliveries." Here, the driver paused and shuddered. "Now I realize that if it were not for the heavy rains, I would have been inside the diner with the rest of those poor folks. Oh, by the way, I saw no one arrive or leave the whole time I've been here."

After the man had finished speaking, Howe and Kent thanked him and said that one of the dayshift detectives who was already in route would take his formal statement.

The dayshift watch commander came in early in response to the diner murders. Immediately, he called to inform Kent and Howe that he had called the Pennsylvania State Police and they were sending down an investigative team and forensic expert to aid in the investigation; they should arrive within the hour. Kent and Howe were so tired that they were pretty much numb at this point. Kent suggested that they head back to the station and then home to get some much-needed sleep. But first they wanted to take a quick look at the scene inside the diner— not to step inside but just take a quick look.

They turned away, shaking their heads, but Howe abruptly stop short of the last step. As he glanced down, he noticed a gold-tinged reflection from the edge of the step. It was a spent cartridge. He reached down and with his pen and slipped it inside of the cartridge casing. As he picked it up, he realized that it had a familiar look. He pulled a plastic bag from his pocket that contained the casing he had picked up at the scene of the missing truck. Kent saw the two shell casings as well. Then they looked at each other and smiled, but they were too tired to pursue this clue at the moment.

As they prepared to drive away, they received a phone call from

FBI agent Cole. He had received the email, but resolution of the photos of all the Chinese personnel from the "missing-truck" mess did show up well on his phone. He was in route back from Washington and would stop at the office and take a look at the photos on his office computer. Cole recommended that until he had a chance to run them through the facial recognition equipment, that they back off and contact him before they confronted any of the other Chinese personnel. That was a strange request, to be sure, but they were so tired they just agreed and left it at that.

The detectives had just arrived back at the station when the dispatcher at the fire station number 34 called about a fire of suspicious origins and two victims who had been discovered at the site in a most curious condition: their hands and ankles tied with thin copper wire. Naturally, they wanted a detective on scene. Within five minutes, a 911 dispatcher called about a robbery and homicide at a pawn shop. Kent and Howe realized that dayshift was very short on personnel. They told the watch commander that they would come in to handle those cases *after* getting some sleep.

The two black sedans arrived on the outskirts of Hulmeville at 3:22 am as Cue directed them to the warehouse area. The rain was letting up, and the moon was finally appearing from behind the clouds. The cars pulled into the parking lot, just around the corner from the loading area. Wei warned Cue not to try anything crazy; otherwise his brother would suffer the consequences. Cue was, of course, still unaware of the fact that his brother's life had ended some time ago. Wei instructed Chin to ensure that his men had at least two full magazines just in case there was another prolonged gun battle. The group followed Cue around the corner to the personnel door. Pointing to the large number of cars parked nearby, he commented that the people who had been invited to look at the equipment must be here already.

As they approached the door, Wei and the rest of the group hung back, out of the range of the surveillance cameras. Wei asked Cue about the leader was, what his name was, and what he looked like. Cue pressed the doorbell and one of the guards inside looked through the small peephole in the door. He recognized Cue and radioed King Leon to ask whether he should admit him or not.

King Leon wondered why Cue had returned, but thought that now was as good a time as ever to eliminate a possible witness to the theft of the truck. As the guard opened the door he let his weapon swing down by his side. At that moment, the unit leader accompanying Wei pulled the trigger on his pistol and dropped the guard with one shot to the center of his chest. The use of the silencer and the group's distance from the main gathering meant that no one was alerted to the entry of Cue, Wei, and the rest of Chin's team.

Wei asked Cue where the other guards might be located. Cue indicated that they had just come through the warehouse entry /exit door and the rest of guards would be on an elevated catwalk that surrounded the bay where the truck was likely located. As they approached the truck bay, the noise from the conversations covered up the footsteps and the clicks issuing from release of the 'safety switch' on the men's weapons. A couple of the men moved in front of the group with instructions to take out anyone they sighted. The two men quietly turned the corner and took aim at the two guards on the catwalk.

With two quick *pops*, the guards went down. Surprisingly, the conversations had become so loud that no one was aware they were under fire. Wei and the rest of his team quickly came out with weapons raised as Wei shouted to the group to drop to their knees or they would be shot. A group of three men were standing by the truck; either did not hear Wei or did not believe him, thereby continuing to just stand there. Wei noticed them still standing; without a second warning, he pointed at them and with a short burst from his men's machine guns, they dropped where they had been standing. "There, that should be sufficient to show all of you that I'm serious," Wei said in a stern and demanding tone, as the rest of the attendees gaped at him in terror. "So the rest of you be quiet, or else!"

King Leon saw Cue standing with Wei's group and decided that he had been double-crossed by the sleazy little bastard. Incensed, he charged through the crowd, yelling in Spanish that Cue was a dead man. Cue tried to warn King Leon that this was not his doing, but before he could finish his sentence, Wei pointed at the King as he emerged from the crowd, and with another short burst, King Leon was hit in the shoulders and upper chest, which threw him back to edge of the crowd and into some trash cans. In the end, the King had met the same fate as BT. Now, there was a deathly silence in the room. Having gotten his point across, Wei said, "If you want to live you will do exactly what I say." Again, he was met with silence, so he smiled at the crowd and then said, "I think we understand each other now, I'm sure we can work things out!"

With the demise of the King, it was now clear to everyone who was in charge. Wei's men quickly positioned themselves so as to have clear lines of fire, while others got to work shutting down the sprinkler and security systems. Two of Wei's men moved to the truck's location; as one climbed behind the steering wheel, the other opened the truck bay overhead door. After opening the door, the truck was moved outside and the overhead door was closed behind it. As the truck moved out of the loading bay, the right rear tires left bloody imprints on the concrete as they passed through the pool of blood where the first three men had been shot. Two of Wei's men came over to him and whispered into his ear that everything was set. Wei took a moment to look around and then put his hand in the middle of Cue's back to shove him into the crowd of unlucky invitees. Then, Wei nodded again, and the machine guns opened their rain of bullets upon the crowd. Within seconds it was over and only a mass of bodies remained.

A few men, such as Cue, had tried to make a run for the exit but had gotten no more than a couple of steps before being cut down. Wei walked over to Cue's body and looked down at him for several seconds before turning and signaling for everyone to get back to the vehicles. Then he ordered the driver and personnel of the last sedan to quickly finish up here and follow the truck back to the house. Their instructions were to set the place and bodies on fire to cover up what had happened, which would hopefully slow down whatever official investigation would ensue.

Presently, they gathered up what they thought were small barrels of flammable liquids, presumably gasoline, and poured it over all the bodies and the surrounding structure. As fate would have it, only one of the small barrels contained gasoline while the rest had low-quality diesel fuel. Wei's team moved out on command as the last man fired up a couple of road flares and tossed them into the fuel-soaked pile of bodies. As the flares made contact with the gasoline, the whole area burst into flames with an explosive roar. Wei's men jumped into the sedan and headed back to the house in South Philly. Wei was sure that by the time the local fire department arrived, the whole complex would be a blazing inferno. As the gasoline burned off, the low-quality diesel was very slow to ignite and mostly sent up thick clouds of dense black smoke. As luck would have it, a police patrol car saw the dark smoke clouds against the slivers of moon light glowing against the smoldering portion of the warehouse. The fire trucks arrived quickly and with little effort put out the fire, thereby exposing the true nature of the ghastly incident that had taken place a short time ago. The chief of police was awakened by a call from the fire chief regarding what they had found at the warehouse. The police chief made quick calls—first to the state police office and then to the FBI office in Philadelphia.

About the time the fire department was putting out the blaze at the warehouse, the once-missing truck was back in the driveway from where it had been stolen a few hours earlier. Wei and Ling departed for their hotel some time before five in the morning. It had been a long and trying day, but in the end they had managed to clean up the mess the O/T unit had allowed in the first place. Wei was now more convinced than ever that his personal involvement was key to a successful outcome of the big plan.

It was just fifteen minutes past five in the morning when senior FBI agent-in-charge Tim Cole reached the agency field office; he was back from his two day stint in Washington. He had planned only a short office stay, just long enough to place some classified documents into the safe and check his emails. He was quickly going through the emails when he stopped again to peer closely at the photos sent to him by the Philly PD. He just stared at one of the photos for several seconds before reaching for his raincoat. As he searched the raincoat's pockets, he wondered if it could be possible, if the man in the photo on the screen would match the photo of the Chinese man that Steve North was seeking. He held the photo next to the emailed photo…and said to himself, "by God, it's the same man!"

A quick text with the accompanying photo to North's phone drew a quick response. Though he badly needed some sleep, North said that he was leaving DC immediately and should arrive in Philly by ten in the morning. His text also requested that Tim use his position as agent-in-charge to arrange a meeting with the police to appraise them of the whole situation, and to get them to back off— in the interests of national security, of course. Agent Cole said that he would do as North requested and then headed for the office sofa to catch a couple hours of sleep before the meeting at the SE Precinct Headquarters.

It was nine fifty in the morning when North arrived at the SE Precinct

Headquarters. He was quickly escorted into a private conference room. When he entered the room, Agent Cole stood up and introduced him to the Precinct Captain Simpson and detectives Kent and Howe. Captain Simpson said he appreciated the Major driving all the way from DC to get to the meeting, but expressed some hesitation at any hint of taking his officers off the investigation that might include the Chinese man in the photo! North listened intently to the information that Kent and Howe had collected. The Captain then added that a couple more "incidents" could be linked to this man and the "operation" that he appeared to be deeply involved with. The press was hounding the SE Precinct Public Affairs Officer for more information! He was currently feeding the press the old line that it was still too early in the investigation to have any concrete leads, but the incidents looked to be "gang related." The Captain put down his cup of coffee and leaned forward to make his point, saying, "What have you got for us that would be a valid reason for us not picking up this guy and squeezing him for information until his eyes pop?" Then he picked up his coffee cup and leaned back in his chair, waiting for North's response.

North had been going over what he could and could not share with the police as some of the information he had at his disposal would certainly be considered highly classified. To the extent to which other countries and agencies were involved in this situation made the whole thing even trickier. North took a long thoughtful pause, then a sip of coffee, and began with why the case must be appropriately handled in order to reveal the true extent of Wei's intent and goals. "Given what I know thus far, his actions could lead to what I believe could be major loss of life and property here in the United States!"

"I know you have your local issues to deal with, but if we step in too soon, some of the aspects of the operation that this man is heading will likely be driven underground, meaning we will not be aware of, or prepared for the death and destruction this man or the government he works for are prepared to inflict on the people we are sworn to protect," North said in an even tone. "I can tell you that I've been involved in an ongoing trail of events that I'm sure point to this man and to his government. These events involved several murders overseas and other actions that—given enough time and the right circumstances—will lead us to the heart of what he is planning and prepared to do in the service of whatever this operation requires. I must warn you that his preferred reaction to those that stand in his way is almost always lethal. I assure you that what I do know and can relay to you is his resolve to execute his mission regardless of who or what might be in his way. I have knowledge that he spares no one, has killed men, women, and children, and even slaughtered their family pets! I realize that you are under pressure from several stakeholders to crack cases as quickly as possible, but in this case that would not mean the best outcome for your city, the country, and maybe even the world. I have already told you more than what I should have, but I desperately need you to trust and to give me, *us*, more time to fully understand the plan he is here to execute!"

As North finished speaking, everyone was silent. At that moment, all they shared were looks of disbelief. After a few more seconds, Agent Cole spoke up. "I can confirm his position with the NSA.I have known and served on active duty with North for many years in the Marine Corps; his current rank gives him the perfect platform to understand and link the civilian and military aspects of the case that we're currently pursuing. So I can assure you that if you trust him on this, you will not regret it."

Kent was the first to speak up. "I wouldn't give a rat's ass about trusting the NSA, but a fellow Marine? Now, that's good enough for me. I say we leave the hook in the water, so to speak, and see what else we can catch." Captain Simpson looked at Kent and Howe for a minute, as if marshalling his thoughts together. Then he said, "I think the gang-shootout-over-territory storyline should hold up a little longer. Okay, let's keep the information active and flowing in real time!" North asked if he could ride along with Kent and Howe to the house from where the truck had been supposedly stolen. "Okay," replied Howe in a nonchalant voice. "But first we have three other crime scenes to look at."

The first location was a partially burned apartment with two bodies. As they pulled up in front, the two detectives immediately scanned the area looking for security cameras that may have recorded any questionable activity. At first they missed it, but upon climbing over some trash cans, they noticed a camera mounted over the neighbor's garage apartment. Howe sent one of the uniformed officers to acquire a copy of any recordings from last evening. They ran the tape as soon as the officer came back with it. The quality of the recording was poor, but it did show several men coming and going. Yet their faces were not clear enough to identify them. But when they watched through the tape a second time, one figure stood out, his distinctive colorful Hawaiian shirt giving him away!

No one said a word; they just looked at each other. A few seconds later, one of officers from the fire department's arson investigation team came over and tapped Kent on the shoulder, saying, "There's something you need to see." He led the three men over to what was left of the two individuals who had been burned up in the fire. He pointed to their hands and feet; they were tied to the chair by thin copper wire. "That must have really been painful," the inspector commented. When North saw the copper wire, he knew it was the signature of the same team that had butchered Will and his family. Howe asked one of the officers to run the address through state records to confirm who lived there. The officer replied, "I don't need to, sir. This is where Cue lives."

"Who or what is Cue?" Kent shouted back. The officer yelled back, "You remember him, don't you? The little bald dude we picked up for trying to hustle teen girls into prostitution."

"Oh yeah, he seemed harmless enough," Kent replied. "I wonder what he could have done to draw the wrath of these guys."

"There's nothing more we can do until forensics turns in its report; let's move on to the pawn shop shootout location," said Howe. "It's about ten minutes north of here."

As they arrived at the pawn shop, dispatch called and urged Kent and Howe to call the Captain right away! Kent and North went inside as Howe got on the call. It was several minutes before Howe joined them inside the pawn shop. When he did come in, he had a very serious look on his face. He came over to North, looked him directly in the eyes, and said "Just what are we dealing with? These two guys you have been trailing…the Captain got a call from the head of the state police to inform him that the Hulmeville city police had received a call from the fire crew about a warehouse fire. They got there only to discover twenty-one bodies! They had all been shot, doused with gasoline and diesel, and set on fire—just like the last location we were at! You weren't kidding, Major! We have got to stop these guys now before they do any more damage!"

"But can we be sure it was our guys?" Kent interjected at this point. "Isn't it a bit early to assume it was the same guys"? Howe looked at Kent and replied, "An early morning jogger spotted two black sedans sitting, engine running, under a parking lot light and heard the men inside speaking in Mandarin Chinese."

"How could the jogger be so sure it was Chinese?" Kent responded. "The Captain asked that very question," Howe said. "The witness had worked in Japan for several years, dealing with several Chinese shipping companies, and was sure that they were speaking Chinese. He also remembers seeing a medium-sized truck leaving with the two sedans escorting it—one in the front and one following behind."

"So the truck was stolen. They found it and took it back by whatever means necessary!" Kent mumbled to himself. "Now you're getting the picture," North spoke up at this point. "Whatever it is they are working toward is so important that they are willing and able to silence, kill, pay off, and—by whatever means necessary—remove all obstacles that may hinder their efforts to accomplish their mission. I hope you now understand if we stop them too soon, I fear we will not understand their main mission, which I'm now convinced will be far deadlier then we can imagine."

With this ominous announcement, they turned their attention to the matter at hand: the robbery of the pawn shop and murder of the shop owner's son. As they entered the pawn shop, it was clear that there had been a shootout. Several bullet holes adorned the wall and there were several more in the stainless steel table top. Howe picked up one of the spent cartridges and immediately saw that it was a match to the one he had found in the gutter at the house in South Philly. The pawn shop owner was sitting by the front counter, very depressed and sobbing over the loss of his son. The detectives introduced themselves and questioned him on what was missing, assuming that it had been a robbery gone wrong. The owner looked up at the detectives and said, "That's what's so strange! When I left around seven in the evening, we had just finished a complete inventory and needed to be verified it in the master accounting book where we record everything we receive or sell. When the inventory is complete, we start a new page for any new acquisitions. That's what is so hard for me to understand: Nothing seems to be missing except for a few dollars from the cash register. I mean the safe door was partially open, but the cash is still in there. It almost seems as though he had received something in the inventory, and then they wanted it back. That's why they ripped the pages out so no one would know who or what was involved in that exchange. Another thing, my son may have not been *the sharpest knife in the drawer*, but he knew you do not open the back door after you close, unless it's for someone you're very familiar with. You see his coat by the back door? He should have just left by the midnight, but he said he had something going that would really impress me."

"Did he say who or what that might be?" asked Howe.

"No, he did not," Junior's father said in between heart-wrenching sobs. "Please catch whoever killed my son! He was all I had!" Howe put his hand on the father's shoulder and said, "We'll do our best, sir. You can be sure of that." The owner picked up his son's raincoat that was lying by the back door to take it home. The raincoat had covered a small bright yellow machine about the size of a large tool box. North's eyes immediately focused on the lettering on the side: It was Chinese. North turned to the owner and asked where and when he had acquired that item. "I've never seen that before and if I had, it would be recorded in the ledger and that would have shown up during the inventory. I have no clue where that came from or what it is."

North nudged Kent and nodded toward the yellow box. "We would like your permission to take the item for further examination as evidence," said Kent. Just then, Howe received a call from Sgt. Barr who was at the diner where the shooting had taken place. Dr. April Farrow, the forensics expert, had concluded her initial review. Did they want to hear her conclusions and preliminary findings or did they want to wait for the report? She had a spotless reputation for accuracy and was able to deliver findings that held up even under the heaviest cross-examination by the best defense attorneys in the business. "We'll be there ASAP!" said Howe. As they headed out the door, North picked up the bright yellow box and placed it in the trunk of the car.

As they arrived at the diner, they noted a crowd of reporters gathered around a petite woman wearing white coveralls. They were throwing technical questions, like time and weapons used, but nothing seemed to bother her until one of the reporters asked the question, "Did you think that you could actually figure out what took place so soon?" She stopped walking and turned to the reporter who had asked the question, just staring at him for a second.

In a stern voice the woman replied, "I'm in charge of the State

Forensics Lab because I know what I am doing and do it better than anyone else, so should you ever question my capabilities or reputation I will never, and I mean *never*, answer any of your questions in the future!" Then she motioned to one of the uniformed officers, snapping out the words "Get these halfwits and morons away from me!"

As Kent and Howe approached the small woman in white, a smile appeared on her face. The detectives had worked with her before and she trusted them. "Ah, two men I can trust, finally! Is this mess going to be your case?" She motioned toward North and continued "is he with you guys?" Howe responded with a thumbs-up sign. Howe asked, "Can you give us any insight into what this guy will do next or the way he tends to think based on your preliminary impression of the scene inside the diner?" She looked down and took a deep breath before saying, "Look, all I can say is that what took place here does not even scratch the surface of what this guy is capable of and he is far from finished!

"Most bad guys do not overkill when they start out, because they do not want to get caught, but this guy doesn't give a shit about getting caught, because what I can tell you is he doesn't think he will ever have to pay for what he has done…which tells me he has gotten away with this kind of stuff in the past. Most importantly, you guys better be careful because you guys could be next!

"Look at this massacre as a gesture, a sort of an invitation, as it were. It reminds me of my brother's research paper where he had uncovered a rather disturbing program the Nazis were working on but that never materialized. It was all in the theoretical stages. The Russians got to it before we could and then in turn passed it to the Chinese. The story sort of dies there—except bits and pieces would pop up from time to time. The latest rumor is that the 'process,' as the Commies refer to it, has found a home and proven very successful when used on those extreme believers of socialism." Here, the woman paused for a while, looked around to check for eavesdroppers, "You should talk to my brother Vince; he used to be a professor of history, but he found things going on at the universities that he could not morally support. Now he has a position at one of those think tanks, so you might as well give him a call. Now, back to the issue at hand... no doubt you're aware of what happened at Hulmeville. From the initial report from the officers on scene, I can say that the same guy is responsible for what happened here."

"Give my brother a call," she repeated. "He may provide you with the insight on what might come next, but I warn you, you may not like what you hear."

"Let's go see if our two favorite suspects have anything new to add to their stories. Hey, North do you want to meet them face to face or hang back?" Kent asked jokingly. "I think it's very important that they think they're only dealing with local law enforcement," North replied. "I don't want them thinking they are being suspected by anyone else. I want to ride along, but I do not want them to see my face. There have been rumors for some time that certain foreign governments have acquired personnel photos and addresses for everybody at the NSA as well as the FBI. I know it may seem inappropriate for you guys, it would better serve us if you both seemed less aggressive and even apologetic toward them—like you might be if the Mayor was forcing you to back off. But don't take it too far. I'm sure that seems like a lot to ask, but we need to have them feel free to continue with their plan. Once I can confirm they're the men I've been seeking, the FBI's surveillance teams will immediately become available and I will have NSA assets at my disposal."

"Kent.... just think of it as though you're back in your high school and you're acting in a play," Howe chimed in. "All you have to do is to be a completely different person! A *pleasant* one for a change!" That comment brought smiles all around.

CHAPTER 5

EYE TO EYE

As the three arrived at the Chinese O/T unit's house in South Philly, the "missing truck" was back in the driveway. Pulling up in front of the house, they saw Wei and Ling walking toward their vehicle. Wei signaled for Ling to stay back as the detectives walked up the lawn. Howe commented, "Well, you were right: The thieves must have taken it for a joy ride and here it is—back where it was, just as you said it would be!"

Kent spoke up at this point with a convincingly apologetic expression. "We're sorry for any misunderstanding; you see, the Mayor helped us understand that you had a tough job running things, especially given the difference in languages and all that!" Wei took a second to look at the new vehicle they were driving, particularly its dark-tinted windows. He commented that there was someone else in the back seat. Howe said, "Oh him, an intern considering a job in law enforcement."

"Yeah, how do you like our new ride?" Kent cut in, trying his best to distract Wei from focusing on North who was sitting in the car. "Our other car broke down just at the right time when we got this new SUV in; I guess it was our lucky day." Because of the angle at which sunlight fell on the tinted windows, North could not definitely confirm Wei was the man in the photo, no matter how hard he strained to look. As the two detectives entered the vehicle, he attempted to peer through the open door, but by then Wei's back was turned.

In a desperate attempt to confirm Wei was the man in the photo, North lowered the backseat window about half way as they were slowly pulling away. North took one long, last look at the photo then looked up and out the window. In those passing few seconds, as the window lowered, Wei had turned and moved closer to the vehicle. As North peered out the window, Wei looked in and for a split second they were looking eye to eye. As the vehicle picked up speed down the street, their eyes followed each other, even as North was raising the glass. North now knew for sure he had finally located the man who had killed a dear friend and his family. He also realized that he had made an error by letting Wei get a good look at him and hoped that the cover story of him being an intern "ride along" would stick.

As they drove away, North looked back down the street and wondered, *Just why a house full of Chinese men would choose to sit in a house with no air conditioning during the hottest time of the year?* North wondered where the street lead to and what was down there. Perhaps sensing his unspoken questions, Kent said, "This area's what's left from housing for the workers and ship builders of World War II, the ones who built the 'Liberty Ships.' They leveled parts of the neighborhood and converted it into dock fronts and warehousing. Nothing special down there, as far as I know."

"Is there any way to access that area without going by the China house?" North persisted.

"Yeah, if you know the right people you can come through a series of gated facilities and approach it from the opposite direction."

"Without being seen by our Chinese guests?" North repeated.

"Yeah, what do you have in mind?" By the time Kent spoke these words, North was already on the phone with Agent Cole. "It's him," North began without a preamble. "We'll need multiple teams, and I'll get my folks moving. You know we are going to need a slew of wiretaps and the best crypto and data encryption teams you guys have. "I'll send you a picture of a piece of gear that I'm sure belongs to our boys, but I don't want to return it until we know what it is for and how it operates. I need the feedback on it ASAP."

Not even ten minutes after North had sent Agent Cole the photo, Cole received a call from headquarters, saying, "As we speak there is a chopper in route from Quantico with an expert on radiation detection gear. When they saw the photo they got very excited, as they had been trying to get their hands on this brand new device for some time. They'll be there in twenty minutes or less."

As North and the detectives pulled into the FBI secured parking area, a couple of agents armed with shotguns escorted them to the building's fifth floor where the experts were waiting. The room contained a live video feed to the DC HQ as well as several other pieces of equipment. As the experts examined the equipment North had brought in, they removed the side panels and exposed a series of circuit boards. They continued to inspect and probe the machine for the next hour.

While the experts worked on the machine, the surveillance teams were working through the details of what they needed to begin their monitoring. When the team of experts was through the device, the four were invited back into the room. The lead technician put the reassembled device back on to the conference table and started his briefing. "You may have wondered what the devil this is. This an amazing little piece of gear. It's a radiation detector, but not just any old 'radtech;' it's so advanced at what is does that it can find the one radioactive needle in a billion haystacks so to speak."

He turned to North and asked, "How did you even come by such a valuable piece of equipment?" North did not reply to the question, instead asking, "What would that piece be used for in Philly?" The expert looked a bit perplexed and replied, "To detect nuclear weapons? That's what it's built for!"

He went on to say, nuclear weapons can be reduced in size so they can fit in a briefcase. Using the proper shielding material in the briefcase's construction, the bomb would be undetectable except by a machine such as this one. "So what does this do that others can't?" Howe cut in. "Well, that's a bit complicated…but to put it simply, this machine measures the frequency of the waves created by the shielding material that blocks the radiation created by the fissionable material that makes up the bomb. Each type of shielding creates a different pattern based upon its construction and the fissionable material, yield, and destructive power of the device. You have given us what we have needed for some time. Now we can build our own!"

Kent asked, "Does this mean they're bringing nukes into Philly"?

"No, they would not," North spoke up. "That would essentially be an act of war, and their whole operation was meant to be more subtle. They were placed there to detect…but what in the rundown neighborhood in South Philly are they trying to detect?" North turned to Kent and asked, "You said you could get me access to the warehouse area further down the street without going by China house, correct?"

"Yeah, but I'll have to make a couple of calls first."

"Okay, then make those calls!" North replied before continuing, "Agent Cole, is there anyone on your staff who can write Chinese? If so I need to see him or her right now." A few minutes later, a man came in, saying, "Hello, Major North, I'm Agent Kevin Chang, and I heard you needed someone who writes Chinese?"

"Agent Chang, I need you to write something on this tag for me in Chinese, something very specific, but not too neat. Write the same message I have written here on this piece of paper, but on that blank tag, understand?"

"Yes sir, I understand. In Chinese. On this tag you just gave me."

Watching this curious scene unfold, Howe asked North what he was up to. "First we need to get this machine back where it belongs—with our Chinese friends. Second, I need to figure out what they're here to detect."

"Just how do we get it back in their hands without raising some concern on their part?" Kent asked. North replied, "Now, that's the easy part; someone will just carry it up to the truck and leave it there. One of the sentries will come upon it and return it to wherever it was supposed to be—it's that simple."

"Ha...did someone put some liquor in your coffee when you weren't looking? Why do you think that will work?" Howe asked in disbelief.

North's reply was simple and straight forward. "In Chinese, the tag says 'This equipment has been checked and calibrated. Return to designated location.' And I'm betting one of those men will do just that: follow instructions! Do you really think any of them want Wei to ask them why they had left such important piece of equipment lying around. So I'm betting they don't want to complicate their lives again with putting up with another visit from the madman Wei. So they'll just do what the tag says.

"We'll get one of the smaller and much faster patrolmen to sneak up by the truck, place it on the ground, and run like hell," Howe replied. "Now that you put it all together, that sounds like a good idea after all. I've got just the patrolman in mind for the job. I'll have him pick up the device and make sure he understands what exactly we want to happen. We can count on him and he knows how to keep his mouth shut."

At this point, Kent returned from attending a phone call. "Okay, everything is set. We can go all the way through to the other side and not have to pass the China House."

That night, the three men were at the last locked gate. Beyond that, at about 600 yards further down the road, was the Chinese O/T unit's house. There had been nothing remarkable for the last quarter of a mile, but looking down the road, they noticed that behind some tall trees sat a non-descript building that did not look like a typical warehouse. Its 14-ft concrete and barbed wire–topped walls and reinforced entry /exits piqued North's interest. A very small sign over the personnel gate read "International Security and Transfer." Since North had never heard of them, he scanned the NSA records to see what they were and what they dealt with. To his surprise, he found that the lease to the building had been secured by the US Air Force and DARPA (Defense Advanced Research Projects Agency). Just why they had this location confused him; per his understanding, they always chose rural locations. As he approached the front gate, he could see a uniformed guard behind the thick bulletproof glass. North often glanced up toward China House to ensure no one could see him. The guard asked, "What can I do for you, sir?" North showed his NSA ID and requested to enter the facility. The guard said, "Sorry sir, but you're not authorized to enter."

North began to say "I am deputy—" but the guard finished his sentence for him, saying, "Deputy Director China Intel Unit! Yes sir I know. The guard asked him, to move on. When North looked at the guard's face, he could tell that the man meant business, so he quietly backed away and returned to the car. Kent asked if everything was okay, but North did not reply. In fact, North did not say anything else until they got back to precinct HQ.

Based on the recommendation by the forensics expert he had met at the diner, North placed a call to The Washington Institute, a think tank located in rural Bucks County, just outside Philadelphia. North requested a meeting with Vincent Farrow, visiting professor in the History and Classics department. "He could meet with you over breakfast for about an hour, starting at 7:45 am tomorrow, otherwise he is due to fly abroad and would not be back for ten days. Shall I confirm that meeting for tomorrow, Sir? Yes, OK, your meeting is confirmed." North turned to Kent and Howe, "I have a breakfast meeting scheduled at the Washington Institute tomorrow morning;

are you interested?" They both nodded their heads and said they would pick him up at half-past six the next day.

After checking out the warehouse area beyond China House, North arrived back at his hotel room, as he sat down to relax, there was a knock on the door. North was not expecting anyone, he pulled out his pistol, looked through the peephole…and saw an old friend from many years ago.

"Dan Kelly, you old bastard you!" he exclaimed, opening the door. "What's the occasion?"

"Grab your coat," said Dan. A tall thin man, with red hair and a firm handshake. "I know a little Italian place, and you're gonna love it!" As they walked down the street, they talked about when they had first entered the Marine Corps. They talked about family and friends. Dan said, "What did you want at the warehouse in South Philly?" North was shocked. "How did you know I was visiting a warehouse?"

"How did I know?" Dan replied with a dry chuckle. "Because that's one of my operational facilities. You see I work for a branch of Air Force Intel, mainly dealing with ways for creating deception and misinformation. Should conflict break out, our enemies will be targeting classified facilities, such as the warehouse on the South Riverfront that they believe is housing advanced weapon systems. But in reality, it's just a decoy structure meant to draw their attention away from a location that holds 'real' weapons."

When Dan finished explaining, North briefed him on the Chinese team he had been pursuing and the nuclear detection gear that they had discovered. Oddly enough, his old friend did not seem at all surprised. "We've known about all that for some time," said Dan. "Because of your clearance level, I can paint you a more complete picture. No doubt you've heard that we've been working on a hypersonic cruise missile as well as on shrinking the size of nuclear payloads. Well, we've had those two in the bag for some time now. We have reduced the size of the nuclear warhead payload down to the size of a football, with a yield of anywhere between five and ten kilotons. Also, with the latest improvements, we have cruise missiles approaching speeds of 6200 mph. The missiles also have redirection capabilities. Suppose you fired two missiles at a target two minutes apart. Then if the first one gets the job done, by the time the second one gets there you can redirect it to another target."

"Now you can guess what comes next: Somehow the Chinese found out about it. Appears to be a high-level leak from the White House, which we're still looking into. That really set the Chinese back on their heels. Then a couple of senators started talking about giving Taiwan some of the mini-nukes along with the cruise missiles. Well, that sent the Reds into orbit, and they've been paranoid from that point on, even though the administration has denied that they would even consider it. Shortly after that fiasco, we got a strange report of the Chinese buying up farms near the bases where we stored the mini-nukes and advanced cruise missiles. We think they're purposely tracking where we store them, primarily to ensure they know whether or not we've made good on our promise not to supply them to Taiwan. So yes, we're aware of their monitoring efforts."

"The Chinese use what they refer to as Observation and Tracking units. As a cover, the O/T units actually monitor day-to-day weather conditions, air particulate levels, effects of solar flares and other such issues to provide relevant climate change data, when needed. They compile that information and ship it off to Princeton University for climate change research. However, their main goal is to ensure Chinese target specialists keep up on America's advanced weapons locations in the event of a war breaking out. More recently, they have really been concerned that we would sneak out some of those advanced weapons to Taiwan. So, essentially we keep playing a cat-and-mouse game. My job is to keep them guessing so they stay busy chasing ghosts."

"But why let them continue to operate?" North asked.

"By keeping the O/T units engaged and occupied, we control what we want them to know," Kelly responded. "My operation actually directs them *away* from where we really house those systems. We've moved them from time to time, so currently the Reds are monitoring locations that only house decoys, including the Philly location."

North asked, "Why would they monitor a location where you have no weapons?"

"We know they have a reader that can detect our smaller warheads in transit, so we crate up mock cruise missiles and warheads that are tuned to activate the O/T's 'reader' device and fool it into thinking there's an actual warhead inside the canisters. We move them from time to time, as an exercise, just to keep the Chinese O/T units from getting too lazy. In fact, our Philly location is long overdue for a drill."

North leaned in and asked, "So for a drill, you just load them up, truck them out to an air force base and fly them out?"

"Yep, that's it."

North said, "I may need equipment like that in the near future… for an exercise."

"Really, that would mean we would not have to conduct one. How many of each would you need?"

North thought for a second before saying, "How about twenty-five of the mini-nukes and a hundred of the hypersonic cruise missiles?"

"Great, I'll put in an authorization release for those for an NSA exercise, on your signature. I usually turn to McGuire AFB over in Jersey because it's close by, and they keep a reasonable number of C-17 transports on hand. Plus they know how to handle the canisters to make it all look real."

"One more thing, if you do use the McGuire AFB, just call Col. V. Adams. We've got it all scripted out, and he can take it from there," Dan stood up and clapped his hands, saying, "Well that's it in a nut shell. Now you're one of only a handful who know what game we're playing, just to keep the Chinese guessing. Anyways, got to run, Steve. It's been great to see you again; I just hope we'll have more time in the future. Now I'm off to Alaska!"

It was almost eight in the morning when they arrived at the dining hall of the Washington Institute. Inside, they saw a tall, curly-haired man in a dark grey suit reading the Wall Street Journal. Once he looked up, he motioned for the three to join him. They introduced themselves, and after ordering coffee for each of them Professor Farrow asked what he could do for them. "My sister called me with an update on the situation you're involved in. I'm not sure how I can help, gentleman. I'm not a profiler of people—that's more in her line of work—I'm concerned more with how governments can perhaps incite or embolden their citizens to commit actions that, in some cases, may be well beyond what we'd consider appropriate."

"Actually that's more to the point," North cut in smoothly. "Given what Wei has done so far, do you have any insight on how far the Chinese will let this guy go to achieve their goal, whatever that might be?"

"Let me provide you with a frame of reference…."

"The Declaration of Independence and the Constitution are monumental examples of the triumph of classical thought of higher visions of what man can achieve as an individual."

"My point…in 'our classical perception of society,' individual or personal responsibility, or accountability are not deferred. In other words, your acts always come back to haunt or define you. As an individual, for your future, bound to reflect, consider, held accountable and answer for 'your' decisions or actions, good or bad. Not so for the political left and I choose to use that term to include socialist, communist, progressive elites-- who believe that individuals must surrender themselves for the greater good of society, with ever-diminishing room for individual expression. So rather than holding themselves accountable, the group or society as a whole now bears that burden. So the individual identity of a person or more often a mob committing an act we might find inappropriate, is now spread out, to the point where the individual is no longer held accountable, so long as the sin is generally reflective of the elites in control. Like in China were during Mao's Cultural Revolution, the children were turning in their parents for any perceived error against the society. Or in the late 60's when millions of Chinese starved to death due to mismanagement and blind obedience toward leaders who, like the rest of their society, felt no moral obligation for the famine they had caused and fostered."

"Through personal responsibility and effort, the United States has contributed more to peace, prosperity and security than any other nation in the last two hundred years. Yet, individual differences in ability, interests, motivation, beliefs, and drive are foundational for much of America's success are only acceptable to the left only so long as the outcomes for all individuals are equal. Rather than promote and encourage those traits that have proven successful, there is an ever growing drumbeat to conform. What all of that boils down to is, if you favor conformist and reject the individual, you will find it difficult to punish the mob, so no one is held accountable or gets punished.

"Often religious values assist society in controlling individual actions. It is fascinating, the left generally hates religion, but they effectively use the Judeo-Christian teachings and code of ethics to induce guilt and shame or convince people that unless they go along with the left's societal programs and beliefs, then they're not living up to their religious values.

An odd thing about this whole process is that the 'the hard core' left and its followers, as I refer to them, still adhere to all of the trappings, benefits, and pleasures they get from what that 'sin-laden' society has created, even while they 'campaign' against it."

"Since he (Wei), feels minimal pain or remorse, and is certainly not held accountable for what he has done or will do for attaining their version of society, he will stop at nothing. I would say that if Wei's leadership approved what he has done or will do here in the US, then there's no telling what they might be up to in the future!"

Howe spoke up, "That's a pretty big leap, don't you think?"

"He apparently feels what he has done so far is justified against the end goal, whatever that may be. So it would seem to me that if he has participated in or directed the killing of at least thirty people in a very short time, he did so with a much larger goal in mind. I think that you'll uncover many more threatening aspects of his overall operation before it is over and done. And if he's successful, the casualties so far will pale compared to the numbers if they succeed. Good luck, gentlemen!"

As they walked out of the institute, Kent commented, "I think that was out there a bit." Then, turning to North, he asked, "Did you find out anything about that other building?"

"Nothing I can share," replied North. "Let's get back to the FBI office; I want to make sure the surveillance teams are up and running."

Soon after they arrived at the FBI office, the detectives departed for the precinct HQ for a meeting with Captain Simpson.

CHAPTER 6

PEELING BACK THE LAYERS

"**W**e got a hit!" shouted one of the members of the electronic surveillance team (EST). North waited to hear what they had picked up. "Wei just contacted Professor Nelson Lo, a senior climatologist at Rutgers University," replied Agent Santos headed up both the physical and electronic surveillance teams (popularly called "PEST"). "We'll get the complete transcribed conversation to you shortly, but in a nutshell, Wei contacted him to confirm an upcoming meeting of contacts that the professor is putting together. Shortly after that phone call, Wei made another phone call to someone at Teepee mini mart #36 in Spray Beach, New Jersey."

Even though North was impatient to see the transcripts, days of pursuing Wei and his men had taken a toll on him, so he dozed off for a few minutes—only to be awakened by a call from the CIA South American Chief Walt Allen. "I've got some good news and some very bad news," Allen began without preamble. "Our inside operative informed us that the head honcho for the portion of Leong's operation that will be conducted or controlled from the hotel is scheduled to arrive on flight 472 out of Madrid in forty-eight hours. Sealy wanted to know if you want us to pick him up from the airport itself or give him some rope."

North's reply was immediate and clear. "Do not touch him; just

ID and observe! There have got to be more players than just him, and I want them all!"

"The other piece of news is that our inside man stumbled across another ripple of whatever overall plan they're working on. The bad part is that it's already underway, and we have no good way to deal with it. From what we can tell, Leong had made an agreement with the Cuban regime to briefly recruit and train upwards of 300 men from Cuba, Haiti, and Venezuela to cross into the US via the southern border, along with all the other illegals, and on a given date, destroy certain transportation infrastructure. But with the border being so open, it would be near-impossible to ID, let alone apprehend, them. And on top of that, the administration has been for some time secretly flying illegals to different cities in the US, so that alone will create major problems. Sealy is trying to restore communication with an old contact in Cuba with the hopes that they can get him more information on the 300.

"Furthermore, the Venezuelan President's dealings with the cartels have revealed that they are paid with funds through an account set up by Leong and funded out of the Chinese embassy in Caracas. The Mexican cartels are paid to facilitate, intimidate, and coerce hundreds of thousands of Latin Americans into migrating through and overwhelming America's southern border. This gives a convenient cover to drug traffickers and potential bad actors entering the US. We're also picking up from our bank-monitoring folks that this operation may have connections with other overseas terrorist groups planning to ramp up illegal immigration across the US southern border from African and Middle Eastern countries—with the intent of eventually provoking social unrest across the nation. Sorry for the bad news. But that is not the worst of it: Our guy on the inside is dead."

"Are they onto us?" North was quick to ask.

"Fortunately no, the agent had a heart attack in his garden at home; it's sad and unfortunate, but now we're on our own and flying blind!"

Soon, Agent Santos arrived with the transcripts from Wei's conversation with Lo and the operator at Teepee # 36. The conversation between Wei and Lo yielded just what North had been hoping for: a chance to reveal and expose the deep assets Wei would activate to carry out the operation. North stressed to Agent Cole the importance of PEST's flawless performance during the operation in Beach Haven. "No sweat," Cole replied. "Agent Santos will take care of everything, and you'll be very impressed with the outcome. In fact he has come up with a way to actually participate in the BBQ party that they're having at the Lighthouse State Park." North commented that he seemed a bit older than other agents of his rank. "Ah, but his experience prior to his entry into the FBI has proved invaluable," Agent Cole responded. "He started a roofing company in college and became very successful. Then he gave it to his children and wanted to do something entirely different and ended up with the bureau. He often uses his former business as a cover during the PEST operations."

At this point, Santos came back with some additional transcripts from Wei's conversation with the Teepee operator. "How are you going to get invited to the BBQ meeting using your roofing experience?" North asked him.

Santos replied, "I'm not!"

"But Cole said you were going to somehow participate in the BBQ meeting by using your business background?" North persisted.

"I am!" Santos replied. From the look on their faces, he knew that they were missing something. "Let me clear up any doubts you may have regarding my role at PEST!" he began in a dynamic voice. "You see in the transcripts, when Wei and Lo talked about using the BBQ get-together as a cover for a meeting, Wei asked Lo if children were going to be present, and Lo confirmed that children would be there. In America, BBQs are family events, and there could be as many as twenty children, some as young as four. Then Wei voiced his concern about children being disruptive to the meeting, insisting that Lo come with a plan to minimize or eliminate the children's presence! That's where I come in. In high school and college, I ran a cotton candy concession stand to make extra money; this was before I started my roofing business. My uncle had owned one of those traveling kiddie carnivals that had food courts and games. So on occasion I would help out by working the cotton candy machine. I had a clown suit and a few side games that brought in some extra cash."

"When my uncle decided to get out of the business, he gave me the 'cotton candy' machine and the side games, which I operated for extra cash in high school and my first two years of college. And I still operate it today at community and church functions. The BBQ meeting is going to be held on public land, therefore, it is posted. I would, with your approval of course, approach Professor Lo and offer my services, which are guaranteed to keep the children occupied and happy—and that too at a price he could not pass up on! At least that's my plan!" Both North and Cole gave him a thumbs-up gesture, denoting their approval.

Once Lo finished his phone call with Wei, he started a series of phone calls to all his contacts. PEST efforts were to catalogue all the contacts, ID their family members, and begin independent investigations to check if there was another layer of operatives. Stakeout equipment was already on its way to Beach Haven so the personnel could observe each of the suspects and their families. Teepee #36 was already under constant observation and the FBI hacking team had already broken into the internal camera systems. Cole approached North and said, "We just found out that Wei and Ling have future reservations on flights from Philly to Chicago then on to San Francisco and then back to Philly!" North noticed that this operation that Leong had put together went much further than even he could have imagined.Santos was directed to notify both the Chicago and San Francisco FBI offices that they would need to co-ordinate with North and Cole for future operations related to Wei and Ling.

Cole remarked that he would need the Senior Regional FBI Agent's support to ask for the additional resources and went off to get that approval. After a few minutes he returned with the news that Senior Agent (SA) Albert Argo was on his way to the Philly office. Cole commented they were lucky to have SA Argo on hand to support their efforts concerning the Chinese operation. He was an old hand in dealing with some of the thorny issues during the first cases of the Chinese being accused of stealing technology from US companies. North recognized that he would probably have to lay out everything concerning Leong, the Australian murders, and the Venezuela operation for SA Argo, but if that's what it took to get his full support, then so be it! A call came through from SA Argo who said he would be there within the next hour and that along with a briefing from North and Cole, he would also like a PEST briefing from Santos.

It was approaching six in the evening when SA Argo finally took his seat in the conference room and made his opening comments. "I'm here to listen, but I'll be honest with you Major North, what you're asking for will mean other investigations being put on hold and/or set back by several weeks, based upon what I hear. You have the floor, so make your case and you better have a good one!" But before North could speak, Cole asked to make a few comments. "SA Argo, we recognize your involvement in many other cases that might seem to warrant more resources than what might be required for a couple of territory shootouts between rival gangs. I have known and been friends with Major North for many years, so trust me and hear him out and you will be thankful that he has involved us as soon as he did." Cole's comments were followed by a few seconds of silence from Argo; then he turned his head and nodded for North to begin.

North started with his friend's connection with a Chinese national who had stumbled onto the cover sheet of what appeared to be a legitimate operational order, and which had ultimately lead to the murder of his friend's entire family, including even his two dogs. "I'd originally thought this would just be a case of tracking down a couple of murder suspects. But I'm now certain of a much bigger operation that appears to threaten more American lives, with international implications."

When North finally checked his watch, it was almost eight in the evening. He had been at it for over an hour! Once he had finished his brief, Argo took several minutes to look through the supporting documents before he spoke. "Get me the Director on the line. If he has already gone home, then call him there! We've got a lot of work to do and I want to know where and what that son-of-a-bitch Wei is up to 24 hours a day." He asked for Santos to come into the conference room. Argo looked at him and said, "You have a huge task to get your PEST unit up and running. I will be here tomorrow at 8:00 am for your briefing, got it?"

"Got it, sir!" replied Santos in a firm voice.

At precisely eight the next morning, the meeting regarding the PEST unit status kicked off. The unit had IDed all the locations that the targets, would occupy. Most of the targets, including Wei and Ling, were not expected in the area for at least two to four days. That would give the unit time to work out the details and come up with back-up plans. Santos stressed that round-the-clock surveillance on ten targets and on the Teepee #36 store was going to require all the agents that could be assigned to him. "If you need my assistance to get additional resources, just let me know!" said SA Argo. "Thank you sir, that is what I was hoping you would say," Santos replied.

The PEST status meeting lasted over two hours, and at the end, there was uniform agreement that the operation was going to be a real test, given the fact that the targets' locations were all short-term rentals with other civilian personnel coming and going who were not targets of the investigation. A particularly important task was to determine exactly what part was Teepee #36 was to play in all this. From the monitored conversations, it was clear that it was to be a location that would play a central role in distribution, but of what? That was the big question. Santos remarked that they were lucky that one of the new agents had worked in a Teepee store in the summers and after classes while in college. He was assigned lead for the Teepee location. He had also helped install their security and camera systems in many of their stores since he was majoring in computer science. SA Argo informed Santos he would like regular updates, and daily reviews at 8:00 am and 4:00 pm.

The agents monitoring Wei's phone came into Cole's office to report that subsequent to the finalization of Wei and Ling's future travel plans to Chicago and San Francisco, phone calls had been made to specific individuals. The team had IDed them, and background checks had been run. They handed over the information to Cole and North who looked at the list and commented that Leong had done a masterful job of giving his west coast operatives the kind of background, professions, and locations that would minimize their detection. Two were accountants with small banks, one worked as the CFO for a medium-sized tech company, two worked in the medical field, one in state government, and one was an auditor for a large accounting firm. Their work locations certainly were widely dispersed and called into question just what their mission would be. For instance, four were stationed in relatively rural locations— Yakima and LaCenter in Washington State and Bend and Klamath Falls in Oregon. The other three were in Redlands and San Diego in California and Santa Fe in New Mexico. Their meeting date, time, and location had been set.

As North went over the list, he wondered if they would be planning the same covert activities as the east coast operatives. On August 2, these operatives were scheduled to meet at a little Chinese restaurant in downtown Oakland at eleven in the morning. Wei had directed them to get all of the necessary gear and to secure reservations at their assigned targets, but what the targets were was not mentioned. SA Argo asked if the west coast operatives were under surveillance at this time, and he was reassured that they were. At that point he wanted daily updates. Santos came into the conference room with an update: All PEST units were up and running as of July 17. The first of the operatives was due to arrive at their rental on Long Beach Island the next day at about noon. The rest were due to check in within the following twenty-four hours. Santos had been down there all night, making sure everything was good to go! "It's a madhouse on the island. It's the height of the tourist season, families and kids everywhere, so it was a real challenge, but we are 100% ready to go."

As the operatives and their families started arriving at the location, it just seemed the way it always is on family vacations or outings—pure chaos! Kids wanting to rush to the beach, moms wanting to apply more sunscreen, dads bonding over chilled beers, and so on. The BBQ was two days out, and Lo was very busy trying to arrange for all the food and refreshments. It was then that Lo received an email from Santos offering his "Cotton Candy Concession and Kiddie Games" services for a base price of $300, which would include one cotton candy for each child and one dollar for each additional cotton candy. Soon, Santos informed Cole that Lo had hired him, so he would have multiple cameras operating from the party. During the next forty-eight hours, the PEST units picked up no new information regarding the operation. The families just did what all families would do in such a setting.

The day of the BBQ had arrived and all of the PEST unit was up and ready. Video and voice surveillance units were already in place at the park. By eleven in the morning, everyone was there, including

Wei and Ling. Everyone seemed to be having a good time, especially the kids with their cotton candy and side games. Wei met with each of the operatives and said basically the same thing: He was in charge and if they did their part successfully they would be rewarded; if not, they and their whole family would face his wrath. Once their part of the operation was finished, they were to arrive at the El Norte Motor Inn in El Paso, Texas, as soon as possible and await for instructions to cross over into Mexico and then for additional passage to China. Around three in the afternoon, most of the families, especially the ones with small children, started to leave. As they left, Lo thanked them for coming and reminded them to stop by on the way home and patronize Teepee #36 in Spray Beach, since it was owned by a fellow Chinese businessman.

After the last of the operatives left, the PEST team met for a briefing of everything that happened at the BBQ event. To a man, they were all somewhat shocked that they had not picked up any new details related to the operatives' mission. The only information they had was the Teepee comment Lo had made as the families were leaving. A call was put through to the team set up to watch the mini mart. They were alerted that they might see some of the operatives stop by to pick up snacks or perhaps something else. Sure enough, one by one the operatives arrived at the mini mart and went in. Since the PEST team had hacked the internal security camera system, they could observe not only their arrival and departure, but their activities inside the store. The operatives did nothing more sinister than picking up some odds and ends, snacks and the like. At times, the owner had to go into the storage room to pick up some items that they had apparently run out of on the shelves. As the last of the operatives was checking out, one of the PEST unit members arrived from the BBQ operation.

As he sat down in front of one of the monitors, he almost knocked over his coffee. Something had caught his eye.

Pressing replay he watched the video feed three times but could not connect what he was seeing with what he thought he might be missing. He finished his coffee and was going to get another cup when he slowly turned around and asked the operator to play the video again! About halfway through the replay, he murmured "That's it!" Without saying another word he quickly walked out of the door and could be seen heading into the mini mart. They were able to observe him as he walked up and down the aisles, putting various items into his basket. So far they did not observe anything that could seem out of place. After a few minutes, he went to check out, paid for the items he had picked up, and departed the store. Coming back, he emptied the contents of his basket onto a table and stepped back, saying, "I almost missed it!" The rest of the team looked at him with puzzled looks on their faces. "I worked part-time at a Teepee mini mart while I was going to college," began the agent, "and I remembered how the parent company strictly instructed the franchisees to use or carry only those items that were on an approved list and warehoused by the company. If you violated that policy, you could face a big fine or they might not even renew the franchise lease. So when I looked at what the last guy bought, something stood out. Unless you were familiar with what the stores are allowed to stock, anyone would have missed it. Play the parts that show the checkout for each of the operatives and let's see if I am onto something." After reviewing each operative's purchases, they replayed the PEST team member's checkout. One of the team members reluctantly ventured a guess. "The only thing I noticed was you bought a different brand of milk."

"No, you are incorrect...I bought the *only* brand of milk that the Teepee Corp. allows their franchisees to carry! Notice the carton is basically yellow, but what the operatives walked out with is a mostly blue carton...they each got something that was not supposed to be in that store. I took a close look around and the milk cartons they each walked out with was special, just for them. As I remember it, the blue cartons are an ACE Supermarket brand. Someone in their operation made a mistake and used the wrong cartons. Trust me, I looked all over the store and didn't see any of those cartons. I even looked into the dairy storage locker, pretending to look for a yogurt I knew they didn't sell. And if we look closely, I'm willing to bet that the only thing consistent with each purchase is that half-gallon, blue milk carton!" Turning to Cole and North, he said, "We've got to get our hand on one of those blue cartons!"

"I've got just the two folks for the job," Santos spoke up. "I got them out of prison on an early release about two years ago—on the condition that they were willing to work for us, exclusively. It's a husband-and-wife team who would have never been caught, except they were hired by an Iranian agent to steal a laptop containing classified information on new technology for weapons systems. They got the laptop but couldn't bring themselves to turn it over to the Iranian. So they were in the process of placing it back in the safe when the angry Iranian agent made a phone call alerting the local law enforcement which caught them in the act. Trust me, they are top-notch and can keep their mouths shut!"

"We'll need to get some milk cartons from an ACE Supermarket to replace the ones we will steal from the operatives and we should get the cartons with the same' best-by date' in case they notice the difference. Let's see if we can read what the date is on the cartons they bought, shall we?" They focused on one of the milk cartons that was bought at the mini mart. Fortunately the video was clear enough to make out the 'best-by date,' which was August 29. They were already on the phone to the Black Ops Team (BOT) with instructions to acquire at least one of the targeted milk cartons in the next twenty-four hours. The PEST team put together all the information the BOT would need with regard to the families' names, addresses, their arrival and departure times, and their keys from the rental agency. A request immediately came from the BOT to identify the contents of the milk cartons. Cole turned and looked at North for ideas about what might be concealed in the milk cartons. North just shrugged his shoulders and said, "It could be anything, so be very careful!"

Shortly after North's arrival at his hotel room, a call came in from an excited Allen in Caracas. North had barely picked up the call when Allen exclaimed, "We now know what Chinese are up to. Now we know the name of the leader of the Maria Drive operation. Sealy reported that watching the small airport, just to the east of the city, finally paid off. About one in the morning last night, none other than Juan Pascal, one of the top ten cyber criminals in the world according to Interpol arrived on a private flight from Mexico City. Upon his arrival at the airport he was escorted to the hotel by security personnel. We also found out that he had given the security guards a list of around ten other people who would be arriving in the next few days; we are still working on getting the names and dates for the others. Also one of the workers at the hotel said that they got instructions that all of the communication equipment had to be fully tested by August 27!

So it seems pretty clear to me that this is going to be a major disrupter— where or whatever they intend to target! One last thing: Your instincts were right, and the Chinese must be driving this thing because one of the folks who met Pascal was the security chief from the Chinese embassy. He passed a briefcase on to Pascal. An eye witness stated that when Pascal opened the case, it was stacked with $100 bills! More good news, Sealy is having no problem recruiting men for the attacks on the hotels!"

North was stunned at this information. He had an idea that Leong was up to something in Venezuela but the magnitude of what was shaping up was beyond North's imagination. He reminded Allen to ask Sealy not to initiate anything without checking with him first. Allen said he would remind Sealy not to move without his approval.

North voiced his appreciation for the work that they were doing and promised to fill them in when he had a more complete picture. To his surprise, he had received an encrypted email from Col. Sutherland. It was a brief note detailing top-secret information and photos showing Leong on a visit to North Korea. It also detailed that he had made several other, undetected visits to North Korea in the last few months. Tired from the long days, North just sat there, trying to put the pieces together.

Eventually, he dozed off.

The next morning as North and Cole arrived at the PEST operations center, they were greeted with disappointing news. Though the BOT was ready to go, there was a delay. The agent responsible for acquiring the ACE milk cartons with the same best-by dates as the ones from the Teepee mini mart reported that there were none in the stores in town with that date. Then he had a fellow agent in the Philly office checked in the stores there. That agent reported that the furthest best-by date he could find was August 12. This was followed up with calls to all of the milk processors in the tri-state area. The processors reported that because of the extreme heat waves experienced in their area, they had shortened the best-by dates because of complaints of the milk going sour. Then the agent covertly contacted the processor for all of the dairy products (including milk) for Teepee Corp. Their reply was the same as the others! This latest information posed both a challenge and an important question: How to get milk cartons with that date? And also was there any significance to that date or had it just been randomly chosen for the blue milk cartons? This was going to slow everything down; before proceeding further they would have to assess the level of risk they were willing to take if they decided to use cartons that did not bear the same dates as the operatives' cartons. The same agent who had worked at a Teepee mini mart had a friend who had worked for ACE in college and, after graduating, had taken a job with ACE in their junior management program. This agent said he could try to track that friend down and see if there was anything he could do to assist the FBI. Cole approved his idea and he started making phone calls.

About two hours later, the agent came in with surprisingly good news. He had located his friend from college and as luck would have it, he was now an assistant manager at one of the ACE stores in Atlantic City, about thirty miles from the FBI operation. But there was even better news! On occasion the milk cartons would arrive at the store with their best-by dates too lightly printed or otherwise unreadable. Rather than send the milk back, they had developed a manual process using a hand-embossed print to correct the problem dates. The agent described what they needed and his friend said he would get back to him within the hour. About forty-five minutes later, the agent got a call back from his friend, telling him that there were twenty cartons of ACE milk with a best-by date of August 29 waiting at the dairy office in the store and that he would be waiting for the designated agent to pick them up. Within three hours, the PEST team was back on schedule.

North sat in the corner of the operation center. He was still troubled by a myriad of questions: Was he missing something? Why had the August 29 date come up twice by now? One of the PEST operators came up to North and Cole to let them know that Wei had just finished a phone call to the Chinese liaison in Philadelphia confirming that he and Ling would be flying out to Chicago the next day on a late afternoon flight. Then he had asked the liaison to confirm hotel reservations and the meeting time and location for the Chicago operation. So everything seemed to be set in Chicago. "We have located the destination of the Chicago operatives and are working at this time to have listening devices installed in both the location where the operatives are staying and the meeting location."

"Do we have any indications of what they are planning to do in Chicago or the date of action?" SA Argo asked. He had just arrived back from Washington after meeting with the Director and had said, "I can assure you both that we will get all the resources we need for this operation!" At that moment, the BOT team stopped by to give feedback on what they had observed while planning to retrieve at least one of the milk cartons that the operatives had picked up and substituting them with one of the new ACE cartons. "We believe we could get one of the operatives' milk carton within an hour if we get the go-ahead for our part of the operation. The fact of the matter is we were casing a particular house when the operatives arrived home yesterday from the BBQ. They had all gone into the house and were getting ready to go to the beach. The dad had yelled down from the bedroom on the second floor that he was going to take a nap and wanted his son to go out to the car and bring in the grocery items that he had picked up at the Teepee mini mart and put them away. Well, the other children were yelling at their brother to hurry up. Like most kids he wanted to get to the beach right away, but in his haste he left the milk carton on the backseat, where it still is right now. We observed that the whole family is currently on its way to the local amusement park with some friends. So if we hurry we could make the exchange and have it back to you in very short order."

With this, the BOT received the substitute milk carton and went off. Soon, they came back with the operative's carton and handed it over to Cole. The BOT crew joked that things were not normally this easy and trying to retrieve some of the other cartons, if that was their assignment, would be a much bigger challenge. Cole handed the carton to one of the other agents who was responsible for getting it to Fort Detrick, Maryland, so it could be carefully examined to determine whether it was something to be concerned about. A helicopter was waiting at the local Coast Guard Station to transport the agent and the carton to Fort Detrick. North had contacts at the army labs on base and had asked that they speed up whatever processes necessary to determine if anything contained in the carton was a threat to national security. He got a reply that the lab teams would work around the clock to find an answer to his question! Now they just had to determine the next steps for the local operation. So the focus now shifted to Wei's Chicago operation and what it was up to. North was assured by SA Argo that the PEST unit was standing by for the meeting scheduled the next day.

At this time, one of the PEST operators came to North and Cole with somewhat questionable information that they had picked up while monitoring phone calls the operatives made while at the beach. It seemed that two of the families had made reservations for flights to Texas. One was to San Antonio with a connecting flight to El Paso and another directly to El Paso. What was most interesting was that they both had a departure date of August 29. *What can I be missing?* North thought to himself again. On a hunch, he asked Cole to check with the Border Patrol to see if they had caught any illegals trying to cross the border with explosives. To his surprise five such individuals, eventually identified as Cuban nationals, were encountered at approximately three in the morning on August 2. Three were captured and two were killed in the ensuing gun battle. Though there was no explosives on their person when they were apprehended, eight pounds of C-4 along with initiators were found in the bushes nearby. Cole said he would have an agent there within the hour to question them. But the Border Patrol Officer had bad news. A lawyer from one of the immigrant rights groups and an attorney with the DOJ had gone to court to have the men released, stating that the Border Patrol had no proof to hold them in jail per the administration's new guidelines. The attorney reassured the judge if released he would have them back in court the following day. The judge released the three men with orders to appear in court the next day! "Well you can guess what happened after that," the agent continued. "The three men have never been seen again." As per the information that Border Patrol passed onto ICE they were headed for Denver, but we should take that all with a big grain of salt!"

"That's not good news," said North. "It seems to confirm the Intel that Leong had made some sort of pact with the Cuban regime to have some disrupters come across our southern border during the same timeframe as the other actions were planned! Professor Farrow might have been more accurate than we had originally thought."

The BOT team was eagerly waiting to hear back from the Fort Detrick labs, as the results would indicate the extent to which they would need to speed up acquisition of the operatives' milk cartons. As North waited to hear from his friend at the labs, he picked up the latest file on Leong and Wei's Chicago operation. Having the listening devices in place was paying off. So far, they had found out that there were five men involved in the Chicago area operation. They had been actively discussing the plan they were to follow. The men had been recruited by local criminal figures to do a job for an "overseas client." The pay for this task would be $250,000 per man, which they thought was pretty good money for a one-day job with minimal risk of getting caught. Part of the plan was to frame five Chicago police officers in the process. In fact, these men had been carefully selected because each of them bore an uncanny resemblance to an actual Chicago police officer who patrolled the district in which they were to conduct their attack at two in the afternoon on August 29. That was the date and time for a public meeting at the American Legion Hall on Howard Street. According to the transcript of their conversation, many of the civic leaders would be present there on that day and around 200 citizens were supposed to be in attendance.

The targeted building was very old with simple wooden walls and large front windows. They would be able to see their targets and in turn the people inside could easily identify the shooters. The plan also required them to use standard police weapons and to wear police uniforms. After pouring as many bullets as they could into the crowd in the building, they were supposed to speed away and head back to the safe house. As per Leong's plan, their money would have been waiting at the house, but the "new guy," had changed the plan. The ensuing discussions got heated because some of the men would have preferred to get their money and head out in their own direction. But the new guy (whom they would soon meet) had made it clear he was in charge and they would follow his new exit plan. They were to head back to the house, dump the car, and take another one to the small municipal airport just east from their location. From there, a small plane would fly them to El Paso where they could cross the border and vanish into Mexico. The money would be given to them when the plane landed in El Paso. The new guy said he would be there the day after tomorrow for any last minute questions or changes. He also told the men to expect plenty of media coverage, which mean that his idea of flying them out of the area immediately would be safer. One man said, "I just don't like the idea of shooting regular people. Cops and government folks, okay, but murdering everyday folks does not sit well with me!" "Look, we are all wanted for murder and more," said another man. "This is a chance for us to make good cash with minimal chance of getting caught. I don't like it either, but I have no choice and neither do you—unless we want to spend our time on death row!" Then the group leader voiced his opinion, saying, "The guy wants this shooting to start riots here in Chicago and other major cities, and I expect he'll have his wish. All right, let's go out and drive over the new escape route to the airport one more time!"

After hearing this recording, Agent Cole asked, "Should we pick them up today or wait until Wei has met with them?" North gave a puzzled look, saying, "We can't pick them up at all; otherwise Wei will know something has gone off the tracks and that their whole mission is compromised—meaning our whole operation will go to waste. He'll go underground and we'll lose him, and then there is no telling what he might do."

"I can't believe I'm hearing those words!" Agent Cole snapped. "Have you become so fixated on Wei and Ling that you're okay sacrificing innocent lives to catch them? I hesitate to say this but it might be time for me to intervene and take full charge of this operation!" North walked over to Cole, looked him in the eyes, and said, "I wouldn't try that if I was you."

"Look Steve, I know you're under a lot of pressure. Maybe you should pass up on this mission and get some rest. It seems that you're taking this too personally..." Now North's voice went menacingly low, and there was a sting to it as he said, "They murdered—nay, *slaughtered*—a very dear friend and his entire family, so of course it's personal, Jesus Christ! I just go this information an hour ago...I- I need some time to think it through and consider some options, okay?"

As luck would have it, SA Argo had overheard the entire exchange, and he told both of them to stand down for the night and get some rest. He also informed them of the latest news from Fort Detrick—that there would be a comprehensive video update at eight in the morning—and told them that he did not want to see either of them back at the PEST operation center before the 8am update. As North headed out, he realized he had to come up with a solution that protected innocent civilians but did not put their undercover operations at risk of discovery and he needed to come up with that solution by eight the next morning or this whole thing could blow up in his face. As he sat there at his desk, little did he know that his situation was about to get more complicated.

Soon, Sealy and Allen were on the line with bad news. Homeland Security had found out that Juan Pascal had finally surfaced and they wanted Allen to pick him up right away before he disappeared again. "Walt, did you explain to them what we are looking at here, this whole thing is much bigger then taking down some cyber crooks! I'm hesitant to have you provide too many details to Homeland Security, you know how porous those agencies are with classified information. 'Jesus Christ,' the last thing we need is them blowing this whole thing up, just to get some publicity or political grandstanding. I can't go to my boss for her help to get them to back off, she'll most likely would put the 'kibosh' to the whole operation. She would say, much of it is based on 'hunches' and conjecture beginning with two faxed pages in Chinese, photos of two men in a speeding car, somehow connected with murders in Philadelphia and would top it off with, it's just me chasing 'ghosts' in an effort to extract revenge for the murder of a friend. Then to top it off, connecting it to China, would send her into 'orbit!' Currently, there is not enough of a connection between what the FBI is working with here in the US to link it with your operation in Venezuela. I am going to have to ask you guys to carry the ball and persuade Homeland Security to let us play this out a little longer." Allen agreed, "OK, I'll do my best, but if Pascal got away, I'll be in real trouble! Also, the word is there are two more of Pascal's team coming in tonight, we'll get you their names ASAP!" After the phone call ended, North stretched out on his bed and thought to himself, *Another fly in the ointment. Maybe the solution will come to me once I get some rest?* With this feeble hope, he set his alarm, turned out the table lamp, and started to wonder if some of Cole's comments were more appropriate than he would care to admit.

The alarm went off at half-past six the next morning. North pushed the ten-minute snooze button, but instead of going back to sleep, he sat up straight in bed and spent the ten minutes doing research on his laptop. Once he finished his research, he smiled, and exclaimed, "I've got it!" Within ten minutes was dressed and on his way to the PEST center. It was a quarter after seven when he pulled into the driveway of the rental house the FBI was using as its operations center. North was surprised to see SA Argo and Cole were already there. They had scrolled the words "Chicago Options" on a marker board and had several items listed that they had covered with their Chicago office. There were four options that they felt fit the threat and were within their legal authority and limits. Option 1: Arrest them outright; after all, they were wanted fugitives. Option 2: They could have a car thief steal their "police" vehicle the morning of the event. Option 3: Order local authorities to put up checkpoints in the vicinity of the meeting location, under the guise of a recent attempted kidnapping. Option 4: Ask that the meeting at the Legion Hall be cancelled or rescheduled. North listened to each option and the details necessary to execute it. Then cleared his throat and thanked them for the options, saying that he realized they had to do something to protect the public. "Still, I think that each of your proposed options would cause Wei to wonder if someone was on to them," North continued, "because each of those options either reflects back on to the men executing his plan or is an arbitrary action with no specific reason, which I believe would make it likely for Wei to assume that we're on to him!

North begin, "the American Legion Hall, where the meeting is scheduled to take place, was built in 1934 and is due to be torn down next spring. In fact I found out that the company that has the rights to recycle the metal, pipes, and all that stuff has already started pulling wires and pipes from the basement. So, what if, in the early morning hours of the day of the meeting, a fire started in the basement area where the men have been working? The old wooden structure would go up in flames quite quickly and since it is the last and only building on that block, no other structures would be threatened. The meeting would *have* to be rescheduled, most likely to a date after the long weekend. Therefore, it would seem to be beyond the operatives' control or in any way reflect on their ability to get the job done. In this way, Wei will be less likely to suspect that his plan is in jeopardy. Then, later you can move in and quietly arrest the bad guys!"

"Burn down the meeting hall? You're not serious!" Cole said in a low voice. SA Argo spoke up. "Look, I'll be the first to admit our senior FBI leadership has gone astray and made some questionable and even some terrible decisions in the past few years, but I don't think even they would think highly of an FBI field office being involved in arson, and that too of it being public building."

"That's the beauty of my plan," North responded. "I'll take care of getting the meeting delayed so the public is safe. You keep an eye on the bad guys, just in case something goes wrong with my solution. Either way, you get the bad guys, nobody gets hurt, and your hands are clean!" SA Argo and Cole looked at each other, slowly shook their heads, and then nodded in agreement. "Okay, but if anything starts to go south or the public appears threatened or it appears that the bad guys might get away, we will not hesitate to step in," cautioned SA Argo. At that point, one of the PEST operators motioned to him that the live feed from Fort Detrick was about to begin. Agent Santos was standing nearby and had overheard North's plan. Presently, he commented, "North's plan sounds pretty cool to me. I've got some great ideas about how to trigger the fire so it will torch the place in very short order!" Cole gave Santos a stern look and said, "You stay out of this; the burning down of public buildings will be strictly left to Major North!" As North and Cole were walking over to the monitors, the latter remarked, "You know Steve, you've come up with some pretty strange stuff in the years I've known you, but I think this is a first for you…are these the types of things that make you so well loved or, on the other hand, hated by your bosses?"

"Generally they don't tend to tolerate these sparks of genius I come up with!" North replied with a grin.

"Then why do things like this if you know your bosses are going to try to shit all over you?" Cole demanded.

North thought for a second. Then he looked at Cole and said, "One of my old professors from the Naval Academy once asked me the same question a while back. I told him I love this country and took an oath to serve and protect it, but these days, people don't seem to understand or remember the effort and sacrifice of so many previous generations to get us everything we have in the way of collective freedom and individual rights and all the comforts we enjoy. When I think of all that…I just can't bring myself to give less than 110% every day. Sometimes that means pushing back against or challenging the people or thoughts that try to take us down. And sometimes that causes a stir or disturbs the lefty progressives who want us to look like every other country. Many folks now just put their time in and will roll when the pressure comes to bear and not really accomplish anything meaningful. But somebody's gotta be tough! The big boys don't always like the dust that I kick up, but I'm committed to doing what is best for the nation and that means getting results!"

"Good old Steve," Cole replied, shaking his head and chuckling dryly, "a constant in an ever-changing world!"

The feed came through, right at 8:00 am. Fort Detrick was now online. "LtCol. Ball speaking," came a voice on the radio. "Please go to channel two, and secure line."

Then LtCol. Ball asked, "Who is online, anyone not carrying at least a Top Secret with a 'need-to-know' endorsement should not have access to this video transmission. Major North, since you represent the requesting agency, I will start off with my remarks directed to you. When I'm finished, I'll be happy to take questions from any agency present. To begin, the milk carton that you sent over was immediately x-rayed and checked for contaminates upon arrival at our intake facility. The outside surfaces showed nothing unusual. But the x-ray revealed a metal container taking up approximately 80% of the interior volume of the milk carton.

"The next step was to test the liquid that surrounded the metal canister. It turned out to be plain tap water. Then we carefully removed the metal canister and found it to be an aerosol dispenser that would be triggered when a safety pin was removed and the lever turned clockwise once. It should be noted that the instructions, written in

Farsi, were etched into the surface of the metal container. The literal translation of the instructions are 'Under pressure, turn the lever clockwise, one full turn, aerosol dispensing begins in 30 seconds and continues until the canister is empty.' There was also a small note, enclosed in plastic, attached to the top of the canister. Printed on it were the following words in Chinese: 'Remove and destroy this note prior to use.' This note also listed the instructions to operate the canister. The canister itself is made of high grade stainless steel and expertly manufactured. It was subjected to tests to see if there was or has been any leakage. That results were negative! The next step was to check what the container had inside. Of course, following standard protocol, we moved the dispenser to our level 5, extreme bio-hazard lab. Before I go into what we detected, let me tell you this: You were damn lucky you didn't trigger this thing! Following the instructions etched on the dispenser we activated the device. As expected a very fine mist shot into the air to a height of approximately ten feet. When fans were turned on the mist followed the expected airflow patterns."

"Then we followed the protocol of chemical and gene analysis before further testing. From initial results, it appeared to be nothing more than many of the same Covid-19 variants, similar to the original strain that had escaped the lab in Wuhan. So we moved on to animal testing to confirm our anticipated results. Within ten hours, all of the animals went into severe respiratory failure. We managed to save half, with heavy intervention—meaning everything we could throw at it. We were both surprised and shocked by the results with the lab animals. We went over our testing again and again. Covid-19 was lethal for 1-3% of the overall population; our forecast for what was in the dispenser ran closer to being lethal for 50% of the general population and that too at what appeared to be a much faster transmission rate. This is serious stuff, gentlemen! There are folks here shitting their pants and in near panic; where did this sample come from? By the way, we're also running it through our new gene scrambler to try to get a better handle on this bug, because there are still some aspects of the gene sequencing that look odd based on current data. I've reported the results up the chain, as required. So heads up! You'll probably get calls and people are going to want answers."

"Doc, this is SA Argo. Is it possible to get aerosol dispensing canisters like the one you tested?"

"Probably, but I doubt they would be an exact match!"

North spoke up, "If we exchange all of them, that won't matter if they match the one we have, because the only person who would know they have been changed would be the one who placed them in the milk cartons in the first place."

At this point, Cole spoke up, "true, but that'll work only if we can exchange them all!" North, who was already on his way to address the BOT team, said, "That's just what we're going to do—nothing less. Failure is *not* an option!" The BOT team had just got back from the source that provided their fake uniforms from during their illegal activities. They had been casing the operatives' beach rentals and had observed that all but one of their targets had a natural gas meter. So they had decided they would deploy the ruse of NJ Natural Gas employees checking out suspected leaks and equipment performance. On their way back to the PEST unit, they picked up an NJ Natural Gas truck at the FBI yard; it had been used on a case last month. The BOT team listened intently as North laid out the dire situation. "If we just rush in and openly secure the canisters, it would be obvious to Wei that the North American portion of the overall plan has been compromised, which would most assuredly drive everybody else underground."

"Sir, how long before the rest of the substitute milk cartons with the fake aerosol canisters would be available?" asked one of the BOT team members. North said, "I'm not sure, but we're pushing hard to speed up the acquisition timeframe." At that point, Santos entered the room, saying "We'll have the replacement milk cartons with substitute canisters in forty-eight hours or less! Also, I've reached out to a friend who holds a fairly senior position with NJ Natural Gas; he'll provide cover for this operation if he gets official reassurance that our BOT team is legit!"

"By the way, I have another job for you in Chicago if Argo and Cole will approve of using you," North said.

But before he could say any more, an operator rushed into the room, saying, "Major North, you're wanted at the communications center. Fort Detrick is back online and has requested that you be present."

When North joined the call, LtCol. Ball said, "Major North, we just finished our fourth sequencing analysis and have now confirmed the nature of the virus. It's based on the original lab-produced Covid-19 but has been weaponized to speed up the effects on the victim faster and to a much greater degree. That we knew from our first analysis. Then we noticed a minor change, buried deep in the genetic protocol. That variation both amped up the speed and severity of the virus but most amazingly was also a trigger that would program the virus to self-destruct. Essentially, while contained in the atmosphere within the canister, the virus was asleep, for lack of a better term. Once exposed to oxygen it would awaken and wreak havoc on the host body. So we asked ourselves why would you have to suspend a virus' life-cycle? Then we looked again…and much to our amazement, we found a 'kill switch." We ran that scenario through our new quantum computer and it came up with the same answer: As long as the virus was held in sleep mode, the self-destruct clock was not running. Once the virus was released into the air, the exposure to oxygen set the self-destruct clock ticking. So we started to dig deeper and our preliminary data show a self-destruct run time of ten days, add or take away a day."

"So let me get this straight," North cut in. "You have a virus that has been amped up to an extremely dangerous level. Also, this new lab construct is likely lethal for up to 50% of the people that contract it?"

"That's what our tests results indicate, which makes this new biohazard a military-grade bio-weapon, meant to kill large swaths of the civilian population."

"However, once you release it, the virus will follow its programing and essentially commit suicide—in about ten days—and then revert to a less lethal form?"

"Yup, that is our current estimate. Strange isn't it!"

"Surely, getting caught releasing a bio-weapon like that would be considered an act of war, wouldn't it?" Agent Cole remarked. "What do you mean by getting caught?" North replied in a tense voice. "There would have to be irrefutable evidence and considerable public pressure for this administration to do anything. Also, the public has been led to believe that Covid-19 was transmitted from animal to humans, so they would be pre-disposed to think the same thing happened again and the outbreak would have to be so substantial as to cause real panic and bring the public outcry to a fever pitch to move this administration to do something more than shutdown schools and bring back the mask mandate. Those who said that the Covid-19 outbreak was in fact the consequence of a collusion between China and leftist /socialist organizations across the globe were called 'crackpots'. They claimed that it was a test run to see the levels to which the public would tolerate being controlled via media and governmental mandates. So a smoking gun would definitely be required!"

LtCol. Ball asked, "Are there any more questions for me? I've got to meet with a British Major on loan to us from the UK. He has reviewed the data and has drawn some rather odd, even outlandish predictions about the presence and use of what he refers to as the 'suicide switch,' given the ten-day shelf-life of the virus."

"Can we hear what his thoughts are, Doc?" asked North directly. "I don't have clearance to tell you all the things we are involved in, but this current operation is just part of something that could be much more significant, and different perspectives may help us connect the pieces together in a more coherent way."

"Okay, I'll get him over here to the Comm center; it will take a few minutes, but again I want to stress, we deal in science and certainty, and his theory and conclusions or, as I refer to them, *guesses* and *interpretations* are interesting but by no means do we like to spin up stuff we cannot back up with scientific facts. All that said, he's an entertaining guy with lots of wild yarns about what he believes the future of warfare will become! He should be online in a couple of minutes."

Here, SA Argo spoke up. "Correct me if I'm wrong, but given what we know thus far, we still need to acquire and replace the canisters currently in the hands of the operatives!"

"That is correct," Agent Cole replied in a worried tone.

"Major Dunhill online," a crisp voice said then. "Whom am I speaking with?"

"Major North here."

"I heard from LtCol. Ball that you wanted to hear my thoughts on what I refer to as '*Covid-20*.' Why do I call it that? Because of the unique characteristics that have been placed in the virus to get a specific result. And because of the introduction of the 'suicide switch.' Before I provide my thoughts and theories, let me tell you a bit about my background. By profession, I'm a medical doctor with specialized training in the areas of viral and bacterial uses in warfare. I am part of a group that plays the 'what-if' game against the future of limited or global conflict. We have concluded that the reality of global nuclear war is not as feasible an option as some folks think, especially in ways the media likes to portray. What our group has concluded is that given the current make-up of military power in the world, an era of 'tactical destabilization' is more likely. For some time, we have viewed the so-called 'terrorist states' as countries that—because of limited military capacity—must resort to unconventional or limited means to realize the goals, real or imagined, of the military and civil factions in their country. For the most part, due to better cooperation, surveillance, technology, financial controls, and so on, the more powerful nations have marginalized the smaller players into being, at best, the proxy for the former. So, it's beginning to seem that the big players teaming up with perhaps a coalition of smaller countries is how this game is now going to play out."

"So your group's conclusion is that there will be no global nuclear war?" SA Argo chimed in. Dunhill answered, "Not exactly. We conclude that it is not nearly as likely as it used to be, given recent events and our review of leadership traits and psychological profiles. The profiles we have researched indicate that the leaders in left-leaning or socialist governments tend to exhibit similar power perceptions—that they know better and are more important than the rest of the citizens—and to that end, they will not likely risk full-scale war; on the off-chance they might be seen as the fools that led their populace into a perilous situation, where the citizens would seek a new leader—the thing all leaders fear the most. This is true since socialist governments are built around the leader, an individual with less checks and balances, and not so much around concepts or philosophies, with the leader being subservient to these ideals, like it is in the West. In republic/democratic governments, the leaders' actions can be held up to or compared against the concepts that define that country. Therefore, with the checks and balances in place, a larger conflict without additional input or constraints are less likely to be triggered. That leaves us with smaller-scale destabilization as a means to weaken an adversary. And that means instituting a different form of terrorism—no longer by the smaller countries, but the 'big boys.'

"I know that was a long-winded introduction, but it will provide a frame of reference for what I'm going to tell you next. So the future of terrorism is likelier to manifest itself in a way less than obvious or by clandestine means. The goal is to destabilize or weaken a country's resolve to challenge or confront another nation because there is no *overt* act of war—which essentially means that you target the other country in a way that makes it difficult for them to rally their citizens to support 'war-like' actions against the opposing country that's ultimately responsible for problems within ones border. You do things to cause problems within the other country, cover it up, and deny you had anything to do with it! So, let's look at your canister and the virus. What we know: It's clearly part of a Chinese operation; however the canister has instructions etched into the metal surface in Farsi, the language used in Iran. So if the operative follows instructions, he or she would destroy the attached note written in Chinese, and the evidence would eventually point to some country that uses Farsi as their main language. The virus, as you heard from LtCol. Ball, has a ten-day self-destruct mechanism that will return the virus to a much less lethal form. If you did not have the self-destruct gene sequence, hundreds of thousands or perhaps millions of people would die as the virus would continue spreading. But hundreds of thousands of dead citizens and even more that are likely to die would panic the population and force a dramatic response from that country's leadership. But with a virus perceived to be a severe Covid-19 outbreak, devastatingly destructive but limited in duration, there probably would not be sufficient pressure to respond militarily, even if we could confirm who triggered the outbreak. To sum this up, my best guess is China is up to something and it wants Washington to be consumed in dealing with the outbreak brought about by the release of this weaponized version of Covid-19, what I now refer to as Covid-20."

At that point, LtCol. Ball came back on the line with an update. "We have run more tests and data-driven scenarios and have some more information on the virus. This virus will lead to the patient showing signs of infection much quicker than the original Covid-19. We've concluded that it will begin with a spiking fever in as early as four hours after exposure. We have reconfirmed the ten-day self-destruct gene will disappear from the virus and it will revert to behaving the same ways as the Covid-19 virus, that is, a much less lethal form. We have also projected that it would take three to five days before it would be apparent that the patient has taken a dramatic turn for the worst and would most probably be beyond hope at that point. And the virus would still be in its most virulent form. So if you were infected on day one, to day five of the virus' exposure to oxygen, you're in deep shit. However, if you contacted the virus on day eight, within two days, Covid-20 would revert to Covid-19, and conventional treatments and previous vaccines would probably be effective enough to save the patient."

"And there you have it!" said Dunhill. "An immediate disrupter to your country, but short lived and easily explained based on the previous outbreak. The administration would just force you to wear your mask everywhere, cancel school, and force you to get shots. It worked before. They are in control, the media would support the administration's spin on the story, and they will both take credit for saving you. Hell, the Chinese know exactly how you Yanks will respond, since the previous test run was such a success."

Just then, Santos came in with good news. "The substitute cartons have arrived and the BOT team is already on its way to the first target. The replacement canisters are essentially a commercial aerosol air freshener. Great news eh, Major North!" North seemed preoccupied with other thoughts, but he looked up and said, "That is great news! But now, how to convince Wei that there was an outbreak and his operation is still going the way he is expecting it to? He will need to see something in the papers, online, and on TV indicating that a new virus outbreak is developing."

"I have a fraternity brother who holds a fairly senior position at the CDC," Agent Cole said. "Let me contact him and see if he can help us. By the way, the Chicago office just called and is sending the transcribed text of Wei's meeting with the Chicago operatives.

The agent-in-charge said the meeting was short and to the point. Everything still stands as planned. Wei and Ling are currently on their way to O'Hare to catch a flight to San Francisco. Once that plane is in the air, surveillance will switch to the San Francisco office. The meeting with his west coast operatives is scheduled for the day after tomorrow. The San Francisco office is currently tracking all the west coast operatives who are inbound to San Francisco and should arrive in time for the meeting with Wei. The office noted that they have monitored the operatives' phones, online activity, and their FEDEX, DHL, and USPS accounts, yet they still don't have a clue what or where their targets are. The timeline was also undisclosed at this time. Wei and Ling have a scheduled flight departing for Philadelphia the evening after the meeting."

Over the next two days the BOT had success after success in acquiring and then substitute the "milk carton" containing the dangerous virus, for one with a scented air spray, (including re-exchange of the first one sent to Ft. Detrick.). They were down to the last one. "Generally speaking, the replacement process has been a piece of cake compared to some of the jobs we've had. Since the houses were all rentals, the families did not seem to care who we were. We looked official, had letters from the rental agencies, were polite and on time for our appointment, and even helped some of the families move their furniture around. When we arrived at the last target, we were surprised to find they had left early since they had a long drive back to North Carolina."

Cole thought for a second before saying, "I think we could ask the Virginia State Police to set up a roadblock, under the guise of checking the vehicles for drugs. But I will need to let them in on at least part of the story. Getting to that right now."

"Great!" North replied, "that means the BOT can head for Chicago, if the FBI will approve their use?"

SA Argo nodded in approval.

North had just finished a two-hour briefing with the BOT where he had explained the situation and what he expected when they arrived in Chicago. He emphasized the significance of the timing for the meeting hall catching fire and then burning enough so that the meeting would have to be rescheduled, rather than shifted to another location on the same day. Above all, no civilians were to be injured. He also provided them with the necessary contacts for assistance once they arrived in Chicago. As North exited the meeting, he was approached by Cole who said, "Well Steve, the San Francisco office just filed their initial report following Wei's and Ling's arrival in the city. And it did not go quite as planned. If you remember, we had tracked the meeting location and our team had the place wired and fitted out with video surveillance to ensure that whatever they said or did was recorded. The surveillance team tailed Wei and Ling on their cab ride to the restaurant for the scheduled meeting. When the cab arrived, all the attendees were standing in front of the neighboring business. There were also a lot of police vehicles, sirens, flashing lights...you can imagine the scene. It seems there had been a gang shooting, you know, the usual Asian gang stuff. It became clear that the meeting location was out of the plan. Our team followed them to another restaurant just down the street. The place was packed, and we watched as the owner tried to seat them, but there was no tables large enough to accommodate the group.

"At that point the owner showed them into another room and our team lost contact with the group. They exited the room after about forty-five minutes. But the meeting must have not gone very well. Their body language was quite animated and their facial expressions showed very clearly that the operatives were not happy with whatever was discussed at the meeting. They headed to their vehicles or cabs, while our teams followed them to their respective hotels. Wei and Ling exited the room about fifteen minutes later and took a cab to their hotel. We monitored their phone calls, of course, but picked nothing unusual. Wei called the airlines to confirm their flight out to

Philadelphia at nine in the evening. Among the rest, most just called on their families, while two of the operatives talked to their sons and discussed getting their 'Boy Scout' camping badges. They were making a plan to go camping and pick up the necessary gear at one of the big outdoor stores before they left the city. One of the operatives ordered up a bottle of expensive whiskey, apparently looking to self-medicate. The rest either did not phone anyone or made just typical business phone calls. There was one inbound call from the mother of one of the scouts to remind her husband that she had booked a campsite in the Willamette National Forest in the vicinity of Sisters, Oregon. That was the extent of the report. We will get the next update at about 2:00 pm tomorrow."

North replied, "Thank your office for the update, and I look forward to tomorrow's follow-up." After the call ended, North headed to his room for some much-needed rest.

But no sooner had he entered his room when a call came in from Allen in Caracas. "We have hit the jackpot, Steve! In the last forty-eight hours some of the most talented and wanted cyber criminals in the world have arrived in Caracas. We are compiling the list as we speak. It's like the World Series of Hacking. They certainly tried to keep their arrivals as quiet as possible. A couple even came in by sailboat and one came in dressed as a Caracas police officer, but Sealy's people were on to them. One thing you should know is that they have fortified their hotel and increased the military presence with undercover 'special forces' dressed in civilian clothing. As far as we can tell, the systems are up and running."

"One of our undercover phone company operators overheard a phone conversation confirming that everything was tested and ready per the requirement target date of August 27. ' I'm taking a big risk by not sending the list of hackers to my boss, for fear he will not want to wait to play things out, as it were, and send reinforcements down here and capture as many of the hackers immediately! On another note, Sealy's recruitment efforts have been going well. He's confident that when you give us the go-ahead, he'll have enough forces to attack every one of Ruiz's hotels—to mask our primary target. The only thing I'm concerned with is that Sealy's folks might see this operation as a chance for revenge and things could get a little out of hand, so I've requested that he be present at the main target to keep a lid on their actions. How are things working out for your state-side operation?"

"Well, so far so good," replied North. "But the west coast portion of the plan is still up in the air, and we still do not have a clear picture of what they have in store for us. You guys are doing great! Keep up the good work and just let me know if there is anything you need from me in the way of assistance."

Finally, his head churning with a million thoughts, North put down the phone and turned on a late-night movie.

At ten the next morning, North's phone rang, waking him up. It was Cole who let him know that the next operational report had come in early from the San Francisco office. North said he would be right there as soon as he had showered and grabbed a cup of coffee. Upon arrival, North reviewed the report. There was nothing there that would tip their hand as to what they had in mind. Only five of the operatives had made phone calls: Two had called their offices, one had called his dentist, and one had called the reservations office at the Cleveland National Forest to confirm his campsite reservation beginning on August 29, and the last one had called Parker Outdoor and Sporting Goods to confirm if they still had a sale going on at their store. Since the store also carried rifles, handguns, and other forms of ammunition, the San Francisco office had pulled a copy of the receipt to see if perhaps they had purchased a weapon. As North took the receipt, Cole commented," I've already reviewed both receipts and there is nothing that we should be concerned with. It's all normal, everyday camping supplies and equipment." North grabbed a cup of coffee and sat down to go over the receipts himself, telling Cole, "I'll just take a quick look myself."

The first receipt was for a total of $418.55, and the items included a sleeping bag, freeze-dried food packets, flare guns and cartridges, a small hatchet, two headlamps, a small cast iron stew pot, bug spray, camp stool and an instruction manual on what to do if one encountered dangerous wildlife, such as a bear or mountain lion. North took a few more sips of coffee and grabbed the second receipt.

This receipt was for a total of $459.95, and the items included a complete set of camping pots and cooking utensils: an automobile guide on prepping one's vehicle for driving over rough terrain, a guide on how to "read and recognize" the stars in the nighttime sky, a first-aid manual, a box of road flares, bug spray, binoculars, and a four-person tent. North took a couple more sips of coffee, lay the receipts on the table, stood up, and walked outside. Standing there with the noon sunlight on his face, he recalled how pleasant it had been to come to the island when he was much younger. Sure, the place had many more visitors now, but the smell of the salty air brought back some very fond memories. He took another sip of coffee and thought about the fun times when he had gone crabbing with his grandfather and how he usually ended up with several pinch marks on his hands from not handling the crabs appropriately...here he stopped mid-thought. Something he had seen in the receipts was troubling him. But he couldn't quite put his finger on it. A couple more sips of coffee and the cup was empty. He went back inside, poured himself another cup of coffee and sat back down at the table. He picked up the receipts and put them back down. He called one of the agents over and asked, "How long would it take to pull records of credit card purchases and corresponding receipts for each operative for each of their purchase over the last thirty days?" The agent replied, "No more than two hours, because we have already started to compile background information on each of the operatives. I'll give you a holler when I get them together."

Then, North thought he had better alert Kent and Howe about Wei and Ling's impending return to their locale. "Lt. Howe, this is Major North," he said as soon as the detective picked up. "I wanted to let you know that Wei and Ling are due to arrive on the United Airlines flight 651 tonight. We are ending our operation here on Long Beach Island as the last of the operatives left for their home this morning. I'll be back in Philly later this evening. I'm sorry for having to delay your investigations, but we can't afford to rattle their cages just yet! I've noticed in the newspaper you are taking a beating in the press on account of still using the 'gang warfare' cover for the diner murders, so let me assure you that this thing will be wrapping up by the second week of September. At that time you can 'let loose the dogs of war' on that whole crew!"

Just as North was wrapping up the phone call to Howe, the agent he had previously spoken to came in with the record of the operatives' credit card purchases along with the corresponding receipts. The agent had placed them neatly in stacks and North started to go through them, purchase by purchase, receipt by receipt. *What am I looking for*? North thought to himself. *There could be something staring me right in the face and I wouldn't even know what it was!* He kept glancing back at the first two receipts he had reviewed, hoping that some epiphany would lead him to better understand what the operatives were going to do as part of this whole operation. With that part of the puzzle revealed, everything would fall into place. After about twenty minutes, he felt he was no closer to seeing any pattern underlying Wei and Leong's plan. He got a fresh cup of coffee and walked outside. There were several agents loading up the equipment on to waiting trucks as they dissembled the operations center. One of the agents loading up the gear commented that this reminded him of when the family would always go to his wife's parents' home for Christmas, when the children were very young; it was like getting ready for a big camping trip. Just when he thought he had everything packed for the trip, his wife would come up with something else she thought was required. Often, it seemed to him that those items were out of place or not needed, but he had to load them up anyway.

That got North thinking. Perhaps rather than looking at the receipts for each operative separately, he should look for items from each receipt that are alike or related to other items on other receipts. He knew this would take more time, but perhaps that process might prove more productive, because he wasn't getting anywhere by isolating the receipts of each operative. So, he piling receipts according to categories such as household items, vehicles, trips and travel, dental, medical, school- and business-related expenses, and general catch-all items. North had created multiple stacks when Cole walked by and asked if he needed any help or if he would like to have one of their profilers look over the receipts. One of their computer programmers could also write an algorithm to help look for a link between the operatives. North just kept staring at the receipts and slowly shook his head, thinking to himself, *Something in those first two receipts made me think that they were not appropriate or were somehow out of place. If I can identify what that was…then I can look for something similar in the other operatives' recent purchases; it's something that will help identify what their targets are, I'm sure of it.* The two receipts from that morning were focused on camping supplies or equipment. He picked up the receipt for $459.95 and went over the list carefully, trying to imagine something that could be used to trigger an event that would disrupt or threaten innocent people's lives. So, the family likes to go camping. Big deal, its' what a lot of young families do in the summer.

Let's have a look at the receipt for $418.55. Sleeping bag, freeze-dried food packets, flare gun and cartridges, small hatchet, two *headlamps...* and here he stopped. He took a sip of coffee and asked the agent, "Which operative called regarding reservations at the Cleveland National Forest and which operative had received the call from his wife regarding the reservations for the Willamette National Forest?" The agent confirmed that the operative who had gotten the call from his wife was the same operative whose receipt he was currently reviewing. North thought of the time he had spent in Oregon. Much of the time, he had been in the Bend and Sisters area.

He vividly recalled how dry that area got during the summer months and the extreme fire danger it posed. Sisters seemed to be especially prone to fire with all of pine forest that covered the hills. North also did not recall any really large bodies of water in that area. He looked at the receipt again. No large bodies of water, so why would you need a flare gun? Flare guns are primarily used as a signal for rescue or assistance on water. Flares burn very hot, which is not a problem around water, but if you used it around flammable material like pine needles or dry brush, the results could be catastrophic! Every summer for the last several years the western United States had become a scene of fire, smoke, ash, blackened landscape, and charred homes. In some cases whole communities had been destroyed. Since the fire outbreaks had been a regular occurrence, another year of multiple forest fires would probably not raise any more attention than other years. So, playing on that hunch, he now had an idea about what to focus on and look for. He thought to himself, *If I wanted to start a forest fire, where would I go and how would I travel so as to not raise suspicion while starting the fires?* A viable cover to use for escape and, more importantly, effective means to start fires quickly would be of paramount importance. With those points in mind, he started going back through all of the receipts. A little over an hour later, he felt he had enough to prove that his hunch was correct.

As he went through the receipts he added to the list. In the last thirty days, six of the seven operatives had confirmed camping reservations to begin between August 27 and 29 on national or state forest locations, which included the Cleveland State Forest, northeast of San Diego, California; the Willamette National Forest, near Sisters, Oregon; the Wenatchee National Forest, near Wenatchee, Washington; the Modoc National Forest, near Alturas, California; the Bitterroot National Forest, near Boise, Idaho; and the Stanislaus National Forest, in the California, Sierra foothills. Three of the six operatives who had additional reservations booked, for August 31-September 2, campsites in the Los Padres National Forest, north of Los Angeles, California; the Rogue National Forest, near Medford, Oregon; and the Tonto National Forest in Arizona. Although North could not find any evidence that the other operatives had any additional reservations, he was sure they would be engaged in the same activities. He also found that of the seven operatives, five had purchased flare guns and additional cartridges, and one had purchased road flares. Shooting off the flares during the bright sunlight hours of the day would make it difficult to see them. The operatives could literally shoot them off as they drove through the forest. Another point that led North to believe his hunch was correct was the timing of the reservations. The timeline to start the fires aligned within the August 29 "window" for the other phases of the operation. He was now sure that part of the operation was to turn the western United States into an inferno. The operatives had the perfect cover: the family camping trip with mom, the kids, and even the family dog.

For a while, North just sat there, pondering his next step. Both the east coast pandemic and the Chicago Massacre had been dealt with in ways that would make it appear that the operational objectives had not been compromised. You could plant stories on social networks, in newspapers, and on the radio about people getting sick and dying from a new variant of Covid-19. In Chicago, if the meeting hall where the targeted group was supposed to meet, burned down, Wei won't suspect outside intervention or blame his hired assassins. But, when a forest was supposed to be engulfed in flames and everybody can see it's not, you can't fake it. *I do not see an alternate solution*, North realized with mounting horror. *If I tell my friend Cole, the FBI will have to intervene and most likely arrest the operatives and then Wei will know the operation has been compromised. He might even have a back-up alternative that could be something much more lethal that we are not prepared for.*

For a long time, North tried to think through the implications of letting the operatives continue with their assigned tasks, but he failed to come up with anything solid. By now it was almost seven in the evening and he was feeling exhausted; he needed more time to consider how his decision could affect the outcome of the entire investigation. He would sleep on it. As the agents were working on their final checklist of shutting down the operations center, North gathered up all of the receipts, mixed them up, and placed them in the same folder in which the agent had given them to him. He picked up his list which showed all the evidence he needed to confirm what the operatives were planning and shoved it in his pocket.

As he was getting up to leave, Agent Cole walked into the room and yelled over to North, "Steve, want to go get a beer to celebrate what I think was a pretty successful operation? By the way I noticed you pouring over those operatives' receipts; did they turn up anything interesting?" North ignored the second part of the question and said, "Not today, buddy. I'm heading straight for the hotel and taking a hot shower. I'll see you the morning for the drive back to Philadelphia." With that, he walked out the door. SA Argo had been standing nearby and commented to Cole, "It looks like the wear and tear is beginning to take its toll on Major North."

Cole turned to SA Argo and remarked, "I've known Steve for over ten years, ever since Quantico, so trust me when I say this: He has not changed. He always gives 110%; if he promises something, you can bet he'll deliver. Unfortunately for him, his bosses have not tended to tolerate that level of passion, drive, dedication, and smarts. Frankly, I think his bosses feel threatened that he would show them up. I don't think I ever told you but he graduated from the Naval Academy with a degree in Electrical Engineering. But his first love has always been plants. In fact he went back to the University of Alabama and got his PHD in—get this—Paleolithic and Neolithic Botany. Sometimes I just think he is too hard on himself…but thank God he is! At least for the rest of our sakes. See you in the morning."

At eight the next day, Agent Cole pulled up in front of North's hotel in a black Chevrolet Suburban. North was seated on a bench outside; he walked slowly to the vehicle and got in carefully, so as not to spill the two coffee cups he was carrying. As North was closing the door, Cole gave him a tense look and said, "I just heard from the San Francisco office, and we may have a problem. It seems that they had two rookie agents observing one of the operatives' houses and they may have blown their cover. They were supposed to be two carpenters who were part of a remodeling crew working on a house one door down and across the street. Apparently, one of the agents got hot so he unzipped his coveralls which revealed that he was carrying a weapon, his service revolver. It just so happened that the operative was returning from his morning run and unfortunately he saw the pistol.

"The other agent saw that the operative was startled and had stopped suddenly once he had noticed the exposed firearm. Trying to salvage the situation, the agent said, in a loud enough voice so the operative could clearly hear, 'Jack, I don't care if this is an open-carry state or you have a concealed weapons permit, I have warned you not to bring your gun on the job, you crazy Second Amendment extremist!' Then, turning to the operative, he remarked, 'Ever since he stopped a robbery at a mall back in Lubbock, Texas…I think he sort of sees himself as Wyatt Earp or some movie actor. Sorry for startling you! I assure you he will not bring it to the jobsite again.' The operative seemed to be fine and remarked, 'It takes all kinds of people…I guess if he has a permit to carry, its fine with me. Just don't let my wife see it. She'll freak out; you knows how moms get!'"

Having finished the report, Cole said, "I think we're okay for now, but I wanted you to know about the incident."

That's just the opening that North was hoping for! So far the FBI was still looking to figure out what the west coast operatives had for targets. North had spent the night trying to devise a strategy that would allow him to persuade the FBI to back off at least the physical observation teams, thereby decreasing the likelihood that WCU's mission would be uncovered. "Well, I for one would feel more comfortable if we dropped the direct surveillance of the operatives at this point and focused on the wiretap and online communications instead," North responded. "Didn't I hear you and SA Argo discussing this very issue before you made the assignment to the San Francisco office? In fact, I must strongly recommend that a course of action be taken immediately. Do you want me to speak with SA Argo, or will you?"

"No, I'll handle it!" responded Cole. North was somewhat relieved, but he still felt that they were not out of the woods yet, and that the other officials could still make the connections between all of the camping trips. But at least, the field agent's slip-up had bought him some time.

Once back in Philly, North set up a meeting with Captain Simpson and Detectives Kent and Howe at the South Philadelphia Police headquarters. He wanted to get the latest update on their investigations to see if there was anything else they might have uncovered that would provide greater clarity to Leong's overall plan Leong. Forensics Chief Farrow and her team had done a very thorough analysis of both the diner and warehouse murder scenes. In doing so they had discovered a blood sample on the doorknob at the diner, on a chain used to prevent turning off the water valve to the sprinkler system at the warehouse, and on a broken hacksaw blade. She had presumed that the blood on the doorknob was from a botched effort to jimmy the lock on the door. The blood sample from the chain most likely came when the bad guys attempted to cut the lock used to keep the chain that controlled the main valve to the warehouse sprinkler system. Though the blood samples were very small, her team was able to confirm that they came from none of the victims of the diner or warehouse slayings. With no firm evidence, there wasn't a prayer of getting a court order requiring any of the Chinese nationals to provide blood or saliva samples. "Once this operation is completed and portions of it are made public, I am sure you will be able to get a court order to get DNA samples to confirm the Chinese O/T personnel were involved in those two murder scenes," said North. He asked them to hold off a bit longer, not wanting to draw additional attention toward the O/T location. North finished with, "I really appreciate how flexible and supportive you guys have been, given all the public pressure on you to solve these crimes. I want to assure you that the national security is at stake and I hope that in the end we can declassify enough of the operation so you can see the part you played and appreciate just how important your efforts have been!"

As North was leaving the police headquarters, he received a call from Cole. "I just received a call from SA Argo about needing some assets from the Philadelphia office for additional security detail; the aim was to cover the arrival of a high-level delegation from China on, August 28 and their departure on, September 1. "I have a friend, Watson Parr, at the State Department who works the Japanese desk and we were going to host a BBQ that Sunday," continued Cole. "But he has been told that he has to be at work that whole weekend, because, and get this, the Japanese Foreign Ministry is hosting a Chinese delegation during the same timeframe in Tokyo. Also, his counterpart told him that the request was a complete surprise given the present state of relations between the two countries. What really concerns me is the dates of the scheduled meetings. I understand there are a lot of parts to this puzzle, but I still don't have a clear picture of where this is heading. I will give you a call if I find anything new. I've got another call coming in, so got to go!" Before North could respond, Cole had dropped the call.

At this point, North was fighting a headache and this latest news only made it worst. What was their next move? *I'll reach out to Col. Sutherland in Sydney to see if his contacts inside have picked up anything new and let him know that I have tracked down and confirmed that the two men from the photograph had murdered Will and his family!*

"Col. Sutherland's office," the secretary said when North called. "I'm sorry, but he is currently in a conference call. Can I take a message or would you prefer to call back?"

"Would you tell him that Major North had called from America? And can I speak with him now?"

"Stand by Major North. I will check."

After a while, North heard the voice say, "Major North, he'll be with you in a few moments. Please stand by, and I'll connect you now!"

"Col. Sutherland, I have some news that I think you will appreciate," North began as soon as the colonel came on the line. "I have found the two men who murdered Will and his family. Currently, they are involved in a major operation here in the States, and this operation also has international implications. You can rest assured that no matter what happens to the operation, the two of them will pay for their crimes, but you won't read about it in the paper or online. They will just disappear!"

"Major North, that is good to know, and I will relay this news to some of Will's closest friends. We really appreciate your efforts to bring this very sad chapter to an appropriate end. Oh, by the way, feel free to inflict as much pain on the two bastards as possible. Is there anything I can do for you, or are you coming back anytime soon?"

North's voice lightened a bit as he said, "Unfortunately no, I've got my hands full with an operation that involves the two Chinese bastards we were just discussing and it's getting more complex as time goes on. By any chance, have you or someone from your country's law enforcement run into or have become aware of any attempts to inflict a mass casualty event anywhere in Australia?"

"Normally, I would consider that an off-the-wall question, but yes we did." North could hear a change in Sutherland's voice. "Why do you ask?"

"I can assume by your response that such an event did not and will not *actually* take place," said North. "What was the plan meant to do and when was it scheduled to take place?"

After reminding North that the information was classified, Sutherland said, "About two weeks ago one of Sydney Police's undercover drug unit member was working on a buy, when one of the regular users comes in. The seller signals his security guys to 'get that broke son-of-a-bitch the fuck out of my sight!' So the security guys grab this 'user' and are about to throw him out, when the guy pulls out a wad of cash. The seller motions to let him stay. While the undercover officer and seller are trying to finish their business, the guy waiting is clearly coming down and in desperate need of getting more drugs into his system.

"So the seller asks the officer to let him take care of the guy waiting and motions this user forward. The seller grabs the cash and starts to count it out and to his amazement, the bills total out to $5,000 dollars. The seller confronts this guy about how he got this much cash. This user smiles and says, 'I will have even more once I get all of Sydney high.' The undercover officer chimed in, saying, 'You're full of bullshit! You're the one that's high.' The guy looked at the officer and said, 'No, really, some guy is paying me to pull a massive joke on all of Sydney; it will be in all the newspapers, you'll see.' Everybody started laughing at this guy, and he stopped smiling, saying, "You'll see and those at Perth too.' The user grabbed his drugs and headed out the door. The undercover officer asked, 'Who in the hell was that?' and the seller said, 'All I know is his last name is Burnett and he works part-time in Sydney's water department, or something like that."

"The undercover officer reported what he heard that night and Sydney's police commissioner turned it over to us. We started to follow and observe this guy and placed video and sound surveillance in his apartment, but it looked as though there was nothing to the story. We were just ready to drop the whole issue when a package was dropped off via local courier on August 2. Written on the package were the words 'Not to be opened until August 30,' but he probably thought that it was more drugs for him. While my team watched, he opened the package to reveal more money, some type of instructions, two large double-layered plastic containers, and a small package of cocaine for him to use 'only after he had poured the large containers of white powder into the city's water system, beyond the filtration system.' And a note attached to the small bag of cocaine said that if the 'joke' was successful, there would be more. But if the joke did not go as agreed, he would be dealt with in a terrible manner.

"Well, you can imagine that the idea of a bag of cocaine just sitting there was too much for a hardened drug addict. The bag sat on the table for about six hours until the video recorded him saying to himself, 'Fuck it' before he cut the bag open, put a tiny bit on his finger, and proceeded to rub it on his gums. My men who were observing this expected him to show the signs they were trained to see when someone uses cocaine, but they saw something very different. Instead of him looking like he was getting 'high,' they said he spun around a couple of times like a child's spinning top and then dropped like a sack of potatoes. The team rushed in from the van where they were observing him, but he was already gone. They gathered up everything, including his body, and have kept everything under wraps as we check out whether or not his comment about Perth was real. I have a team over in Perth and another team trying to track down the courier and hopefully the source of the poison contained in the package that was to be put into the city's water system. I expect we will have much more information within the next 36–48 hours."

"Thanks, I'll give you a call back in forty-eight hours," said North. "One more question: have you heard anything about a Chinese delegation coming to meet with your leadership?" He could hear even more hesitation in Sutherland's voice as the latter replied, "I'm stunned! We just got news of it about an hour ago; why do you ask?"

"I'm still working on a hunch, so I'll tell you later Colonel, gotta go now!"

All the same, North just sat his hotel room, in the dark, trying to put the pieces of the puzzle together. He turned on his desk lamp, took a pad of paper and started to make notes, but the more notes he made, the more he crossed out. He realized he was reaching the point of exhaustion, but knew time was running out as well. He looked at the calendar and saw that it was already August 14, and he still did not have a grasp of what the end game was for Leong's plan. It was clear that he was seeking to impact the US, but did he think that the outbreak of a new lethal pandemic, race riots in Chicago, the western forests on fire, mass border crossings, and a major cyber-attack would further weaken an already anemic administration? North knew that if he took all of the information he had and told his boss of his operation thus far, she would shut everything down and say that he was chasing ghosts, since it would be hard to prove that China was actually the driver of the whole show. *I have already stepped over the limits of my authority, so she would either fire me or have me thrown in jail. I've got to think more clearly and figure this thing out.* With these thoughts, he turned the light out, closed his eyes, and quickly feel asleep.

North was awakened by a call from South America; it was Chief Allen who said, "Steve, I've got some good news and some very good news. Our current list of cyber criminals now totals ten, with the addition of Calvin Wang of Hong Kong and Jeffery Cline of the UK! If we can pull this off and snatch even half of these bastards when this thing is over, it will put a real dent in cyber-crime. I'll say one thing about these criminals: They sure know how to party. The expensive liquor and even more expensive female companion-ship have been nonstop. I wish I could get invited to one of those shindigs. 40-year-old Balvenie Single Malt Scotch, 45-year-old Ma-callan Scotch, 18-year-old Sazerac Rye, George T. Stagg Bourbon, Dom Perignon Rose' Champagne… the list goes on. The receipt for the liquor alone runs into several thousand dollars every day. I'm putting you on notice right now; when you give us the go ahead to apprehend these 'sons of a bitches,' I'm sending Sealy and his crew of cut-throats after them and I'm going straight for the liquor cabinet!

"And wow, the women…well they are bringing them in from all over the world. You know, the real high-class stuff, so clearly they are sparing no expense. This is where having a guy like Sealy on your team pays off. He is actually old friends with one of the pimps that handles some of these international beauties. So Sealy made a deal with him that's going to cost the NSA a small fortune. Sealy said that we, the CIA and the NSA would match his entire take from this event if he could get one of his 'ladies' to plant a listening device some-where on Pascal's nightstand, so that we could listen in on phone calls. Hold on to your pocketbook, because that is just what they did and it paid off. The leader, Juan Pascal, received a phone call from the

Chinese embassy, reminding him that his crew must be ready to go at exactly 11:59 pm on August 28. And that Leong would expect the shutdown or severe disruption of all utilities, banking, stock markets, fuel pipelines, hospitals, power grids, communications, and air traffic control centers, including military operations. However, Pascal's team's services might be needed even during the first stage of the operation, starting on August 27, albeit to a lesser extent. The caller also reminded Pascal that Leong had stressed that Pascal's team must be absolutely careful not to tip their hand and alert the Americans to what will happen before 'phase two' kicks off. It sounds to me that there are two distinct stages in Leong's plan.

"Interestingly, it appears that the US mainland is not to be affected during the 'first stage.' Also wanted you to know that Sealy has a small army ready to go. I will warn you that the folks Sealy recruited really have it in for Ruiz and the government. It will get bloody, but I think that is all we can expect. This regime currently in power has reduced what was a thriving economy to a socialist nightmare in shambles. The leader's 'socialist paradise' promise has people out of work, without adequate food or medical resources, and trying to escape anyway they can. Many of the people that signed up for Sealy's army have suffered greatly because of Ruiz and they want revenge! I just hope Sealy can keep them on a leash. So that is the latest from down here; you got anything I need to know?"

North's comments were immediate and very appreciative. "I couldn't have picked two better guys to handle the situation down there than you and Sealy. When this is over, you'll have to introduce me to some of those expensive liquor brands."

As North set his phone down, he now had another variable to put in play. The division of the overall plan into stage One and stage Two was a new twist to be considered, since the August 27 date had surfaced before only in connection with having the tech system tested. North thought it might be a good time to engage with a Japanese counterpart now that he knew a Chinese delegation would also be meeting with high-level Japanese government officials. Last year he had met and gotten to know a member of the Japanese Interior Service, Jetsui Kozan. And Jet, as he liked to be called, was a senior deputy. North could tell immediately that Jet had the same level of intense dedication toward Japan that North had toward America, and that is probably why they hit it off. North felt if he could touch base with Jet, just maybe he could provide some additional Intel to help him more clearly understand Leong's "big picture." North's call to Jet was a brief one, for Jet didn't have any Intel. So, at the end of the day North was still stumped.

Eventually, North fell asleep at three in the morning, after several hours of tossing and turning from trying to piece this whole show together into a coherent and logical plan that would provide him with the means to anticipate what Leong was going to do next.

North was awakened by the sunlight coming through the curtains he had left open the previous night. He sat up on the edge of the bed, rubbed his eyes, and looked at his Rolex Submariner. "Almost ten," he muttered out loud to himself. "I have to get some coffee and get moving." But before he even got up, his phone rang, and it was Allen again. "Steve, I don't know if this is important or not, but I thought you should be aware that some more hackers have shown up. From listening to Juan Pascal's conversations with the Chinese embassy, we had assumed that all of his team had arrived. However, there was an incident that took place in front of the hotel that got our attention and may provide you with intel you could use to figure out the big picture. At seven in the morning, a small van pulled up in front the hotel, or 'hacker central,' as we now refer to it, and unloaded four Asian-looking guys. While they were unloading their gear, the undercover security guard on duty saw what was taking place and motioned them to get back in the van and leave. When the four men either ignored their orders or did not understand Spanish, they were wrestled to the ground and handcuffed. We could not make out everything that was said, but we could hear one of the men mention Pascal by name. That brought a response from the senior security officer on duty; he phoned the seventeenth floor, saying that he needed to speak to Pascal.

"Pascal was evidently still asleep, probably recovering from the previous night's festivities. He took the call in his bedroom, and we were able listen to the conversation between Pascal and the security officer at the front of the hotel. The officer told Pascal that the men they had in custody were part of his team, to which Pascal replied, 'Bullshit, my team is assembled and up here!' Then he slammed the phone down and we assume he tried to go back to sleep. At that point, a police van pulled up in front of the hotel—most likely to haul off the four detainees. One of the detainees must have known some Spanish, because the officer removed the handcuffs to permit him to make a phone call. About five minutes later, Pascal was awakened again by his phone ringing. We listened in as a senior officer from the Chinese embassy explained that the four men currently detained were in fact a late addition to the operation. Pascal was incensed that he had neither been informed nor consulted with on these additions to his team. The embassy officer explained that the men had been added at Leong's instructions. He also added that the four men would not be directly involved in stage Two, which begins on August 29, but would be resources if he chose to utilize them. The four men were there expressly to commence operations at midnight on August 26, when stage One kicks off. 'What the hell are you talking about? stage One, August 27...I've never heard any of this before!' The embassy's officer's response seemed to surprise Pascal; after his outburst, he was informed that 'he did not need to know.'

"Pascal was told that he had to make room for the four hackers and to provide assistance to them if necessary. Pascal said he did not understand why the four new men were so important, as his team was already top notch and could handle any challenge. Now get this, he was told that 'Leong has full confidence in your team, but the four 'North Korean' hackers have specialized targets that they have been working on and that are critical for stage One's success.' At that point Pascal hung up on the embassy officer and called down to the security officer to escort the four new members to the seventeenth floor. North Korean hackers…I wonder how they fit into the overall plan, interesting, eh? Well, Steve I'll give you another call if anything new pops up!"

After Allen hung up, North just sat there in his underwear, re-membering that Col. Sutherland had shown him photos of Leong during several visits to the North Korean leader's residence over the past eighteen months.

After showering, North grabbed a cup of coffee and sat down at the desk. He picked up his notes, stared at them for a long time, and then proceeded to rip out all the pages and start over with a fresh clean page. He knew time was running out but he needed to find out their next move. At the same time, if he alerted a lot of others about what he had uncovered, their actions would in response cause a chain reaction that would tip their hand and show the opponents that North and his team were on to them. Leong was a devoted chess player and, it became very clear, a keen student of Sun Tzu's *Art of War*. With that in mind North started to list the things that were most obvious to him.

1. Leong was a long-term strategist who was quite adept about anticipating the countermoves of his opponents.

2. The secrecy of the plan was so important that he was willing to risk an international investigation by murdering a hotel manager and clerk in Singapore and the entire family of an Australian intelligence agent.

3. Leong had started to set this up as long as twenty-five years ago, when he had started to place deep cover agents in both Canada and the US.

4. This plan must have been sanctioned at the highest levels of the CCP to have acquired funding and approval for its international scope.

5. The current administration's perceived weakness has emboldened the CCP that now is the time to execute this plan.

6. Xi must have given the green light once he had become President for life.

7. There is a coordinated plan to affect life within the US, to cause death via the Covid-19 variant, riots in response to the large-scale massacre that was planned for Chicago, extensive forest fires in the west, destruction of infrastructure, an ever-increasing flow of illegals at the southern border, and nationwide shutdown of critical services via hacking. None of these would have been directly attributed to Chinese involvement.

8. Leong had planned that these internal problems would absorb the public's time and attention, thereby putting added stress on the current administration.

9. Since all of those calamities would not be directly attributed to the Chinese, the public would be less likely to demand retribution or confrontation with China.

10. At first, everything seemed to be solely led by the Chinese, but now it appeared that the North Koreans were involved too.

11. The North Koreans had clearly targeted South Korea for unification of the Korean peninsula.

12. The Chinese kept demanding that Taiwan be recognized as part of China and would do whatever is necessary to make that happen.

13. The Chinese had been aggressive in building up and modernizing their military, as quickly as possible.

14. America and its Pacific allies finally recognized that the notion of benign neglect toward China has had the opposite outcome than what they had hoped.

15. China now saw a closing window of opportunity before the US and its allies would put together a unified strategy that would reduce or make less effective China's efforts to displace American global influence with its own.

16. North Korea had been viewed in the past as a necessary buffer to protect China's southern flank, but recently it had been more of a distraction and headache as well as a financial drain to its own needs.

17. North Korea's constant agitation and renewed friction with South Korea meant that the military positioning of US forces required a greater presence and readiness than would be normally necessary.

18. China had become aware that Taiwan had sped up its top secret nuclear weapons program.

19. The US had repeatedly maintained that it would not provide nukes to Taiwan, but the Chinese have never trusted that pledge, which is why they had deployed monitoring teams like the one in South Philadelphia.

20. Whatever was going to happen, North Korea would kick off part of the plan on August 27 and China was targeting August 29 to do the same.

21. China was sending secret high-level delegations to the US, Australia, and Japan at the same time.

22. China's long-range missile silos were not operational yet.

23. The US had a deep commitment to defend South Korea.

24. The US had said it would defend Taiwan but had not specified its level of intervention.

25. The timing of the Chinese operation was scheduled to align with an extended US holiday and, most importantly, only sixty days before a presidential election.

CHAPTER 7

CLEAR AS MUD

North leaned back in his chair and stared out of the window, thinking that if he were playing chess with Leong, he would likely want to draw his opponent away from where he would plan his important moves. Leong would want his opponent to engage his initial moves while he would move his other pieces into place for the main assault. If Taiwan was the main objective, a North Korean assault and invasion of the south could be the stage One. Because many of the smaller US military bases were close to the border, the North Koreans would likely overrun those bases in short order. Those bases or camps act as a trip wire, and the casualties would be very high. Once that happens, US forces would swarm the Korean peninsula and it would get very bloody. The concentration of US military would continue to build into an overwhelming force that even Kim Jong Un knew that he could not defeat. So, Leong's trip to Jong Un's palace was intended to reassure him…but of what?

Kim must have been promised that if he attacked South Korea, China would back his play. If such a notion were true that would violate Leong's chess-like theories of misleading his opponent to conceal his true intentions. The invasion of South Korea by North Korea would, in very short order, see a high concentration of US military assets, so if one wanted to look for targets, such a scenario would provide a target-rich environment, essentially a kill zone that China could easily attack from different directions, particularly from several of its newly established bases in the South China Sea. That may have been what Leong had promised Kim Jong Un, but again, that seemed too obvious a ploy; North decided that there must be another move that Leong has planned for.

The obvious move for China would be to persuade Taiwan to join China or face an invasion, which Taiwan could never resist since the US would be engaged in war on the Korean Peninsula, Australia was too distant to react in a timely fashion, and Japan had limited striking power. The arrival and timing of high-level Chinese delegations would decide if they would be in position to negotiate or threaten due to America's heavy engagement in an ongoing Korean conflict. So the secret delegations could put an ultimatum to the US, Australia, and Japan to back off of their commitment to Taiwan or else they would take Taiwan by force and engage all three countries in a bloody conflict. Such an option might force the US to consider the nuclear option. But given the current administration's "lack of backbone" in dealing with tough issues, the thought of a nuclear war would prove to be too formidable. So Leong and Xi are betting that the US will fold under the pressure, while their other plan would affect the US population with the impending cyberattacks, newer Covid-19 virus, and so on. None of the problems could be positively attributed to the Chinese either, thereby making it difficult to make a public case in favor of going to war with China. This would also result in very unhappy American voters, just before a major election. Leong had set up the chess board pretty much all in China's favor, using North Korea and its regime as the pawn to be sacrificed in stage One. And if the US and its allies did not agree to back off of their support of Taiwan, then an invasion would be necessary—which brought them to stage Two. Still, that is guess work at this time!

Such arrogance! North thought. A plan like this would cost hundreds of thousands of lives, and all for what? Just to reinvent a Chinese dream: by eliminating an ethnic Chinese democracy less than hundred miles from the mainland and protecting CCP's tight hold on power, with Xi as the new supreme Emperor. The more North thought about it, the more incensed he became. The best option was to inform his boss. But first, North would run his theories and conclusion by Allen. After a forty-five minute explanation from him, Allen arrived at the same conclusion and agreed with North that passing the information to Director Case was the appropriate course of action. North asked Allen if the North Korean hackers ever left the hotel.

"Yeah," replied Allen. "Every day, at about five in the afternoon, they pile into a cab and go to this little café. Just like clockwork."

"Tomorrow when they go to the café, they will meet an unfortunate end when they are caught in the middle of a botched robbery attempt and killed in the crossfire," said North with a steely glint in his eye. "Or at least that's what will be reported; I want them out of the picture, got it?"

"Got it," Allen replied. Then North said, "For the record, if you do not get any other contact or guidance from me, tell Sealy to attack the hotel at 9:00 pm local time on August 28."

Allen responded, "Will do and good luck. You're riding a tiger, be careful and don't get eaten."

North began typing frantically on his laptop, piecing the puzzle together as he understood it. Unfortunately Leong's plan still had a high likelihood of success, given the current administration's failure to exercise international power diplomacy, even though some of the major threats to the American public had been mitigated. As North continued to put his report together, he kept thinking about all those lives of US military personnel that would be lost and the people of Taiwan who might be betrayed and given over to a regime that would no doubt destroy their lives to restore an outdated dream of a dictator.

Soon, North needed to take a break. As he walked out onto the courtyard of the hotel, it was still very warm and very humid, but the stars were bright and it was quiet outside. He tormented himself with the thoughts that he must do something to change the outcome; surely there was some power within his grasp to deter the upcoming course of events. If Taiwan had just a few nukes, it might make Leong and Xi rethink their plan. North also needed to even the score with Wei and Ling for the murders they had committed. As he sat there on a bench in the courtyard he noticed an Air Force C-17 transport pass overhead, probably headed for McGuire AFB, across the Delaware River, and into the Jersey Pine Barrens. That reminded him of his conversation with his old friend Dan Kelly concerning the use of the imitation nukes and hypersonic cruise missiles housed at the warehouse in South Philly. Dan had cleared North to use up to twenty-five of the fake nukes and up to a hundred of the fake hypersonic cruise missiles in a NSA sanctioned exercise.

North reached a decision. Tomorrow morning he would call the White House and attempt to get clearance for a NSA exercise outside the US. Then he would pay a visit to Col. Adams, the point of contact for the loading and shipping of the fake nukes/missiles. North thought to himself, *If we can make the Chinese think that Taiwan has received twenty-five small nukes from us and positioned them for use, that might be enough to derail any potential invasion of Taiwan and shorten the incursion by North Korea.* The more North thought about the scheme the more he liked it. At least if it did not work, he had done what he thought was right, even if it got him fired or worse. He also realized that he was reaching far beyond what his position called for and that the worst-case scenario here could mean prison time. As he finished typing his report, he thought to himself, *The Director is going to go ballistic.* He smiled and sarcastically thought how he always seemed to find a way to endear himself to his bosses. Then he realized he needed to rest and wanted to review the report one more time before he sent it to her. North decided to review it in the morning. He also planned to touch base with Cole on his plan and alert Kent and Howe that he might need their assistance in dealing with the Chinese nationals at the South Philly house. He wrote a note to remind himself to call the White House before he did anything else. *Tomorrow I'm going to throw a wrench into Leong's well thought out plan,* North thought to himself as he started to drift off.

At six the next morning, North made a call to a secure number located on the third floor below the White House; the objective was to obtain a Level 5 clearance code required to conduct security exercises outside the continental US. He sensed it might be a long shot, given the requirement of a security review by the White House, because it was an operation that was to involve China.

"Last name and number, sir?" asked a staff officer.

"North. 3439610."

"Very good. And the clearance code phrase?"

"Day light falcon."

"You are cleared, Major North," the officer replied. North spoke, "I would like to speak with the senior clearance officer on duty and this is urgent!" The staff officer on the call said, "Major North, that is not possible at this time; he is currently giving a high-level brief. However, I could pass a message on to him, if you'd like?"

"This is very time sensitive," insisted North. "I need a clearance number as quickly as I can to conduct and test an operational concept with three C-17s being sent to Kadena AFB, Okinawa."

There was a pause before the officer replied, "Major North, after reviewing your clearance profile, I can see that you do not need any further levels of approval. Your profile, A-1b, indicates that I can assign an operational clearance code/number for your exercise without any further review because your position gives you that authority. I have a code/number for you sir; would you like it now, or do you still want to talk with a senior clearance officer?"

There was a long pause and the officer said, "Major North are you there?"

"Yes, yes…I'm still on the line." North's voice was hesitant at first, then firmer as he said, "Yes, I would like clearance code number."

"Are you ready?"

"Yes, go ahead."

"The code is NA, that's November Alpha, 341823. Did you get that?"

"Yes, November Alpha 341823."

"That is correct Major North. Now I just need the name of your exercise."

North thought for a few seconds before saying, "Operation Dark Star."

"Let me confirm this for the record, 3 C-17's to Kadena AFB, Okinawa, NA 341823, Operation Dark Star, got it."

"Could you answer a question for me," replied North. "When did the requirement for a senior-level review for operations in the far east get lifted?"

"Lifted? Sir, we have not had that requirement in effect since…at least eighteen months."

As the call ended, North was wondering why his boss would try to mislead him into thinking that he would need special clearance and would also be unlikely to get it for an operation taking place in the far east. But he didn't have the time to mull over this now. North grabbed a cup of coffee and started the drive from his South Philadelphia hotel room across the Ben Franklin Bridge and on to McGuire AFB in New Jersey. As he drove, he dialed up the number for Col. Adams, whose function was to control much of the US Air Force heavy-lift air transportation requirements for the northeast. "This is Major Stephen North, Marine Corps. I desperately need a meeting with Col. Adams," he said when the call connected. "Please tell him that Dan Kelly must have probably spoken with him about me. I'm on the road right now and should be at your front gate in about forty minutes…"

"Standby, Major North," said the voice before silence ensued for a couple of minutes. "Major North, he has a meeting at ten this morning but, can see you at eleven. When you arrive at the main gate, let the guard know you are here to see Col.V. Adams, I will have them give you an escort to Col. Adams' office in hangar number 22."

"Great, thank you!" North replied. When he found his way to Col. Adams' office, he was promptly offered a cup of coffee. "Thanks for meeting with me sir, I believe Dan Kelly spoke with you about giving authorizing me to conduct an exercise utilizing the imitation nukes and hypersonic cruise missiles that are currently stored in a warehouse in Philadelphia?"

"Yes, Major North, he did just that and he also told me you're a good officer, but you can go out there with some, shall we say less-than-conventional thinking. Is that an accurate account of your character?" North smiled as he said, "Yes sir, Dan knows me pretty well!" "Major North, just so we understand each other, I'm a by-the-book kind of officer!" Col. Adams responded sternly. "However, Mr. Kelly also informed me that you are quite dependable and valuable when it comes to out-of-the-box solutions to difficult problems. So just what problem are you looking to solve?"

"Col. Adams, I'll get right to the point," began North. "I've been tracking information that indicates that if I can execute the proposed operation in the next twenty-four hours, we'll have a chance to prevent a war." Col. Adams had been drinking coffee, and at these words, he stopped mid-sip, and his jaw dropped open; he looked as if he had seen a UFO land in his front yard. He glanced down at his desk, took another sip of coffee and said, "Well, that is certainly out there. You do have an approved operations number?" "Yes sir, but I need this to happen in the next 24–36 hours and I will need to be on board the lead C-17 when it takes off."

Col. Adams called in his Operations Officer, LtCol. Owens and asked him to run the exercise approval number. The officer returned and confirmed that the number checked out. Col. Adams motioned for the officer to take a seat as North explained what he exactly he had in mind and the time he wanted the shipment to be picked up. Col. Adams went over a very detailed procedure that he and Kelly had developed to ensure that the warehouse location and the shipments to and from it remained secret. He added that this procedure had to be followed to preserve the secrecy of their counter-operation.

Two hours later, North was on his way back to Philly and confident that Col. Adams would follow the script. North knew that he had to ensure Wei and Ling would be aware of the shipment and that they would take the bait.

As soon as North arrived back in Philly, he called Agent Cole and asked him to be at precinct headquarters for a meeting with Simpson, Kent, and Howe at one in the afternoon. Walking into the precinct offices, North had to remind himself to be careful about what he said at the meeting. Although Agent Cole had a top secret security clearance, Philadelphia's finest did not, so some of the details would have to be omitted when they were briefed about the activities scheduled for the next 24–36 hours. As he walked through the officers' room, he noticed the weather report that was being broadcast on the screen. Another hurricane was heading up the eastern seaboard and it looked that North's timetable for the operation might need to be adjusted.

North had planned about an hour for the briefing. Using the available chalk board he began by describing the overall plan. Even though parts of his plan could not be discussed, Simpson, Kent, and Howe were surprised to hear that North wanted the police to make as much noise and commotion as possible to draw attention to the fact that there was a large shipment leaving the government facility just down the street from the Chinese O/T outpost in South Philly. North stressed that at six in the evening, the city's transportation personnel should start blocking off the side streets with barriers with signs posted all along the street where the outpost was located, stating that the street will be closed to all civilian traffic from 9:00 pm to 3:00 am to make way for government shipments. That should provide adequate time for the Chinese O/T unit to locate and confirm the likelihood of a shipment coming from the warehouse they had been posted to monitor.

At this point, North turned to Howe and asked, "Do you still have Wei and Ling under surveillance and can you confirm their location at this time?"

"Yes, we continue to monitor their location on a 24-hour schedule," replied Howe. "Today they spent most of their morning at the Chinese embassy and are currently in route to the Mayor's residence for a late lunch with the Mayor and a couple of the area's state representatives."

"Excellent," North commented. "It's critical that they remain local and can be reached by their South Philly outpost leader, once the barriers start going up. I fully anticipate that both Wei and Ling will want to be present to observe and monitor the shipment as it leaves the warehouse. And I'm positive they will want to shadow the shipment to its destination. Before I forget to mention it, excellent work getting the portable monitor returned, by leaving it in the bushes by the driveway! They would never suspect that the police ever had it in their possession. A total of eleven flatbed truck/trailer combinations will depart McGuire AFB at approximately 8:00 pm; they'll accompanied by a New Jersey State Police escort in route to the government warehouse in South Philly.

"The NJ State Police will stay with the trucks until the state line.

Once they enter onto the Ben Franklin Bridge, the police escort will disengage, and the convoy should be met with and escorted to the warehouse by Philadelphia city police units. Loading of the eleven trucks is anticipated to be completed by just after midnight. The trucks will then depart by the same route by which they had arrived. They have been briefed to drive very slowly through the neighborhood to provide adequate time for the Chinese to monitor and confirm that it is indeed the shipment they have been assigned to monitor and report on. City police will escort the trucks to the state line, where the NJ State Police will pick them back up, for the return escort to McGuire AFB to be loaded on transports and onto their destination. Once the trucks leave the neighborhood with their cargo, all of the road barriers can be removed. I would respectfully ask that you do not move to arrest any of the Chinese until I inform you that the operation has ended. I hate to have to be the bearer of bad news, it would be best if both of you detectives stayed away. If you think about it, why would a classified shipment call for the presence of two veteran detectives? I have some further points to discuss with Agent Cole, so are there any questions or points that need further clarification?"

"Are you sure that we will not need the SWAT team tonight?" Kent asked. North smiled as he said, "I'm 98% sure there won't be any gunplay tonight; our opponents have a vested interest in keeping things low key, so you can keep your machine guns and flame-throwers in the trunk!" At that, they all laughed.

"Lastly, I may not see you for some time as I'll be accompanying the shipment to its destination, if everything goes as planned! Thank you all for the support and hard work! At this time I have another meeting to discuss other classified items."

"Major North, just what is being shipped out on those trucks?" asked Howe.

North smiled and replied, "Sorry, but that's classified. However, I assure you the public is not in any danger."

Later, North met Agent Cole who said, "Steve, I hope to God you know what you're doing. This whole thing could blow up in your face and it would be a real doozie. I'm glad I'm not in your shoes. You know this thing you have about saving the world is not going to always work out in your favor and even if it does work out, the big boys will take all the credit!"

"Thanks 'mom' for your concern," North replied in a teasing voice, "but you know me: Once I commit myself, it's 110% all the way! By the way Agent Cole, I would advise you to alert your San Francisco office to arrest all the members of the Chinese WCU."

Cole looked surprised. "Just what for?"

"For conspiring to set fire to state or national forests, if there is such a law. Upon review, I noted that many of them had bought flare guns and additional flares. But if you check where they are going for camping, there are no large bodies of water nearby, so, why you would need a flare gun. At the very least you need to pick them up and hold them so they cannot contact Wei. Several forest fires have already been triggered by lightning strikes and are burning out of control, so Wei will think that they accomplished their assignments."

Soon, Agent Cole was directing the San Francisco office to quickly but quietly pick up and detain members of Wei's WCU. While North was still working out the details, Cole asked, "So what is the plan? And how deep am I going to be sucked into it?"

"The way I figure it, once Wei and Ling get the word about movement from the warehouse, they will want to initiate the tracking process to confirm that it is in fact being shipped to another location. This means that they will most likely shadow the shipment to the air base to confirm that it is loaded and they will note the aircraft numbers, so that other O/T units will be on alert I need you to follow them and keep me appraised of exactly what they are up to. I anticipate that once they detect that the canisters contain the nukes and missiles, they will call the embassy, which in turn will notify the homeland of the movement. The message will then go out to other O/T units in order to confirm where the cargo is unloaded."

"How can you be so sure that Wei and Ling will even get close enough to confirm that the canisters are being loaded, let alone get the aircraft numbers?" asked Cole.

"Good question," North commented. "Col. Adams and I took a quick ride around the perimeter of the base and found a couple of good vantage points that would work in their favor and provide a clear view of the unloading from the trucks and transfer to the air-craft. Col. Adams said that normally the transfer and loading of cargo would be done on the north side of the base, but for this operation, they will conduct the loading on the southern side because we needed to make it easier for Wei and Ling to witness what's taking place. The first vantage point they will use will allow them to follow the trucks to and from the main gate to the hangar area. However, if they want to get a clearer view of the loading process they will need to move further east on the perimeter, where a little tavern is located. They will approach the east end of the parking lot and going maybe 15–20 feet through the pine trees will give them an excellent spot from which to view the loading of the cargo. The tavern is called, 'The Last Stop' and it should be closed by the time they arrive. Since the parking lot should be empty, you will have to use binoculars and a laser speech reader to observe their activities from a distance. And keep me appraised of what they are doing. I'm leaving for the base in about thirty minutes and will be in the driver compartment of the lead truck travelling to and from the warehouse. From there, I will accompany the shipment to its final destination—on board the lead aircraft—so it's likely that I will not see you for a while. Be safe and thanks for all of your help!"

At the Chinese embassy, Wei and Ling's meeting with the local security chief was interrupted by a call from the south Philadelphia O/T unit leader. He informed Wei about the ongoing barricades and street closures. Wei conveyed the same to Ling, and they quickly headed for the O/T unit's location. By the time Wei and Ling arrived at the outpost, the members were busy calibrating their equipment to confirm what was being shipped from the warehouse.

CHAPTER 8

THE BAIT AND THE PAYBACK

North arrived at hangar 22 on the McGuire AFB complex at three in the afternoon. Col. Adams had arranged for him to get some rest in an unused office toward the rear of the hangar. At eight in the evening, the Operations Officer said that Col. Adams wanted to speak with him one more time before the operation kicked off. During the ensuing conversation, Col. Adams went over the details with North one more time. "Okay, once the trucks arrive back here with their cargo, the three C-17s will be on the ground and available. Once loaded and cleared, departure time is anticipated to be 6:00 am.

"First fuel stop is at Travis AFB in California. The layover for refueling and aircraft check will last approximately two hours. The three aircraft will depart for Hickman Field, Hawaii, the next leg, and the same refueling scenario will be repeated. The final leg involves air refueling about half-way to Okinawa. Remember you lose a day flying in that direction, so it will be late August 26 at this point. Flying time will be approximately seventeen and a half hours, a total of twenty-three hours for the whole journey from McGuire to Kadena AFB. Once you get the cargo to Okinawa, do you have a plan to get it to Taiwan? You said it is imperative that you be on the lead aircraft… that too has been arranged. So, does that about cover it?"

North nodded and added, "Yes sir!"

At this moment, the Operations Officer stuck his head through the doorway and said, "The convoy is ready to depart and the state police are waiting outside the gate to escort you to the state line." The three men shook hands and North departed. Outside, he climbed into the passenger side of the lead truck and nodded to the driver to begin. Once on the road, North made some last-minute phone calls. His first call was to the duty officer at the warehouse to let him know that the trucks were rolling and make sure that they would be ready once the trucks arrive. The duty officer acknowledged that they would be ready and the load has been pre-staged to ensure minimal delay.

Next, he called Agent Cole for an update on the current location of Wei and Ling. "I'm currently on the third floor of the abandoned house just up the street. I can clearly identify Wei and Ling currently in conversation with the O/T unit leader. There has been a lot of activity since the barriers went up, and I'm positioned to trail Wei and Ling should they chose to follow the convoy on its return to the Mc-Guire AFB. I have confirmed with Captain Simpson that the convoy will have a police escort from our side of the bridge and back. So, do you think they will take the bait?"

"I'm positive. Wei impressed me as the type of person who does not leave *anything* to chance. He will want to ensure that the cargo is loaded and on its way. You should plan on following them, but once again…they must not know they're being watched." After this, North called back to the base and asked the Operations Officer about a possible weather delay due to the hurricane coming up the coast. The officer said it appeared that the hurricane had stalled on the North Carolina outer banks and should not pose a threat to the anticipated timeline. About thirty-five minutes later, the convoy was approaching the Ben Franklin Bridge, and the NJ State Police escort peeled off as the convoy started across the bridge.

North could see the flashing lights of the Philadelphia city police cars ahead. Once the convoy entered the South Philly neighborhood, he asked the driver to slow down. North wanted to ensure that Wei and Ling got a good look at the truck doors, which had the typical government markings and "McGuire AFB" painted in large letters. He wanted to make sure that Wei and Ling knew where the trucks had come from and where they would return to. As the truck that North was riding in passed the Chinese outpost, he rolled down the window to see if he could confirm that Wei and Ling were standing on the porch with the rest of the Chinese operatives. As North scanned the crowd, he noticed Wei at the exact same time that the latter noticed the man in the gray truck; their eyes locked on to each other and neither North nor Wei looked away until their line of vision became obscured by some bushes.

As Wei sat back down in his chair, he thought to himself, *I have seen that face before*…but he could not recall where.

One by one, the trucks cleared inspection and entered the front gate into the government compound. To North, the hours seemed sluggishly crawl by. It was one in the morning when the last canisters were loaded onto the flat beds before being tarped and tie down thirty minutes later. North and the government officer on duty had carefully observed and counted the number of canisters that were loaded. As each canister containing the fake nuclear warhead was loaded, a device in each of those canisters was triggered so it would emit a radioactive pulse that mimicked the normal isotope leakage typically present if an actual nuclear warhead were present in that canister. North was betting that the Chinese detection equipment would be able to "read" the radioactive signal given off by the canister, thereby convincing the O/T unit that nuclear warheads were in fact being transported along with the hypersonic cruise missiles. To convince the Chinese that the cruise missiles being shipped, he had instructed two of the truckers to temporarily "short tarp" their load, thereby exposing the outline of a missile detailed on the side of a missile canister. Eight trucks were loaded, tarped, and ready to go. North again asked the driver to drive very slowly through the neighborhood. As they passed the Chinese outpost, a man ran from the O/T truck that contained the detection gear, and he was waving what looked like a printout. North could see Wei scolding the man for his outburst. As North looked in his side mirror, Wei signaled something to Ling as they both made their way to their car. North gave a sigh of relief; it seemed that they had taken the bait.

North called Agent Cole to let him know that Wei and Ling would in fact be tailing the convoy back to the air base. Cole acknowledged the message and said he was headed for his car. North was glad he had asked for the police escort. With their sirens and flashing lights, there was no way that Wei and Ling could lose the convoy in those early hours. The convoy arrived back at the main gate at three in the morning, and it was followed closely by Wei and Ling, who in turn were followed, at a safe distance, by Agent Cole.

Cole called North, "Just as you predicted, Wei and Ling pulled off the road and into a little clearing by the main gate. Wei has a small pair of binoculars that he's using to follow the trucks. He's waving his arms at Ling; I guess he's signaling at the latter to hurry up and get back in the car. Now, they're leaving the clearing and pulling out onto the main road and heading east. They just passed the little tavern. We're about a quarter mile past the tavern, and they can see the loading taking place and even see at least two of the C-17s' aircraft numbers."

After a short pause, Cole continued. "It appears that Wei has just completed a phone call. Wei and Ling are now shaking hands and Wei just patted Ling on the shoulder; looks like they are celebrating. Wait a minute! Now Ling is pointing in the direction of the aircraft where the loading is ongoing. Wei seems pretty upset about something; he just threw the phone at Ling. Looks like they are leaving. Now he is pointing at something on the ground…oh it's the phone. Ling has picked it up and is following Wei back to the car. They are in a big hurry—I guess because it appears the loading is near complete. Wei is first to the car and is taking over the driving and is apparently about to leave Ling behind. Hold it! He's waving at Ling to hurry up. He must have seen something he did not like."

There was another pause before Cole exclaimed, "Wait a minute! They are turning around and now heading west. It's a good thing I was lying back in my seat as far as I was; otherwise I think they would have been suspicious of another car on the same road at this time of the morning. Now hold on…they are pulling into the empty parking lot at that little tavern. They are going back into the bushes to have a better look. Steve, I've got a feeling they saw something Wei did not like. He seemed pretty calm and happy after his phone call. Then very shortly after that he seemed to lose it, for lack of a better term. I think you better take a quick look at the final stages of loading and see if something is amiss."

"I'm on my way," North replied tersely. As he headed for the south gate, he glanced back to the personnel who were loading the final batch of canisters. To his horror, he saw that the axle to the loading carts had apparently broken, and the canisters were precariously leaning over at a steep angle. In fact, a few of the canisters had fallen off the cart and three had even broken open. From where Wei and Ling were positioned, they would have been able to see the contents of the canisters. The loaders were picking up pieces of what was supposed to be a 3500 lb. cruise missile and putting it back in the canister and then the two loaders would pick up the canister by hand and place it on a new cart to send it off for the final loading.

North was beside himself. No way could two men lift a 3500 lb. canister between themselves. And the canister marked with the radioactive placard had spilled its contents and was being picked up by men dressed in their regular uniforms and not special hazmat suits. It was then that North knew Wei had figured it was all a show. He went speeding out of the south gate, hoping to intercept Wei and Ling before they could contact the Embassy. Agent Cole saw him racing toward the little tavern and quickly followed. North yelled into his phone at Cole, asking if he had observed Wei speaking on the phone. Cole replied that he had not.

North pulled into the parking lot, at some distance from Wei's vehicle. He got out of his vehicle and walked briskly toward Wei's car; as he passed Wei's car, he heard voices coming his way and glanced down into Wei's vehicle. There, lying on the front passenger seat was Wei's phone, right where Ling had left it. The windows were down because it was a hot and humid summer night. North quickly glanced around, reached into the car, and picked up the phone. But as he reached in, his vehicle keys slipped from his shirt pocket into Wei's car and slid down between the seats. North frantically reached down and around the seats to locate his car keys, but came up empty. The voices were getting closer, so North made a dash for the side door of the tavern that was being propped open by a mop bucket. Before disappearing inside the tavern, North turned around to see if the men had spotted him. The second he turned around, Wei caught a glimpse of his face.

Wei was stunned, that was the face he had seen in the truck, and now it came back to him...that was the same face he had seen in the window of the black Chevrolet Suburban that the detectives had been driving. Wei just stood there for several seconds. "What's the matter?" asked Ling. Wei turned to Ling and said, "Get the phone out of the car." After searching for a while, Ling turned to Wei and said, "I know I left it right here on the seat, but now I can't find it!" Wei slowly turned to Ling and said, "I know where it is!" Ling seemed confused and said, "What do you mean? I know I left it right on the seat, but it's not there now, so how would you know where it is?"

In response, Wei looked at Ling and just started walking to the side door of the tavern.Ling had no choice but to follow. Inside the tavern they looked around and called out to see if anyone was around, there was no response. North had left his radio in his vehicle. He wanted to use Wei's phone and was frantically trying to guess the user code, to no avail. As he looked around for a phone, all he came upon was an old-style payphone, but he had no coins. He knew that Agent Cole would soon be at this location, but did not know how long that might take. So in a desperate attempt to find a way out, he headed down a dimly lit hallway— only to come upon an exit door that was chained and locked. Pushing on the door with all his might achieved nothing except making a lot of noise.

Wei and Ling cautiously entered through the side door. As they looked around, they could hear some rather loud noise that sounded like chains clanging against one another. Ling asked, "What exactly are we looking for?" Wei put his hand on Ling's shoulder and said, "Be careful; I have a feeling that the man we are pursuing would stop us if he can, and we cannot let that happen."

On the other end of the hallway, North realized that the door was too tightly secured for him to open. So he headed for the next door up the hall. As he was about to enter through that door, Wei and Ling turned the corner at the end of the hall. Even though it was just a quick glance, their eyes locked again, this time in a steely glaze. The door led to a storeroom and North could see a window in the darkness. As North headed for the window, Wei entered and turned on the lights.

North noticing the bars on the window, took a deep breath, and turned around. Seeing his adversary face to face, Wei said, "I want my phone! Now!" North smiled and said, "Oh this phone?" before bringing it out with a flourish. "It doesn't work anymore," he said firmly, before slamming it against the wall. As the pieces of Wei's phone fell to the floor, Wei's expression did not change a bit. Instead, he smiled again and said, "This is not going to end well for you."

Wei looked at Ling and nodded in North's direction. North took a step in Ling's direction and said, "How do you want to die?" Ling's understanding of English was not that great, but he understood the gist of North's statement and stopped moving toward him. Wei looked at Ling again and nodded in North's direction, this time more firmly. Ling took two steps and stopped after North said, "Hey there big guy, please tell me how you want to die or I will decide for you!" Ling's expression changed and he looked again at Wei as he stopped moving toward North. Wei was getting impatient, so he looked at Ling and in a stern voice said, "Kill him!"

As Ling again started to move toward North.North responded by putting his hand up and said, "Stop! Since you have not told me how you wish to die, I will make the decision for you." Wei and Ling looked at each other in disbelief. North was a shade over six feet and in great shape, but Ling had defeated some very capable opponents in the past and was quite confident that he could defeat North. Ling took another step toward, North who then reached into his pocket, pulling something out, shouted, "Okay then, you're going to die by pencil!" Wei and Ling looked at each other; they were completely dumbfounded. "That's right," North continued. "You're going to die via a very sharp, brand new, bright yellow, American-made pencil. You see I've done it before—not with this particular pencil, but with one just like it! You of course realize there's very little obstruction if you poke a sharp object, like through the ear. However, in your case I will jam it in through your eye and deep into your brain and you'll be dead before you hit the floor. Think about it: What's between your eyelid and your brain. Nothing that would stop a very sharp object, such as this pencil, right? And just think how painful it will be for you if I don't get deep enough on the first lunge. And if I do not get through on the first try, I might try again for the other eye, but by then the pencil point might be a little bit less sharp, so going in, it will hurt even more. Even if you survive, just imagine how you will look with a pencil in your eye!"

At this point, Wei had grown tired of the conversation and Ling's lack of action. He reached into his pocket and pulled out a switch-blade, looked at Ling, and said, "Let's get this over with; there's important work to be done." Then in a clear loud voice, Wei said, in English, "My friend, now *you* are going to die!" Just as they started to move toward North, the door kicked open and an NJ state trooper fired his revolver into the ceiling and said, "Drop the knife and do not take another step, or I'll drop you!" Wei dropped the knife and Ling took a couple of steps backward. Standing beside the trooper was the bar manager who had called 911. Agent Cole soon arrived and presented his FBI credentials. He asked the trooper if he had called it in yet. "Haven't had time," the latter replied. Cole explained to the trooper that this was a highly classified operation and he should not call it in. As Wei looked on in disbelief, North presented his NSA ID to the trooper. "Officer, we both have diplomatic passports," Wei cried out. "You have no right to hold us and I demand you let me contact our embassy immediately or you will be in the center of an international crisis." The trooper looked at Agent Cole and asked, "Is this guy telling the truth?" Agent Cole replied, "I'm afraid he is!"

"So should I let them call their embassy?" asked the trooper.

"No," shouted North. He walked over to the bar manager and said, "Get me a chair, some heavy gloves, and a roll of duct tape, right now!" The bar manager just stood there.

"Didn't you hear what I said?" North repeated imperiously. "I'm in a bit of a hurry, so go get me a chair, gloves, and duct tape, right fucking now!" This time, the bar manager was stunned and replied, "You can't talk to me that way!" North knew the planes were probably waiting on him. So he walked over to the bar manager and said, "Okay, pretty fucking please, get me the chair, gloves, and duct tape before you make me do something to you that I would probably regret." That ensured that the bar manager took less than two minutes to return with a chair, a pair of heavy leather gloves, and a large roll of duct tape. Then North told the bar manager to go home and forget everything that he may have seen or heard tonight. "And if I hear that you have repeated even one word about what you have seen or heard, I will make it a point to make your life unhappy. You see," North pointed at Wei and Ling, "these two wanted to kill thousands of our fellow citizens with a very lethal strain of Covid-19, so what do you think of that?"

The bar manager pointed to Wei and Ling and said, "They were really going to do that?"

North made the sign of the cross over his heart and replied, "Swear to God! They had it all planned out but we stopped their little game and gathered up all of their dispenser bottles before they could use them!" The bar manager gave Wei and Ling the middle finger before turning around and walking away. On his way out, he stopped and yelled, "Just lock up after you're through, okay?"

"Will do," responded Agent Cole.

Wei looked at North with wide eyes and said, "You're lying!" In a moment, North had grabbed Wei by the arms, and using nearly half the roll of tape, secured his arms and legs to the chair, pasting a final strip over Wei's mouth. "You say I'm lying, eh? Well we just got finished arresting the owner of Teepee #36 on Long Beach Island, where you had your little BBQ. We've collected all of your dispensers of the lethal virus you had concocted, there will not be any massacre of Americans in Chicago, and most of your fire-starters are being picked up as we speak. Be that as it may, I'm here to finish some business regarding some murders you had committed, not too long ago, in Australia. You might remember a nice little family that ended up dead because of you and that big guy out in the hallway." North put on the heavy pair of gloves, took a step back, and used up all his pent-up rage to throw a punch at Wei's jaw. Wei's head snapped back and he immediately lost consciousness.

Suddenly, Agent Cole and the trooper heard a blood-curdling yelp from the storeroom. But it was not Wei, but North who was shouting, "Motherfucker, that fucking hurt!" The trooper opened the door just far enough to see North walking around, shaking his right hand. The trooper asked if he was okay. All that North said in response was, "That son-of-a-bitch has a really hard jaw." With that, he went over to the sink in the corner of the room, grabbed a glass and filled it halfway with water, came back and threw it at Wei's face. Then North removed the tape covering his mouth. Wei spit out blood and at least three teeth onto the floor. Then he just stared at North and said, "America's time is coming to an end and you cannot stop it!"

North smiled and said, "Well, we'll see about that!" He took a step back and landed a punch to Wei's mid-section and then another punch to the other side of Wei's face. Wei's head snapped back again under the force. Again, North let out a yelp, saying, "Your jaw is too hard for me."

The second punch to Wei's jaw had splattered blood onto North's face. North came out of the storeroom, shaking his right hand. He headed up the hallway to the restroom. Agent Cole and the trooper assumed North had had enough…but they were wrong. They heard an odd noise coming from the restroom. In less than a minute, North exited the restroom carrying one of the heavy porcelain lids that covered the water tank behind the toilets. As North walked by, the trooper asked, "What are you going to do with that?" Without saying a word, North just slammed the door shut behind him. They heard North say, "This is for Will and Peggy." Then there was a large thud, but this time the scream came from Wei. Then the two men outside heard North ask, "And how is your other knee?"

Then North's voice got louder as he shouted, "This one's for their two wonderful children," before Cole and the trooper heard another loud thud and another loud scream. Inside the storeroom, North raised the porcelain lid over his head and brought it down on

Wei's groin with such force the lid broke into three pieces—which the men outside could hear hitting the floor—but this time, there were no screams, just loud moans. North noticed a box of rubber gloves on one of the shelves in the storeroom and took two out. He came out of the storeroom and looking at Ling, took a deep breath and said, "I wish I had time for you but I do not." He took off the leather gloves, threw them on the floor, and put on the rubber gloves before turning around and walking back into the storeroom. As he passed the trooper, he pulled the revolver out of the trooper's holster in one easy move. Before the trooper could react, North was back in the storeroom.

The trooper started to move toward the storeroom to retrieve his revolver, but Cole grabbed him by his elbow and stopped him. The trooper turned and looked at Cole, but the latter didn't say a word; he just slowly shook his head, with a look that conveyed "Do not even try to stop what is about to happen."

The door slammed shut and less than five seconds later, two shots rang out. As the door to the storeroom opened, they could see Wei's lifeless body still slumped in the chair. One shot through the forehead had blown off part of his skull, with blood splattered all over the wall behind him. The other bullet had gone through Wei's chest. North walked out of the storeroom right past both the trooper and Agent Cole and before they could even react, he stood within three feet of Ling and shot him in the forehead. Ling's head lurched back and he slumped to the floor, dead. Revenge was served!!

Without another word, North slipped the revolver back in to the trooper's holster. The trooper, who was still in shock, said, "You-you just murdered my two prisoners!" North carefully took off the rubber gloves, walked over to the kitchen area, turned on the gas burner, and laid the gloves on top of the lit burner. The gloves vaporized in seconds. North turned off the burner and said, "The planes are wait-ing for me; I must go now." At this point, the trooper grabbed North by his arm and said, "You're not going anywhere! I'm afraid I have to arrest you for murder."

North looked the trooper and said, "Don't worry officer, we won't tell anyone that you murdered your two prisoners, will we Agent Cole?" The trooper turned towards North with a very confused look! Agent Cole followed with, "You know Steve, I don't know why he shot them, but I'm pretty sure they were trying to escape! Don't worry officer, your secret is safe with us." The trooper was speechless. The trooper looked at North and said, "I don't think I can go along with this charade; you shot them and that's the truth."

"Oh really?" North remarked. "When the slugs are examined, the report will confirm that they came from your revolver. Oh and by the way, the only person that will show gunpowder residue on their hands will be you. Oops, that's right, I torched the rubber gloves I was wearing and the gunpowder residue with them! Besides, those two men were part of an operation that would have murdered thousands, maybe hundreds of thousands of your fellow Americans, *and* those bastards killed one of my best friends, his wife, and their two kids."

"You still should have let me take them in," the trooper persisted.

North looked the trooper in the eyes and said, "Given their diplomatic immunity, once the Chinese embassy sprung them from jail, they would have slipped out of the country and they would have never paid for the sins they committed." The trooper still seemed reluctant until North commented, "By the way, besides killing a good friend and his entire family, they killed the family's two dogs." At that, the trooper looked up and said, "Did you say he killed their two dogs?"

"Yup!" said North. Now, the trooper's face changed completely. "If I had known that, I might have shot them myself! You guys can head out; I have a couple of cousins who are connected to some of the mafia crowd. I'll call them and they will have this mess cleaned up before dawn and our two dog killers will find themselves in a shallow grave somewhere in the woods, where no one will ever find them."

North and Cole thanked the trooper; then, North headed back onto the base and Cole headed back to Philly. Once back on base, North went straight for the loading area. He was waved onto the lead C-17, and they were cleared for takeoff.

At about the same time that the lead C-17 was lifting off the runway, the black bag team had just finished wiring the American Legion Hall where a local civic meeting was scheduled to take place in the afternoon. After they were done, they packed up their bags and exited through a basement door. Five minutes later, they were parked about three blocks south of the hall before launching a two-foot-wide drone. The sun had not come up yet, so it was difficult to make out shapes in the pre-dawn hours. Consequently, they switched to infrared on the drone's camera. Before they pressed the button to start the fire, they wanted to use the infrared camera to scan the building and ensure that there was no people inside and so that no one would get hurt. Once the scan was finished, they pressed the ignite button, and on the drone's video feed, they could just make out muted flashes as the flares ignited. In less than ten minutes, the ensuing fire had engulfed the entire basement area and the first floor. With their mission accomplished, the team retrieved the drone, turned off their equipment, and headed for the little motel where they were staying; it was about thirty miles south of Chicago. There would be no mass murder of innocent Americans that day—meaning there would be no riots the day after as well. The meeting would need to be rescheduled to a later date.

Later that afternoon, the local FBI units raided the rental house where the team of hired assassins was now packing up to get out of the area. A shootout soon commenced, and by the time it was over, four of the five assassins lay dead at the scene. The lone survivor was on his way to the hospital in critical condition. The local FBI office listed one agent as dead from gunshot wounds and another admitted to a local hospital in a critical condition.

At the same time, SA Argo had received clearance to issue a nationwide alert to all law enforcement agencies to be on alert to the potential threat posed by 300 Cuban trained saboteurs that crossed the southern border and were sent to destroy infrastructure in the US.

CHAPTER 9

PLAYING HIS HAND

The C-17s were now at a cruising altitude of 28,000 feet and headed west. North was catching some much-needed rest when one of the C-17's loadmasters shook him and said, "You have a call coming in on our classified communications line." North rubbed the sleep from his eyes and went over to the comm board and answered the phone. "Major North here." There was no response so he repeated, "Major North here." A few seconds passed. North turned the volume up and pressed the headset tightly to his head. A voice came sputtering over the line. "Steve, can you hear me? It's Allen here!"

Then the transmission improved and Allen's voice became much clearer. "I have some good news and some bad news," said Allen. "You don't have to worry about the hackers targeting the US and shutting down or disrupting communications, electrical grids, gas lines, and so on."

"I know," responded North. "I wasn't worried about it; Sealy's army was going to attack the hackers' hotel on the evening of August 28."

"Remember I said there's good news *and* bad news? The bad news is that one of the local rabble-rousers threw a big party and well, everyone got fired up. Sealy was out of town, so they decided that now was as good a time as any and attacked all of Ruiz's hotels last night. The little army destroyed all the hotels using mainly Molotov cocktails. You might remember that they stopped all construction on the new high-rise hotel, except for the top three floors which were to be used exclusively as 'hacker central.' Somehow, connecting up the building's central sprinkler system became a task of much lower priority. So, when Sealy's army attacked the hotel, no one ever informed them of the non-functioning sprinkler issue…well you can perhaps guess where I'm heading with this. The fire got quickly out of control and raced up toward the top floors, where the hackers were residing. The city only has three firetrucks with ladder systems that would reach the top three floors, and they were blocked from reaching the new hotel by the exploding vehicles that Sealy's army had placed on the roads. So the Internal Security personnel decided to call in a helicopter to remove the hackers from the roof. As our luck would have it, the weather was rapidly changing, leading to a squall line of violent thunderstorms and high winds. When the chopper arrived, that area was experiencing high winds of 25–35 miles per hour, with gusts reaching up to 50 miles per hour, along with very heavy rain. The chopper tried twice to snatch some of the hackers and their guests from the roof. On the third attempt, a strong gust of wind forced the chopper down—too close to an antenna tower. Its blades caught in the tower and it crashed into the hotel roof, creating a massive fireball. By the time the backup chopper arrived, the whole roof was an inferno. As far as we can tell, no one survived.

"Rumor has it that a couple of the men jumped, hoping to be caught by some bystanders holding blankets to catch any jumpers. But the blankets couldn't withstand the pressure created by the velocity of their fall, and as you can probably guess, they ripped and there was quite a mess on the sidewalk. We have information that the Chinese embassy sees this as a Venezuelan internal matter, noting that there was no outside influence. We still have the four North Korean hackers on standby, and we'll see what we can get out of them. I'll be completing my operations report before the end of the day, and I'll copy you. That's the latest from my end. Good luck on the rest of your 'adventure'!"

"Please do me one last favor Walt," responded North, "and forward the report to FBI Agent Cole as well; I'll send you his email address." North considered the fact that since the Chinese embassy in Venezuela saw this accident as a local matter, it should not cause Leong to suspect that North and his team were on to them, meaning there was no need for a change of plans or timeline. The C-17's loadmaster approached North again, saying, "Sir, in thirty minutes, we'll be landing at Travis for our first refueling stop; you'll need to buckle your seatbelt for the landing. By the way sir, refueling protocol requires all personnel to exit and remain off the aircraft until refueling has been completed. If you're interested, there's a little sandwich shop near the refueling depot that you might visit if you're hungry. A little over two hours later and the lead C-17 was taxing down runway 3N at Travis AFB in California. The other two C-17s followed close behind.

Major General Robert Williams, the Commanding General of Fort Detrick and LtCol. Ball, who was the head of viral research at the research lab on base, arrived early at the personnel transport offices at Fort Detrick's on-base airport. They were awaiting their flight to Atlanta for a secret meeting with senior staff at the CDC. The purpose of their visit was to relay the data and test results from the lab's review and observation of the Covid-19 variant that they had removed from an aerosol dispenser, supposedly from a Chinese source. Normally, a video conference would have been enough, but the Covid-19 variant sample they were bringing signaled an ominous breakthrough in the field of gene splicing and editing. For a long time, rumors had been circulating among conspiracy theorists that the "first" Covid-19 was a test to see if the "system" could handle a new pandemic and what the US response would be toward China in that scenario.

In some circles, it became clear that this was another step in shaping the future battlefield, where patience and preparation would be key elements. Major General Williams and LtCol. Ball were both seated in the waiting room when a captain approached them and let them know he was to be their pilot and a Beechcraft King Air was available to transport them to Atlanta. The flight from Fort Detrick would take about two hours. The purpose behind Major General Williams' presence at the meeting was to bolster the request for the CDC to issue an "alert" that the presence of a very lethal variant of Covid-19 had been detected on the east coast, and that caution should be exercised. In the secret meeting, the general was looking for the CDC notice as a way of convincing the Chinese that their efforts to start a new pandemic had been at least partially successful.

When LtCol. Ball presented the data and test results, the CDC senior officials were shocked. One of the CDC's highest-ranking members said he must now concede that his original conviction that the Covid-19 virus was a naturally occurring virus that had come out of one of the so called "wet markets" in Wuhan must be erroneous. LtCol. Ball said, "What I'm most concerned about was that when we ran some of the naturally occurring evolutionary scenarios on the virus, we found that the automatic self-destruct switch failed to activate, so the virus maintained its lethality indefinitely."

Pausing for a bit to let the significance of his words sink in, LtCol. Ball continued. "China's propensity toward engaging in a viral nuclear arms race will eventually spill over onto the smaller players, encouraging them to get into the 'game,' so to speak. In the end, they will be over their heads and create something they cannot control—for which the whole world will pay the price!" At the end of the meeting, the Director of the CDC said that he would call an emergency meeting at eight the next morning. Then the Director asked if the President had been informed. General Williams stated that a meeting had been scheduled with the President and the National Security Council for nine that evening. After the meeting, the two men headed back to the airport for their flight to Washington, where they would prepare for the evening's meeting with the President and NSC.

North could feel the plane banking and saw the loadmaster approaching. "I know we're coming into Hickam Field, so I've to depart the plane while it's being refueled, right?" said North.

"Very good, sir!" exclaimed the loadmaster. "By the time we are through with the flight, you'll be like one of the crew!" North glanced out the window and thought how he would just like to get off here and avoid the unknown in terms of what would happen if he couldn't get the pilot to divert to Taiwan. He said to himself, *I'm too deep into the game now; I have to see it through!* In the two-hour window he had while the plane was being refueled, he found an empty chair outside the sandwich shop on post and just enjoyed the peace and quiet, which he knew would soon be replaced with tense and challenging encounters. He wondered just what good would come of his actions and hoped that an expanded military conflict could be avoided. He felt that this would be an appropriate time to send his report to the director. But something in the back of his mind caused North to hesitate, yet he couldn't quite put his finger on what it was. He was just ready to doze off when he heard his name being called and the voice sounded very familiar; it was the loadmaster. "We're ready to load up, Major North!"

North got up with some reluctance. In less than ten minutes, he was back on the plane and they were waiting for clearance to take off. The other two C-17s followed close behind. North was getting used to the aircraft engine's noise and the constant air turbulence. The constant hum of the engine actually made it easier for him to fall asleep. About four hours later, he awoke to some quick movements of the aircraft. From the look on North's face, the loadmaster could deduce that he wasn't sure what to make of the sudden jolts. The loadmaster came over to North and said, "Major North, nothing to be concerned about! We're starting our mid-air refueling!" North looked at the loadmaster, smiled, and said, "Am I supposed to exit the aircraft while it is refueling?" The loadmaster smiled and replied, "Only if you want to!" After the mid-air refueling was completed, North wandered onto the flight deck to get an idea of how much longer it would be before they touched down at Okinawa. The pilot was LtCol. Oscar Adams of Omaha, Nebraska. He was into his twenty-first year in the Air Force and seemed very interested in finding out more about North's objective behind running this NSA exercise and bringing all that gear so far. Wouldn't it just have to get shipped back? The co-pilot was Major Mac McDonald who was in his fifteenth year as an Air Force officer. He was a bit more direct about making his point. "Don't get me wrong," he said jovially. "I very much appreciate the fact that you're conducting this exercise, because it gives me a chance to get some flight hours, and my wife appreciates it because she gave me a foot-long list of items she wants me to pick up in Okinawa. But, on the surface, it would appear to me to be a waste of taxpayer money… so what gives? C'mon Major, you can tell us. We both have top secret security clearances." So North detailed his plan to the two men. Mac almost choked on the sandwich he was eating and shouted, "Holy shit, you've got a damn big tiger by the tail. I'm glad I'm not you!" Then just to put a cherry on top, North confided that he was 98% sure North Korea would attack South Korea in the next 24–36 hours. Then within forty-eight hours of North Korea invading the South, it was highly likely China would conduct an invasion of Taiwan. The flight deck got very quiet after North's last prediction.

About the time North was doing his best impression of Nostradamus, the high-level Chinese delegation was landing at Washington National. The members of the delegation had been handpicked by Leong and approved by the CCP's central committee. Their objectives for the secret meetings were known only to them and had not been presented to their American counterparts. The delegation for meetings with the Japanese negotiation team had arrived eight hours earlier and the delegation supposed to meet with the Australian counterparts were due to land in the next two hours. The Japanese, Australian, and Americans teams continued to exchange messages, but the Chinese delegations remained tight lipped! The first scheduled meeting between the Chinese and American delegations was to begin at nine in the morning on August 28. The meetings were set up with the understanding that none of the topics discussed in the meetings or even the fact that the meetings ever took place were to be made public. Some of the American delegates speculated that the Chinese were going to demand even more concessions from the three Allies on oil rights off Vietnam, fishing rights in the Philippines, and more square miles of the South China Sea in which to build their man-made islands.

North realized time was short and he would somehow have to find some way to have the C-17 transports change their course from heading to Kadena AFB on Okinawa to Ching Chau Kang Air Base, southwest of Taipei, Taiwan. He knew the 12,000-foot runway would be sufficient to handle the C-17s. What he didn't and couldn't know was if the C-17s would be permitted to land without the proper pre-authorization normally required. He picked up a flight bag he had brought with him and made his way up to the flight deck. Once inside the cabin he very quietly latched the door lock. Then he casually asked Mac about the course the flight would need to take if they were going to divert to Taipei. Mac turned around to see North holding a Colt .45 model 1911.

"Get a load of Mr. Save-the-World here!" Mac commented to LtCol. Adams who turned around and seemed to ignore what was happening. "What course—" began North again, but Mac interrupted him, saying "The one we are on and have been on for the last ten minutes."

"Yeah…right after you hijacked the flight!" Adams interjected. "Now put away the pistol. Oh and by the way you forgot to put the clip in the weapon."

"No I didn't forget," replied North. "I just didn't want it to accidentally go off."

"You know you're going to go to prison for a very long time, right?" said Mac. In a very low voice, North replied, "I expect so."

"Oh, you can bet on it!" said Mac. "Are you dead certain that what you have uncovered about Leong and his plan requires something this extreme on your part?"

North sat down. "I'm still uncovering new aspects and angles of the plan as it unfolds. From the beginning, and given the time I had, I have reviewed several of Leong's published papers and some that are classified. Leong's way to victory is not just knowing his opponent, like reading about his education, experiences, and so on. Because of your top secret security clearances, I can share with you the latest info I have received. I gained access to a study that the Brits managed to get out of China, just before they turned Hong Kong over to the mainland, in 1997. Leong was the author, and the article was titled 'Sun Tzu, 1995 update.' Simple enough, heh? The study took Leong's previous work to an extreme. The CCP-funded endeavor, which took years, had Iranian and Russian scientists write multiple programs that allowed the CCP to run complex simulations, based on the experiences and psychological profiles of targeted individuals that would predict their likely responses to a given set of circumstances."

"Well, that sounds like a recipe for disaster," LtCol. Adams commented in a low voice. "The Chinese have created a scenario where they think they can predict the actions of our leadership based on a set of circumstances they have created, hoping to ensure a favorable outcome—to the point where they're willing to risk war over Taiwan?"

"Given this plan and where it appears to be headed, that's what it looks like currently," replied North. Mac stated, "Well Major North, I'd guess they hadn't counted on you?" LtCol. Adams said, "Back to the matter at hand. Once we penetrate Taiwanese airspace, what makes you think they will let us land, let alone off load these worthless canisters?"

"I'm working on that," said North.

"You'd better hurry; we're only about two and a half hours out, and they will soon ask us what we are doing and what our plans are."

"Oh boy, that's Kadena regional control advising us that we're off course," exclaimed Mac. "What do you want me to say?"

"For the time being just acknowledge that we received their info and thank them," said North.

"That answers the next question I was going to raise: When are flights 2 and 3 going to question just where the hell we are going?" LtCol. Adams cleared his throat, "Flights 2 and 3, you must have noticed that our current course is taking us to Taiwan, rather than Okinawa. Now that we're nearing our destination of Ching Chau Kang Air Base, I can reveal that this flight is actually part of an NSA-approved, classified mission to deliver our cargo to the Taiwanese military. This mission has been kept secret to the point that even some of the operational units of the Taiwan military may not be aware of our impending arrival. So, you may hear dialogue between Taiwanese Air Control, myself, and Major North. What you will hear may raise concern. Follow my instructions to the letter. This is LtCol. Adams, out!"

At this point, Mac looked over at Adams and said, "This will be an adventure that we can tell our grandkids about...right after we get out of prison! How many years do you think—"

"This is Air Traffic Control, Ching Chau Kang, you have entered our military air control zone. We have no record of your flight being cleared to enter Taiwanese airspace. Please alter your course or declare an emergency!"

Mac looked at North and said, "Time to play your cards if you got them. What do you want us to do?" After another twenty seconds, the message was repeated! "This is Air Traffic Control, Ching Chau Kang, you have entered our military air control zone..." Adams turned to North who shouted, "We declare an emergency!" Adams said, "You know the next question they will ask: What is the nature of your emergency?"

"Tell them you have a person with a gun who has threatened to kill the crew if he does not get to speak with Clinton Tsi, a member of Taiwan's National Security Forces, and to deliver the cargo we have on board!"

"Ching Chau Kang Air Traffic Control, this is US Air Force Transport, Charley Zulu three niner niner two zero declaring an emergency and requesting immediate clearance to land. We have a passenger with a gun who has threatened to kill the crew; he demands to speak with a man named Clinton Tsi, a member of your National Security Forces, immediately. I repeat, this is US Air Force Transport, Charley Zulu three niner niner two zero declaring an emergency and requesting immediate clearance to land, also requesting clearance for two other aircraft in our flight!" Adams turned to North and gave him a look.

Just then, they received a response from the other end. "Charley Zulu three niner niner two zero, what is the nature of the cargo you have on board?"

"The nature of the cargo is classified and can only be discussed with Clinton Tsi of your National Security Forces, or another senior member of the National Security Forces."

At least thirty seconds passed before a reply came. "Charley Zulu three niner niner two zero, you and the two additional transports are authorized to land under your emergency declaration. Fighter jets are being dispatched to act as escort. For initial approach, turn to heading 270 and on command to 182 for final leg and then to 129 for runway 11N. Once you land, follow the runway escort vehicle to pad 7a and then turn your engines off. You must remain with your aircraft until given proper clearance; I say again, you must remain with your aircraft until your status is determined."

"Well, they are not going to shoot us down, at least not right away," said Mac with a shrug. Adams replied, "Roger that!" to the Air Traffic Control office, while Mac relayed the news to the crew on the other C-17s.

Less than twenty-five minutes later, the three aircrafts were on the ground and following the escort vehicle to pad 7a. The engines were turned off, and the wait began. As the crews looked out from their aircraft, they could see at least eight military Humvees, each with an M2 machine gun mounted on its roof. It was now a quarter of an hour since they had begun their wait. LtCol. Adams was becoming impatient with the delay. He turned to North and said, "Major North, I would really like to get this shit unloaded and if they don't want it, that is okay with me. I would just really like to get moving so I can get back home for my youngest daughter's birthday. This year, Labor Day and her birthday fall on the same day, and we are planning a really big BBQ-birthday combo and I have to man the BBQ. It's going to be a tight enough timeframe for me to make it home. Of course, the way our luck seems to be going, and if your predictions are correct, those fuckers in North Korea will probably start something and we will get stuck over here."

Just then, the radio buzzed with a voice saying, "Charley Zulu three niner niner two zero, Security Officer Tsi has arrived." It was followed by a firm voice that said, "This is Security Officer Clinton Tsi; who wants to speak with me?" Mac handed a headset to North who said, "This is Steve North; you and I met at the 'Joint Security Conference' in Sydney last October. I was representing the US Marine Corps and gave a presentation on China's international maritime goals. And hopefully, you'll remember we had dinner with an Aussie Marine and his wife."

There was a short pause before Tsi's voice announced, "Of course, dinner at that little seafood café, yes…Steve, of course I remember. But I must say, you caused a lot of concern with your unannounced arrival. I hate to tell you but you couldn't have come at a more tense time…but I cannot talk about that now. What's with the unannounced visit and the three aircraft?"

"I need to discuss my reason for being here in private and time is of the essence!" North replied. "I will come out to the aircraft," Tsi responded. "Classified information does not seem to stay classified very long inside these walls. I'll get an escort vehicle to bring me to your aircraft." The ramp at the back of the aircraft was lowered. Five minutes later, Tsi came walking up the ramp. Tsi and North recognized each other immediately and shook hands. As Tsi walked further into the C-17, he could not help but notice the markings on the canisters as he passed by. Tsi stopped and looked back and forth as he saw the Cruise missiles and nuclear warheads. For a long moment, he just stood there and said nothing. Finally he turned to North, saying, "What the hell is going on? You have a transport loaded front to back with—if I'm reading the labels correctly—hypersonic cruise missiles and nuclear warheads that go with the missiles!"

"Not just one transport, but three!" interjected North. At this point, Tsi had to sit down before he looked at North and said, "Are you nuts? You cannot hope to get away with stealing this stuff. And I can't be a part of this; I have to call the base security!"

But before the panicked man could say anything else, North cut in. "Clinton, what you see is actually an illusion; they are not the real thing. Let me explain!"

In the next half hour, North told Tsi everything— starting from Will's letter and the murders, the cover page for Leong's plan, tracking down Wei and Ling, Leong's hacker plot with Venezuela, the Chinese operatives in America tracking the transport of nukes and missiles, external attempts to cripple and confuse America with an internal pandemic and riots, right up to the plan of attacking Taiwan just days after a North Korean invasion of South Korea and concentrating US troops and ships for easier targeting by opening up a two-front war. North went on to explain how he had studied why China had pushed so hard to keep Taiwan from getting even one nuclear weapon. The Chinese felt that without America's interference, control of the airspace would eventually be theirs. But to conquer the people of Taiwan a large surface assault and troop invasion is necessary.

"So either during the embarkation phase or the assault phase, the landing force could be turned back or significantly reduced by just a few small nuclear weapons," said North as Tsi listened intently. "And the acquisition of moderately effective cruise missiles with conventional warheads could also act to deter a surface invasion. This presents the option of an airborne infantry option. However, the effect of a nuke explosion in the air on electronic equipment is well known and heavily loaded airborne troop carriers are not very agile in avoiding incoming missiles. But due to China's influence in the United States, your country has been denied those military assets. And, no matter how much I believe Taiwan should be able to protect itself, I could never provide you with the real thing. However, if we can convince the Chinese leadership that the likelihood of their success is greatly diminished due to the fact that you are now in possession of a hundred advanced hypersonic cruise missiles and nuclear warheads to go on the missiles, they just might blink!

"I'm relatively sure that a Chinese agent named Wei confirmed, via a phone call to the Chinese embassy in Philadelphia, that he had witnessed the loading of hypersonic cruise missiles and nukes onto three C-17s. The question I have for you is this: Can you conceive of a way to get the Chinese to believe that the three C-17s sitting here are the same ones Wei told them about?"

A moment later, Tsi slowly got up and walked to the edge of the ramp before turning and saying, "I think I do, but I will need to present my idea to some senior leadership and that will take some time." North replied, "My friend, time is one thing we do not have much of. I expect the North Koreans to launch their attack within the next 12–36 hours. Once that happens, the timeline for a mainland assault on Taiwan would only be a matter of days!"

Tsi was still pondering over it, so North looked Tsi in the eyes and asked, "What's your decision then?" Tsi took a deep breath and answered, "Things are moving quickly; our intel from the mainland has been confirmed! Squadrons of Chengdu J-7s are moving to the airbases in the front; we are guessing they will be the first wave of attack, essentially meant to draw fire, and will be sacrificed while the following waves will be primarily Shenyang J-15s, Shenyang FC-31s and Sukhoi SU-35s coming from Hulan and Zhangzhou airfields. At the Shantou airbase they have already moved in three new squadrons of Shenyang J-11s. Fuzhou PLA Headquarters has locked down and we currently estimate the first wave of anphibs will attempt to land as many as 10,000–15,000 troops at Taoyuan and 15,000–18,000 troops near Changhua in an attempt to cut the country in half, along with the creation of multiple smaller invasion points. Another 100,000 troops are being staged close to the embarkation points to follow up if the landings are successful."

As Tsi finished speaking, North shook his head and wondered if his efforts would be wasted, and an invasion of Taiwan could not be avoided after all. Just then, Tsi's cell phone rang; he answered with a quick "Yes sir," and then quickly departed the aircraft, setting off toward the main building. As North made his way back to the flight deck, he kept feeling that he was missing something. He kept thinking, *You don't need a Leong to plan a war, especially one that would be so obvious as this one.* He walked in to see that all members of the crew were gathered around the communications center console.

As North entered the flight deck, Mac turned and looked at him. "Well, you predicted it. It looks like North Korea must be smoking dope or something; word is they have moved a significant number of troops to the border with South Korea. Jong Un has issued an ultimatum to the South Korean president that all American forces must be kicked out of South Korea in the next twenty-four hours or he and his People's Army will remove them. And get this...he states that he'll be the savior of the Korean people, by removing the yoke of oppression from their shoulders. He also declared that the Japanese people have not paid sufficiently enough for their sins, so the most brilliant and advanced missile named *Vengeance* will be used to bring them to their knees. Kim went on to say he might spare them the full barrage of missiles if they are smart enough to not insert themselves in Korean internal affairs. Then, believe it or not, Kim also threatened Australia with a missile attack!"

The assistant loadmaster turned to North and asked him if he had ever been up by the DMZ in Korea before saying, "Do you think we can hold them back." North did not really want to answer that question, so he hesitated. "Well, what do you think?" another insisted. North slowly looked up at the ceiling, took a deep breath and said, "I don't think those little outposts, Camps Red Cloud, Stanley, Hovey or Market, stand much of a chance. However, the North will never prevail once the US forces are fully committed."

"Sir, then why would he...you know, Kim Jong Un...why would he choose to risk it all?"

"I do not have a clue. I've often wondered why the citizens don't rise up and remove him. But, you can see what early indoctrination can do to people's thinking. Unfortunately, if Kim goes forward with his threats, it is going to get bloody, very bloody."

Mac looked up at North and asked, "Well, what do we do now?" North's reply was terse. "We wait."

In the main underground bunker of the People's Liberation Army's headquarters, Leong was pacing the floor. He was doing his best to hide his growing concerns about lack of confirmation of the North Korean hackers shutting down various South Korean systems such as the railroads, gas lines, and communications and power grid systems. He had made several calls to the Venezuelan Internal Security chief about the status of the four North Korean hackers who were sent there at Kim's request. He had counted on the failure of those systems to provide an edge for his ground troops, and his Generals had worked this point into their invasion plans. Kim's operatives in South Korea had called Leong several times, asking when they could anticipate the failure of those systems to kick in. Leong had told them to count on the failure shortly after 3:00 am, just to get them off his back.

And now, Leong was getting impatient with the lack of information from Venezuela. He placed a call to the embassy security chief, ordering him to find out what was going on and to check on the hackers. Just then, Leong was handed a message from the embassy security chief in Philadelphia. It was a message from Wei. The South Philly outpost had detected the movement of compact nuclear warheads and hypersonic cruise missiles. Wei said he had observed them being loaded into three C-17s. Wei had only included one tail number: Charley Zulu three niner niner two zero. Leong stuffed the message into his pocket, went back to the communications center, and asked the officer in charge to try to get the embassy back on the line. Ten minutes later, he was notified that they had the Philadelphia embassy back on the line. Leong asked for Wei, but the embassy communications specialist said that they had been trying to "raise" him for several hours, with no luck. Leong asked the man to locate Wei as soon as possible and was just stepping out of the room when one of the comm operators waved at him from across the room. They had the Venezuelan embassy security on the line. "What have you got for me?"

"I'm afraid you're not going to like it," replied the voice from the other end. "I have Jose Hernandez with me; he does investigative work here in Caracas for the embassy. I called him and asked him to swing by the headquarters of the Internal Security Directors and see what he could tell us." Then Hernandez was put on the line, and in a heavy Spanish accent, he said that upon arrival at the Internal Security Headquarters, he had asked to see the Director. The staff on duty said that he had left for his home several hours ago. "So I drove directly to the Director's home," continued Hernandez. "When I arrived I noticed trash, clothing, and household items scattered all over the place and the front door ajar. I drew my gun and walked inside, carefully calling out for anyone who might be there. No one answered! So I continued on into the house and eventually ran into the old gardener, I asked him—"

"Stop, just stop, for God's sake just get to the point, man!" Leong shouted into the phone.

"According to the gardener, the Director had gathered up his family and some personal belongs, cleaned out his safe, and left for parts unknown." Then the embassy security chief came on the line, "Unfortunately there is more to report. A rebel group with a longstanding battle with Ruiz attacked several of his hotels tonight. I decided to call and check on the hackers myself. I dialed the numbers, I heard neither a ring nor did I get a busy signal…I got nothing, just a dead line. So I sent one of my guards down there to check on their status. He called and told me that it will take longer than usual, as the rioters have blocked many of the roads with burning tires, cars on fire, and the like. I will call you once he reports back to me."

Leong slammed the phone down, muttering, "I wonder what else could go wrong!"

Almost five hours had passed since North had met with Tsi. It was getting pretty warm and the crew was getting restless. They had just finished some meals that had been provided by the Air Base dining facility. It wasn't burger and fries but they enjoyed it just the same. A few of the flight crew personnel were new to overseas cuisine and struggled with the chopsticks, but it was tasty food, so they didn't complain. Just as North was finishing up, Tsi arrived at the back at the aircraft. He motioned for North to step outside. When North came outside, Tsi offered him a smoke, but he declined. Just as Tsi was getting ready to light one for himself, one of the crew waved his hand at him, then drawing his finger across his throat. "I guess that means 'don't light up,'" said Tsi before getting down to business. Tsi carried a clipboard with several sheets of papers on it. Tsi moved closer to North and spoke in a much more muted tone, "The Generals think your idea has merit and it is worth the gamble. In order to have the deception succeed, we must support the opportunity you have provided. We have built a support program that will further convince any spies that the shipment you just delivered, is real. On the clipboard, there are fictitious assignment orders covering the distribution of both the cruise missiles plus the mini-nukes and to what military locations they are being sent. It will be robust enough to convince anyone. For instance, the top sheet assigns: two warheads and five cruise missiles to Tianao Air Base; next, three warheads and five cruise missiles to Hsinchu Air Base and the list continues. Each truckload will have a brown sealed packet addressed to and only to be opened by the base Commanding Officer. We are projecting that we will need upwards of thirty flatbed trucks to pull this off."

Lastly, as we are loading these canisters from your aircraft to our trucks, the loaders, under strict officer supervision, will be applying placards that require personnel handling this cargo to have radiation detection badges, to reinforce the presence of radioactive materials.

At this point, Tsi paused to study North's expression before continuing. "You're probably wondering why go through this whole sham. We know there are some traitors and spies among our personnel. We have recently confirmed that we have one traitor right here at this base who could be watching this pad right now. In this case, we think we can use him to our advantage. He just happens to be the base transportation officer, Col. Lim. We recently uncovered how he gets his information out and we think his confirmation that we have acquired these weapons may be just what we need to convince the mainland that any attack on our island will be met with devastating results to their forces! You may have provided us the 'greatest weapon, that is not a weapon.' If we can convince them that strategically, they cannot totally defeat us, then we will win by default! As Sun Tzu would say, we will 'win the battle before it begins!' My country owes you a debt of gratitude it can never fully repay…you are a patriot to America *and* Taiwan, Major North. Thank you. I should like to visit you in America once we have a safe future and all this is behind us."

"Tsi, if you come to the States, you will probably find me in Kansas," replied North.

"Is that where your home is?"

"No, that's where Leavenworth Prison is located," North replied with a dry chuckle. When Tsi looked bewildered, North followed with, "You see I had to break some rules to make this happen and you know what happens when people break the rules…they have to face the consequences."

"Yes, I think I understand what you are referring to," Tsi said glumly. "I am very sorry to hear of your friend and his family suffering at the hands of those two assassins. You know Major North, I do not understand America's reluctance to fully support the Republic of China as an ally; after all, we are a thriving democracy. On the other hand, mainland China has never once, in its great and glorious 5000-year history, ever embraced democracy."

North and Tsi shook hands. As Tsi departed he said in a low voice, "I have a rat to catch; I must finish baiting the trap!"

CHAPTER 10

THE RAT SNIFFS THE BAIT

Col. Lim arrived back from a meeting in Kao Shun and noticed three C-17s at pad 7a. He took the binoculars out of his desk drawer to see what was going on, no movement occurred. Then he called in his second-in-command LtCol. Chu and asked, "What are the C-17s doing here?" As the base transportation officer, he had not received any advance notice and was considerably upset about it. LtCol. Chu said that their arrival had surprised everyone and that he was even more surprised when State Security Forces had asked for thirty flat-bed trucks, as soon as possible. "I assumed it was to off load the cargo that the 3 C-17s." As Lim mulled over this vexing development, Lt-Col. Chu exclaimed, "Oh, look Col. Lim, the first of the trucks are headed out to pad 7a!"

At that time LtCol. Chu was handed a note by one of his subordinate officers. "Hmm," he began with a frown, "this is a notice from the base Commanding General; it says, 'As of 9:00 pm, the base is closed to all traffic and personnel. Until further notice, no one will be allowed to enter or leave this base without special authorization from the General or the chief representative of State Security Forces. Also, "the cell phone blocking signal system will be activated, immediately." The base phone rang, and the enlisted clerk answered. "Yes sir, I will pass the message on to him!"

Putting the phone down, he said, "Col. Lim, the Commanding General has scheduled a division meeting of his senior staff at 11:00 pm to implement 'Operation: Game Changer.'"

Darkness was starting to set in, so by the time, Lim made his way to pad 7a, troops were starting to set up floodlights and had taped off the area. Wanting to get a closer look at the cargo canisters that were being unloaded, Lim started to lift the orange tape, but he was quickly stopped by one of the armed guards. Col. Lim identified himself and said he wanted to make sure that the loading was being done correctly. He again started to lift up the tape and again, he was told he could not pass. Only this time, the guard drew his pistol as he repeated his warning: "Drop the tape sir, and step back."

Lim was incensed. "Who's in charge?" he demanded. A voice from inside the nearest aircraft said, "I am." A man walked out of the aircraft. Col. Lim stood there as he looked at someone who appeared to be very young to be in charge.

"I am Clinton Tsi, State Security Force," said the man, "and you are attempting to enter a restricted area, Col. Lim!" Lim noticed that Tsi was wearing a radiation detection badge and so were all the other men around the aircraft. Lim asked him why he was being denied access to the area. Tsi looked at Lim with a steady gaze and just said, "That will be explained at the Commanding General's meeting."

As a hesitant Lim turned to walk away, Tsi planned to set the bait. He shouted to one of the loaders that he was going to the restroom and would be right back. He took his clipboard, lifted the tape, and walked to the restroom near pad 7a. Once inside he made it a point to lay his clipboard on the sink by the nearest toilet stall and close the door. Lim followed close behind. Quietly Lim picked up the clipboard and slowly lifted the cover sheet to reveal a lengthy list of bases where shipments of new, American hypersonic cruise missiles as well as a significant number of small-yield nuclear warheads were due to be deployed in anticipation of a mainland attack. There was a list of fourteen bases on the first manifest and there were two more pages of bases that would receive a specific number of each type of weapon. There was a timetable attached regarding operational readiness. That timetable indicated that in less than twelve hours after distribution, readiness would stand at 50% and by twenty-four hours, it would be at 100%. Shocked, Lim dropped the clipboard into the sink.

Tsi called out, "Who's there?" Flushing the toilet, unlocking the stall door, and stepping out, only to find no one else around. He picked up the clipboard and then went to the base security, video monitoring office. He wanted to see what the video camera that he had secretly installed in the restroom had captured. To no surprise, the video showed Col. Lim looking through the papers on the clipboard. *The rat has taken the bait*, thought Tsi with some satisfaction, *Now we see what he does with it*!

No more than ten minutes had passed when Col. Lim showed up outside the Commanding General's office. He caught the General's aide-de-camp and explained that he had stopped by the pharmacy on his way back from Kao Shun and picked up some much-needed medicine for his wife, who had been very ill. He needed to get the medicine to her as soon as possible. He explained his home was only a ten-minute drive from the base and that he would easily make it back for the 11:00 pm meeting. The aide said he would pass the request on to the General.

This is just what Tsi had hoped for. Lim had taken the bait and would now pass the bogus information to his handlers at PLA headquarters. The General's aide called Col. Lim and said, "The main gate has been notified that you were granted permission to leave the base and to expect you back within the hour. Before leaving the base, he jotted down three C-17's tail numbers. Lim was out of the door in a flash and on his way to his house."Tsi called the undercover unit monitoring Lim's home. Lim had no idea that he had been discovered to be a spy for the mainland. The moment he arrived at the house, he explained to his wife what he had seen and that he would send a message to his contact at PLA Headquarters. He also reminded her to be prepared to flee to their safe house when the fighting started; he would join her there. He also wanted to show her how to operate the microburst transmitter, if he needed her to pass on more information. The actual transmitting antenna was part of a metal sculpture by the edge of a koi pond in their backyard. It took Lim less than five minutes to set up, go online, transmit messages, and receive confirmation before tearing down and putting away the equipment.

Once all this was done, Lim dashed out the door and was on his way back to the base.

What he didn't know was that Security Forces had an outstanding black bag team that had managed to locate the transmitter unit and install a retransmission unit prior to the transcrypto scrambling section of Lim's communications transmitter. Once the send key was pressed, Security Forces could read what he had sent. They relayed the message to Tsi. "Major Development: Three C-17s carrying American hypersonic cruise missiles and surface- and air-burst new mini-nuke 10-kilo-ton warheads. Number: 100+? 50% operational in 12 hours, 100% operational in 24 hours, 23:00 brief by CG on operation 'Game Changer,' greatly elevated risk to surface invasion, airborne units, increased risk based upon initial distribution of new systems. Aircraft tail numbers: Echo Lima Zero Two one two five Zero, November Foxtrot niner two two seven seven, and Charley Zulu three niner niner two zero. End message."

Tsi was jubilant. Things could not have worked out more in their favor. *Now if we can just keep this ruse under wraps, a lot of lives will be spared the horror of war.*

Meanwhile, the mainland PLA Intel operator who read that message noted that the sender had failed to assign an importance/priority code to the message, so he called over one of the senior Intel operators for guidance. As the senior operator got closer, he just started to shout, "Not you again! What do you want now?"

"Well," the junior operator said reluctantly, "The message seems important, but the sender did not assign a priority code." The senior operator said, "What's the standing rule? If the sender did not think it was important enough to assign a priority code, then what do we do?"

The inexperienced junior operator said, "We stamp it 'Routine' and place it in the appropriate briefcase." And that is just what he did!

On the other end, Lim had just walked into his office when he got a call from one of his officers. The "on-duty," Base Transportation officer, Captain Lee, called to inform Col. Lim that one of the trucks had damaged an axle when it hit a curb on its way out the front gate. It was one of the trucks that was loaded with gear from the C-17s. It had broken down and a long line of trucks was stacking behind it. As the Captain was finishing his conversation with Col. Lim, the military police by the front gate were yelling to get that "damn" truck fixed and out of the way. Col. Lim told the Captain to get one of the forklifts onsite and transfer the load. The Captain replied, "I tried but the unloading crew will not give one up until they finish with the third aircraft."

"All right Captain, I'll be down there in five minutes," said Lim. As Col. Lim made his way to the front gate, he passed Tsi who stopped and turned around, calling to Lim. "Where are you headed? The CG's briefing is in ten minutes."

Lim replied, "I'll make it to the briefing shortly; I've got a broken truck issue, one of those with the cargo from the C-17s." Tsi stopped in his tracks, turned, and started to follow Lim. He observed Lim from behind the front gate guard shed and eavesdropped on the conversation between him and the Captain. The replacement truck arrived just as Lim was approaching. The Captain yelled at his men to get going, and they began stripping off the tarp and started removing the shipping canisters by hand, one man on each end.

Observing that a two-man team could lift the canisters by hand caught Lim by surprise and he just stared. The Captain came running up to him and said, "I'm sorry I called you. If I had known the canisters were this light I wouldn't have wasted my time trying to get a forklift. Just after I had spoken with you, one of the drivers came over and said, 'You should ignore the labels that list the weight as 3500 pounds. These only weigh about 200 pounds.'" Lim walked over to one of the canisters and tapped it with his knuckles; it sounded like a hollow log. The Captain then proceeded to tap one of the nuke canisters; it too had a hollow sound. The nuke canister's weight was posted as 457 pounds; the Captain demonstrated that he could lift the canister up with little effort. The Captain said that as per the drivers, "all of the canisters were like that, like someone forgot to include the actual cargo item." Tsi now knew that the cover had been blown and he could see that Lim was processing what he had just seen and heard. Lim realized that the whole show, the three C-17s, the canisters and the accompanying paperwork was nothing than an illusion, an elaborate deception. Lim patted the Captain on the back and complimented him on getting the trucks rolling. Then he started to walk at a very brisk pace in the direction of the main buildings. It was three minutes to eleven at that point, and Lim was not heading for the CG's briefing, but his office. Tsi realized that Lim knew there were no weapons on board the trucks, meaning Lim would somehow have to get the word to the mainland that the threat he had warned them of, was now proving to be false. Tsi called on his radio to his assistant team leader who was planning to take Lim into custody after the briefing of operation "Game Changer." There was no time to lose. Tsi ordered his assistant team leader to take Lim into custody as soon as possible. He authorized lethal action to prevent Lim from escaping or making a phone call. The team broke into a dead run, trying to catch Lim before he could reach his office.

The assistant team leader saw him at the end of the hall and called out to him to stop or they would shoot. Lim disregarded the request to stop and pulled out a PPK .32 pistol and fired two shots at the team. The team returned fire and continued their pursuit. Lim made it to his office. Tsi had called his office and told the clerk to hold Lim, that he was a spy. When Lim burst through the door to his outer office, the clerk grabbed him and tried to hold him down. Lim broke loose and shot his clerk twice in the chest. The clerk slumped to the floor, without a sound.

Then Lim ran behind his desk, picked up the receiver, and quickly punched in his home number. He could hear the phone ringing, then a lot of noise as the security team arrived in his outer office. His home phone continued to ring. "Hurry up, pick up the phone!" Lim muttered desperately. That very second, a member of the security team dove through the door, raising his shotgun… but Lim fired first.

The bullet hit the man just above his left eye and he crumpled to the floor. The second man fared better. Lim fired first, but his shot missed the mark, hitting his opponent in the shoulder. Before that team member fell, he fired one blast from his shotgun. That blast hit Lim in the right shoulder and knocked him back, making him drop his pistol and the phone receiver. The team leader stepped into the doorway, lowered his shotgun, and finished Lim off with two shots that nearly removed Lim's left shoulder and part of his jaw, slamming him up against some cabinets, and then pulling a stack of bookcases down as he slumped to the floor.

At his home, Lim's wife was just finishing up prepping for tomorrow's dinner and had to wash and dry her hands. After she was done, she headed for the phone that was still ringing. In Lim's office, everything had gone quiet. One dead and one wounded, but they had kept Lim from telling his wife that the whole act was a lie.

She reached for the phone and said, "Hello, Lim's residence," but there was no response. She repeated, "Hello, Lim's residence." The team leader picked up the receiver off Lim's desk and gently placed it back on the stand; the line went dead. On the other end, Lim's wife hung up the phone and went back to her efforts to prepare the next day's dinner. Soon, word got out about the shootout and Col. Lim's death. But the actual message being passed around was that Col. Lim had been under the doctor's care for severe stress and had finally snapped and committed suicide. Tsi called the team monitoring the Lim residence and ordered them to take Mrs. Lim into custody. He felt they still had to continue the deception because there may be more spies that could blow the lid off the charade. After the 11:00 pm meeting, the General was briefed on the circumstances and outcome surrounding Col. Lim and agreed that they needed to continue the campaign of deception. The CG was now on his way to deliver an update to the Combined General Staff at tomorrow morning's briefing for the President and key legislators.

Leong was on his way to see the President when one of the communications operators caught him in the hall and told him the embassy in Caracas was on the line and had an urgent message for him. Leong entered the communications center and picked up the call. It was the embassy security chief. "Sir, I have some really bad news about your team of hackers. They all perished when their hotel caught fire. The hacker operations center— in fact the whole hotel—is a smoking pile of debris." While the embassy security chief continued to talk, Leong set the phone down and slowly walked out the door. He said to himself, *Plans as complicated as this one are bound to have portions that do not unfold as anticipated.* With the hacker resource out of the game, the disruptions to South Korean defense efforts that Kim's Generals had counted on, were out of the picture.

Leong was not sure how much the lack of the disruptions would affect Kim's invasion timeline. The invasion was due to commence in less than two hours. Leong decided that he would withhold the information from Kim and his Generals that any anticipated benefits they were hoping for were not going to materialize. Why bother them with the bad news since they were expendable! Leong entered the conference room and began the update. Xi listened patiently to Leong's current assessment and update on how the plan was unfolding. Once Leong finished his presentation, Xi phoned Kim to wish him a glorious victory. Kim responded with the words "Victorious Together!" With the end of that phone exchange, the Second Korean War was underway.

Minutes later, the Korean Peninsula was again plunged into a bloody battle zone. Little did Kim know that regardless of how his army performed in the next couple of days, he was now playing the part of a pawn in Xi's chess game. Xi asked Leong to confirm the three delegation parties were on schedule to be in place.In the next 72–96 hours they would play a crucial part in achieving his long-term quest.

In the meantime, Tsi headed back to pad 7a to give North an update that North Korea had crossed the DMZ, and the war had begun. It was confirmed that a couple of missiles with conventional warheads had made it to Japan, but casualties had not yet been determined. It is being reported that Japanese government officials and its Military are considering a response. "It has been reported by US satellite Intel that before any more missiles could be fired, a series of US submarine-launched cruise missiles has effectively reduced that launch site to rubble. It looks like at this time both sides are trying to stay away from the nuclear option, if possible, at least during the early stages. It was reported that Chinese officials are publicly urging restraint for all sides," said Tsi.

"Refueling will be complete in the next twenty minutes and we can re-board and get out of here," announced Mac. "LtCol. Adams is currently speaking with Kadena to find out where they want us to fly next." Adams exited the flight line with some papers in his hand. Just then, the loadmaster signaled that the refueling was complete. As the crew made their way back onto their aircraft, Tsi made it a point to shake the hand of every crew member and wish them a safe flight home! As Tsi shook North's hand, he remarked, "What you have done makes you a hero in our eyes and even if you will not have a warm reception when you arrive back in the States... staying here in Taiwan could be arranged!"

"No thanks!" was North's simple reply.

The C-17s were now airborne out of Chin Chau Kang Air Base, LtCol. Adams instructed his flight to go to heading 025, in route to Kadena, US Air Base, Okinawa. Then he briefed the crew on their new mission. "We have been ordered to head to Okinawa, prepare to take on troops and equipment of the 3rd Battalion, 4th Marine Regiment, and deliver them to the Marine Task Force Command at Pohang, Korea. We will be tasked with that mission until further notice."

He turned to North and said, "Just so you are aware, base military police will be there when we land, with orders to arrest you and put you on the first flight available back to the US. Obviously you know that I had to say you hijacked us and then we had no choice but to divert from Kadena to Chin Chau Kang."

"Yes of course, I fully understand." North replied, "I just appreciate you not making me play the tough guy." "We should be at Kadena in about an hour and a half," as LtCol. Adams glanced at his watch, "so Steve, just sit back and enjoy your last ninety minutes of freedom." Before North left the flight deck, Mac remarked, "You know Steve, you actually look pretty calm in the face of the storm that is coming your way. You seem to have a sense of satisfaction and relief about you." North smiled. "I did what I thought was right and perhaps put my country in a better place, strategically, than we were before. As far as I'm concerned the current administration's behavior has only encouraged the adversaries of our country to take risks that actually bring us closer to conflict, rather than decrease the likelihood of it. I am going to grab some rest, while I can. But first, how's the battle in Korea going?"

Adams remarked that the message from Kadena had said that the Allies' air campaign was going well and they expected to have control of the air space in the next twenty-four hours. However, the ground forces are getting hit very hard and the casualties are brutal. As North turned around to leave, he said, in a low voice, "Right now I would give anything to be there on the ground with them!"

Ninety minutes later, the loadmaster touched North on his shoulder. He opened his eyes and the loadmaster said, "You know the routine." As the lead C-17 touched down at Kadena, North looked out the window to see the approaching military police van. As he walked down the ramp, the officers took him by the arm and put him in the van. Within three hours he was on a military transport headed for southern California.

The aircraft transporting North touched down at March Air Force Base. He was immediately transferred to a smaller jet operated by the NSA—all of this in no more than twenty-five minutes from touch down to take off. North could tell they wanted him in back in DC as soon as possible, but he couldn't help wondering, *What's the rush?*

The high-level Chinese delegation arrived unceremoniously at the gate at the Camp David presidential compound at precisely 7:00 am. Since the meeting was scheduled on short notice and meant to be secret, there were no reporters. It was already shaping up to be a hot, sunny and sticky late August morning. After verification, their three limousines were waved through the gate and pulled up in front of the main conference hall. They were greeted by the Secretary of State and the Secretary of Defense. Waiting inside were the other members of the US team: Chairman of the Joint Chiefs, Head of the CIA, Director of the NSA, US Ambassador to the UN, Director of the FBI, Head of the NSC, four interpreters and one member from the White House staff. The Vice President was due to fly in at any moment. Waiting in a conference room down the hall were support personnel. The US team had arrived at Camp David at 6:00 am to get the latest brief on the battles taking place in Korea and updates on the status and movement of China's military assets.

The US team had been briefed by experts who thought the Chinese would be pressuring the US and its allies for further concessions, considering the current crisis. At 9:00 am, the Chinese delegation entered the conference room and sat down at the long table. They had brought a stack of folders which was immediately passed to their US counterparts on the other side of the table. The head of the Chinese delegation cleared his throat and in perfect English asked the US delegates not to open their folders but allow him to finish his opening statement first. He started...

"China had been leading the world for many centuries before the west emerged from the dark ages. We are proud of our heritage and now find ourselves ready and responsible to assume our rightful place, as the 'brightest star; in the heavens. We will not be denied any longer by the western powers who seek to contain us. We wish to move forward in peace, but we will move forward without it, if necessary. Our great leader, Xi Jinping, has given us directions to ensure that you understand that he wills for China to be one, again. Once we start to review the conditions, your President will have exactly forty eight hours to agree or face a state of war. In the folders is a list of what China will bring upon you if you oppose us. However, we also have a proposal of what we will be willing to concede in order to avoid conflict."

Here, he stopped and started reading from the folders that had been handed out around the room:

"If you oppose our efforts to annex Taiwan, then conflict cannot be avoided. We feel confident that the following events will take place:

1. Our initial attacks will leave over 40,000 killed or wounded US military personnel in the Far East.

2. Your three carrier attack groups that are supporting your actions on the Korean Peninsula will be destroyed.

3. China will commit 250,000 troops to support our North Korean brothers.

4. We will sub launch our cruise missiles, fitted with conventional warheads, at Hawaii and Guam.

5. Our submarines will launch cruise missile attacks on your military installations in the Far East.

6. Your eastern coast will soon come under the grips of a new, very lethal variant of Covid-19 that by our estimates will likely kill 200,000 to 300,000 of your citizens.

7. Witness an excessive number of fires in the Western states.

8. You will have riots in a large mid-western city.

9. You will incur infrastructure damage in the south.

10. Large-scale cyber sabotage will bring your gas, electric, and communications grids and other essential services to a standstill.

11. Russia will receive critically advanced weapons systems in support of their invasion of the Ukraine.

12. You have witnessed our military capabilities and should realize we will use them, to include in space.

13. Work specifically to support candidates in the next election to defeat the current administration.

14. Enable, support and fund many more illegal border crossings.

15. Increase funding to US universities and expand programs that promote socialist/extreme leftist doctrine.

16. Publish, in its entirety, a list proving current and past elected and appointed officials, to include family members, outlining the details who have accepted bribes/payoffs from Chinese companies or the Chinese government

17. Expose all elected and appointed personnel who have engaged/participated in sexual liaisons with Chinese prostitutes.

18. If America agrees to publicly support and endorse China's peaceful or, if necessary, military efforts to annex Taiwan, China will concede and agree to

19. Cease all support for North Korea, including weapons, ammunition, medical supplies, intel, food, gasoline, oil, aircraft parts, and so on.

20. Shut down North Korea's electrical grid and fuel pipelines.

21. Disable their medium- and long-range missile guidance systems using the secret programing that we have installed.

22. Give up claims and rights to a large area of the South China Sea, including oil rights off of Vietnam and fishing rights off the Philippines.

23. Give up rights to islands claimed by Japan.

24. Prevent and if necessary provide a proven vaccine that will ensure recovery of those citizens who are affected by the lethal Cov-19 variant.

25. Prevent/ undo the cybercrimes and shutdown/disruptions to essential services.

26. Cease all efforts to affect election outcomes.

27. Deny Russia any supporting weapons in its war in the Ukraine.

28. Cut off funds to groups that push or support our indoctrination programs in colleges and universities in the US.

29. Cease funding leftist terror groups and political candidates in the US.

30. Cut off funding for groups pushing, supporting, and enabling continued flow of illegals at the southern border.

31. Destroy the list of and evidence proving elected and appointed officials with extended family members who have accepted bribes/payoffs from Chinese companies or the Chinese government.

32. Destroy all videos of elected officials that engaged/participated in sexual liaisons with Chinese prostitutes.

33. Take no actions of a military nature towards the US or its allies.

We will be waiting for your reply, but for no longer than 48 hours. You have till 9:00 am on August 30."

After this lengthy recitation, the Chinese delegation stood up, turned around, and walked out of the conference room. As they were walking out, the Secretary of State stood up and shouted, "This is insane! We need more time to confer internally and with our allies!" But the conference room door slammed shut as the delegation left.

The US team sat there, stunned. After a few minutes, the US representatives walked down the hall without saying a word. The Director of the NSA broke the silence. "I don't think we have much of a choice. We have to give up Taiwan."

"I hope nobody believes the concessions listed in their folder," said the Secretary of Defense. "They can't be trusted and are just testing us to see how much they can push us."

"Well they're in a much better position than they were ten years ago, but you have a good point," said the Secretary of State before turning to the Director of the FBI and asking, "What's with the Covid-19 threat and the threats of cyber disruption? You know, the internal US stuff?" The FBI director spoke up here. "As a matter of fact, the FBI has already been involved in dealing with and defeating the internal threats that are listed in this document. However, let me call in the agent who has firsthand knowledge of these threats so he can paint us a better picture of whether or not these are real threats or not. I can have him here in five hours, but before that I'll give him an overview of what we are looking for, so he will have an idea what to focus on. In the meantime, we need an overview from Defense about whether or not the Chinese can do what they have threatened here!"

The Secretary of State said, "Well, I better give the leadership of Taiwan a call. I doubt their President is going to believe this." Turning to an aide, he said, "Get us on the line with the Japanese and Australians to get copies of any proposals they might have received."

"Let's get a copy of the threats and concessions over to the President ASAP!" exclaimed the Vice President. Just then, one of the President's senior re-election campaign managers remarked, "This is going to scare shit out of Wall Street if word gets out; the polls are already not looking good! The voters are already on the fence…I think —"

"Shut the fuck up!" the Secretary of Defense snarled, cutting him off. "This is much larger than any upcoming election issue. And who let you in to begin with? Security, remove him!" When they all got up from the conference table, the Secretary of Defense muttered in a low voice, "Maybe if we hadn't been so focused on using the correct gender pronouns or converting all of our military vehicles to zero-emission ones, we would have seen this coming." Then he commented to the FBI Director, "Looks like some sort of blackmail attempt aimed at some folks in high places!"

"Just what I was thinking," came the reply.

General C.K. Lee was in charge of intelligence for the PLA. He had a growing influence in the CCP ranks and had distinguished himself in guiding the development of the Chinese Air Force and the industries that supported it. He was also in charge of the cyber warfare division. He had assisted Leong in selecting the rising stars in the hacker world in order to have the right people for the cyber-attack unit that was due to operate in Caracas. Presently, General Lee was on his way out of the bunker complex when he ran into Leong. He told Leong he had just come across an urgent message from Leong's man in the States, Wei. Leong seemed surprised as he said, "I've been trying to reach him; I've even sent the embassy chief to try to locate him, but all my efforts yielded nothing. When did the message come in?"

"It must have gotten delayed somewhere," replied General Lee. "Because it's dated at over thirty hours ago and it has got me concerned. The Americans were seen moving some of their newest hypersonic cruise missiles and their new mini-nukes."

"It's been done before," remarked Leong, followed with, "What is your point of concern?" Lee continued, "They have moved that equipment before, but we have always been able to track and confirm its arrival at the destination. This time the equipment has disappeared." Leong seemed to disregard the importance of confirming where the shipment had gone. "I have seen the data and results on both those weapon systems and they are better than anything we have by a long shot," insisted Lee. "The hypersonic cruise missiles go to Mach 9, are stealth embodied, and can fly right up your vehicles' tail pipe and you would not be aware until the 10-kiloton warhead sends you blissfully into the next world. By the way, has the cyber team in Caracas started to crack the firewalls on crucial American systems?"

But Leong didn't say anything; he just walked into the bunker complex. Lee stood there for a few seconds, then got in his vehicle, and drove off for a briefing with some of the general staff. The drive would take about forty minutes, so he had brought along additional messages, even the ones marked "Routine." On the drive, Lee thought he would give the embassy security chief Manuel Cruz a call to see how his handpicked team of cyber criminals were doing. Cruz answered the phone right away, saying, "Yes General Lee, I remember you. The hacker team? Didn't Leong tell you? Everyone, the entire team, died in a fire; there's no one left." Lee thought that maybe the Cruz had misunderstood the question, so he repeated it, slowly. "I am calling to get an update on how things are going for the computer specialists at the Maria Drive location." Security Chief Cruz spoke up, thinking that the phone signal was not transmitting well given the distance between the two. "I understood your question the first time. 'There is no team, gone, perished in a fire!' Apparently, some disgruntled local businessmen got a mob to attack all of Ruiz's hotels and business locations in reprisal for some previous business dealings. The building on Maria Drive did not have its sprinkler system operational, once the building started to burn, there was nothing anyone could do. I had the on-site Internal Security officer check and he confirmed there were no survivors. Is there anything else I can do for you, General?" Lee leaned back in his seat and just stared out the window, seemingly in shock, for what seemed to be several minutes, as he considered the implications of not having a cybercrime team to cause disruption inside America. His driver noticing the General's condition, spoke up! "General, General, is there something wrong, are you OK?" Lee, wondered why Leong had decided to not share that information with him.

Just as Lee's vehicle arrived at the briefing location, Lee leaned forward and told the driver, "turn around and head back to the bunker complex—and step on it." Lee started to go through the rest of the messages marked "Routine." He would quickly glance over the messages and then place them back in the folder. As he was going through the last of the items in the folder, he stopped when he noted 'C-17' in the body of a message. Then he picked back up the note from Wei; it had noted three C-17s and so had Lim's note. Wei's note only had one tail number, while Lim's had three…and then Lee spotted it: that one tail number Wei listed matched one of the three in Lim's note.

*Oh my God, the Yanks have pulled a fast one! Lee thought, horrified. Taiwan now has about a hundred of the newest hypersonic cruise missiles and enough mini-nukes to…*here Lee leaned back and took a deep breath. All this was enough to not only stop an invasion but to create utter destruction for more than just the PRC's Armed Forces. Lee now started to imagine different scenarios: What could happen if Taiwan's military took pre-emptive action using their newly acquired firepower, by misreading PLA's activities as an imminent threat or impending invasion? Leong's plan may have sounded fine when he had presented it. And it may have looked doable on paper, but a series of miscues and failures may lead to an unprecedented disaster. "This thing could easily spin out of control and take on a life of its own," Lee muttered to himself. China's military might need half a century to recover and its people would suffer, more than Lee cared to imagine. The citizens of PRC would look no further than CCP, to blame! The US had waited till the last minute. *Are they setting a trap for us?* He wondered.

Lee thought he must contact Lim to see if he can reconfirm his initial findings. As Lee headed back to the bunker complex, the general staff was being briefed on how the war was going for Kim. The North Korean troops had been effectively stopped east of Seoul and just north of Wonju. The South Korean troops had provided much greater resistance and grit than anticipated. SK troops and resources were coming by rail which enabled them to hold their positions even in light of a concentrated push by NK armored units. Between the South Korean Air Force and the Yanks, it was estimated that they would have total air superiority within twelve hours. Once that was achieved, NK forces would need to fall back as the supply lines will be subject to round-the-clock attack from the air. The NK general staff was calling for major infusion of supplies and air support. They also wanted to know when the disruption of rail and communication lines, due to cyber sabotage, will be effective. A call from the Senior Field General pointedly asked, "When will China announce its support and enter the war."

At this point, Xi looked at Leong, and Leong shook his head. Xi responded, "Inform the NK general staff that we have utmost faith that the NK forces will be victorious. That's all."

It was early on August 30 and General Lee started to receive intel dispatches from embassy personnel in the US, regarding the expected rise in infections and panic related to an expected lethal Covid-19 outbreak on the east coast, riots in Chicago, forest fires in the west, infrastructure destruction in the south, and cyberattacks shutting down power grids, banking transactions and the like. All reports confirmed, that there had been no discernable impact on America's day-to-day activities. Lee called one of his most trusted aides for an update on what US news channels were reporting. The aide called the General back, "other than frequent updates on the Korean conflict, at the current time on 29 August, in the US there was little else to report." Lee commented to his aide "the anticipated negative impacts and major disruptions that had been deemed critical in pushing the US administration to consider withdrawing its support of Taiwan, apparently have failed to initiate or have been 'thwarted' by US internal security agencies."

Lee believed he had no choice but to appraise Xi of what he had now learned; however he would need to confirm the missile/nuke information along with a new operations order from a source planted deep inside in the Taiwan's operations. "General Lee needs to speak with you immediately," Xi was told by an aide. Xi asked the communications specialist to put the call on speaker and then asked Lee to repeat the information he had recently obtained. Xi turned to Leong and asked him, "Didn't all of those computer simulations indicate that the American response would mirror your predictions as part of the plan?" When Leong didn't answer immediately, Xi continued, "You assured me that using deception, dissent, early socialist indoctrination, payoffs and bribes a new pandemic in America, isolating Taiwan, and backing the North Korean invasion of the South…all of this would cause the US to question its foreign commitments. That it would ultimately lead to America and its allies being forced to choose between saving South Korea and themselves or defending Taiwan. I hope, for your sake, that there are no more hiccups."

Then, Xi asked his communications officer to make arrangements for him to address his general staff. Xi cleared his throat before saying, "I'm certain that in the next twenty-four hours, we will see the results for all of our sacrifice and hard work. We shall make our ancestors proud!"

As the meetings continued into the early morning hours, the Secretary of State wanted to know when the FBI agent was going to arrive so that he could brief the team on some of the US mainland threats listed by the Chinese. "He is on his way and should be here in the next couple of hours." The conversation again turned to the big question of whether or not the US wishes to engage in a war of substantial portions to protect Taiwan. Once again, the Director of the NSA led the charge to concede Taiwan to the Chinese. "Give up Taiwan, avoid a conflict that wherein the Chinese would likely prevail due to their geographical location and given the fact that we are already engaged in Korea."

"She continued, China is willing to throw North Korea 'under the bus,' so to speak, thereby allowing the reunification of the Korean Peninsula—a cherished goal for over fifty years. Unless the US essentially arms Taiwan to the teeth, up to and including nukes, they will eventually fall...so why should we go through a nasty conflict when we will likely lose Taiwan anyways? I'm very concerned about the internal threats they are saying we will likely face. The idea of us engaged in a two-front war and these real significant threats to our citizens means that this administration would be doomed in the next election, and then we're all out of a job."

"It sounds like you are more worried about keeping your position rather than helping protect another democratic country," said the Director of the FBI. "Fuck you," she blurted out, "I thought this discussion was about Taiwan, not my position." "It is," he replied, "but it's our job to deal with the internal threats so that America can engage with the rest of the world without having to constantly look over its shoulder." The NSA director stood up and said, "Tell us about what you have done about these so-called threats."

Just then, her phone rang. She looked at the number and said, "This is a very important phone call, and very private, so I have to step out to take it." While she was gone the discussion continued. The Chairman of the Joint Chiefs said, "She makes a strong logical case. However, it sends the wrong message: When it's convenient for us, we'll sell out our friends or neighbors. The people of Taiwan will conclude that we sold them out to unify Korea, and the Chinese military will conclude that we didn't have the stomach or the balls to stand up to them, which will only embolden them in the future."

The Secretary of Defense nodded in agreement, saying, "I'm not thrilled to take on the Chinese, since it will bloody for the both of us. But if we don't take on the bully now, a confrontation will still likely take place down the road. However, sometimes it's best to throw the first punch." The Vice president looked up and said, "You mean launch a pre-emptive first strike?"

"Yes ma'am," the Secretary replied. "Look at it this way: I'm assuming the internal threats they were alluding to were in some way connected to their agents in the US implementing those plans. If that is the case, then they have already attacked us and a response is due."

"But we don't know for sure, do we?" the Vice President interjected. The FBI Director said, "When my agent gets here, Madame Vice President, we will find out for sure!" The NSA Director came back into the room at that point. "I want to go on the record," she announced, "that in my book these threats are real and highly credible and likely to manifest themselves over the next 12–36 hours."

"Not so," Agent Cole chimed in as he stepped through the door. "I am prepared to address each one of the items listed here that could allegedly affect American homeland!" The Director of the CIA said, "I can also add to that discussion!" The NSA Director seemed to doubt whether the FBI or the CIA could readily prove their claims that the Chinese were directly involved in such a major operation and so closely tied to the Korean action. "Oh really, NSA Director Case chimed in!" Agent Cole promptly gave a lengthy explanation on each of the listed threats and how the FBI, with the help of local law officials, had greatly reduced or eliminated the threat altogether. He also provided information that supported the view that the operations were directly connected to China and its efforts to bring disruption to the US homeland. The head of the CIA then presented his information on the cyber threats that had been thwarted, culminating with the deaths of some of the world's most wanted cyber-criminals. After the presentations were finished, the NSA director said, "Okay, so the

Chinese apparently—and I say *apparently*—had a hand in trying to fuck up our daily lives but that still does not excuse us from dealing with the big question before us. Look at what we get if we give up Taiwan in exchange for the lists of concessions they are willing to give us." After listening to the discussion between the US representatives, the Vice President said, "I am going to recommend that we move to DEFCON-2 and prepare for a retaliatory strike, should China attack the US or its military components and/or attack the island nation of Taiwan. Also, the strike should be significant enough to eliminate any further actions on part of the Chinese military. I also want to make it clear that the President has reviewed the contents of the folder and based on the threats and concessions, he stressed that he wants to keep all of the options on the table." The Chairman of the Joint Chiefs just about choked on the glass of water he was drinking. "You mean including the option of accepting the list?" The room got very quiet…and the Vice President said, "Yes, he said to keep it all on the table." The Chairman of Joint Chiefs cleared his throat and spoke, "I cannot and will not speak for the other cabinet, staff or department heads in this room, however after several intense discussions with the Chiefs of all of the Armed Services I believe it is my responsibility and duty to raise our concerns about the actions we are seriously considering. We are currently engaged in a war that had we shown a more robust military and diplomatic engagement policy towards China and our unwavering support of Taiwan our Soldiers, Sailors, Airman and Marines would not be dying as we sit here. The thought of America agreeing…..to even consider to what shakes out as the biggest bribe in history is a recipe for disaster in the future. Keeping this set of conditions in play, on the table, in our opinion gives the PRC a sense that our principles and values are negotiable and dependent, on the benefit offered. Having said that, Madame Vice President, if the President wants my resignation, I am prepared to submit it."

At that point, several of the attendees just looked at each other, but said nothing. After a few tense moments of silence, the NSA Director shouted, "You've got to be kidding!" Everyone around the table looked at her. She said, "I'm sorry; that was not directed at you Madame Vice President. I have just received a message that a top-secret US mission has delivered hypersonic cruise missiles and some of our 10-kiloton mini-nukes to Taiwan, and they are in the process of deploying them in anticipation of a PRC invasion. Does anyone here have any knowledge of this? Speak up!" She went on to say that the weapons had just arrived in Taiwan over the last thirty-six hours. The FBI Director motioned for Agent Cole to bring in the man who had been arrested in connection with hijacking a flight of C-17s that was destined for Kadena AFB in Okinawa and diverted them to Taiwan instead.

At that point, Agent Cole brought in North.

The NSA director looked at North and shook her head, clearly frustrated, "this man has been a thorn in the side of the NSA for some time. Now apparently he has gone rogue on us. I received some information just moments ago, from a source that I cannot reveal, that Major North used his authority to pick up a shipment of hypersonic cruise missiles and nukes from a warehouse in South Philadelphia, loaded on eight of eleven trucks, and moved the shipment to McGuire AFB, where he had it loaded onto three C-17s, and then, as reported by the FBI, he hijacked the lead aircraft and threatened the pilots and crew.

"Upon arrival at Ching Chau Kang Air Base, the hypersonic cruise missiles and mini-nukes were loaded onto thirty flatbed trucks to supply Taiwan's armed forces with weapon systems even though the administration had publicly stated it would not provide those weapons systems to Taiwan."

North's eyes grew wider with every word the NSA Director spoke. Agent Cole leaned over and whispered to North, "Just tell them the truth. It was not a real shipment, just an exercise."

"Major North, you have put us in a precarious position," said the Vice President. "By delivering that cargo, you have created a situation that we can no longer control, whether or not we were going to defend Taiwan, you have now given them the means to engage in a fight that may also draw us in."

"With all due respect Madame Vice President, I believe the opposite is true," North said. Cole nudged North again and whispered, "What are you doing? Tell them the truth." Ignoring him, North continued, "I am sure that if China understands that Taiwan can adequately defend herself, as laid out in Operation Game Changer, they will understand that while China may win, it would at best achieve a pyrrhic victory. But in the process, the Chinese military and civilians alike would suffer so dramatically that the nation would likely never recover. Under the CCP, a dictatorship of extreme levels has come into play, one that somewhat mirrors the 1930s and the rise of Hitler or Stalin. But the people have come too far to go back. Now, they might be ensnared in a war that could put the future of the CCP in jeopardy—all for one man's desire to demonstrate his power. But unless the threat is challenged now, the future looks bad for the whole world."

After this lengthy declamation, North whispered to Cole, "I need to speak with your boss right away. In private."

Cole escorted North to a private conference room so that he might talk to the FBI Director without the other team members overhearing them. At North's request Cole had brought one of the folders that the Chinese delegation had presented. He had just finished reviewing the folder when he heard the door open. The FBI Director came in and took a seat. "For years, there have been rumors that the Chinese had a mole in Washington," began North without preamble, "and most recently, intel leaks have been purported to come from a high-level source within the White House. I now know who the mole is." At these words, the Director immediately sat up in his chair and leaned forward. Cole turned and looked at North, his mouth agape.

"First let me present my rationale for making such a statement," North continued. "When I met with Col. Adams at McGuire AFB with regard to conducting exercise, 'Operation, Dark Star,' which basically is an effort to mislead Chinese intel. The operation involved the shipment of hypersonic cruise missiles and mini-nukes, but of course were empty canisters. He explained a procedure that would assist in maintaining security with regards to location, cargo, and shipment numbers. Depending on how big the shipment was, his team determined the number of flatbed trucks that were necessary, including a couple for backup. Then they would obtain drivers who had proper security clearances and an officer, Captain or above with at least a top secret security clearance to act as officer-in-charge. They knew where they had to go and return. It was never revealed to them what they were to pick up or the number of items to be loaded. So the drivers arrived at the preassigned location. After checking in at the guard gate, they pulled into the yard, got out of the truck cab, and went to the waiting area. A warehouse worker must come out and take the truck into the warehouse loading area. The warehouse loading crew would open up the sealed instructions and proceed to load the flatbed with the appropriate cargo, based upon the instructions from the envelope and then activate a device that would give off a false radioactive signal. The shipping manifest contained the type and number of the cargo they had just loaded. Then they put the manifest with all the appropriate paperwork into a sealed envelope marked 'Top Secret' and handed it to the officer-in-charge. Once the warehouse staff had secured and tarped the load so that no one could see what the cargo was, they then pulled the truck back out into the yard where the operator from the base returned to drive the truck back to McGuire AFB. Once all of the flatbed trucks were on their way with their cargo, they completed the cycle, and the convoy returned to the base. When the trucks returned, they did not go to the aircraft loading area, instead they were routed to a parking lot near the main entrance. The drivers remained in their vehicles until the convoy officer-in-charge is cleared, upon which all of the sealed envelopes were turned over to the senior aircraft loadmaster. Once cleared, the OIC signaled the drivers to exit their vehicles, board a bus, and return to the base they are assigned.

"Then an independent team must examine each vehicle to ensure no information was left behind that would indicate where the loads came from. Once that was done, a bus would arrive with the loading area drivers who would drive the trucks to the hangar where the aircraft was to be loaded. At this loading area, the tarps would be removed and the cargo unloaded, serial numbers confirmed, and the count checked against the manifests before being loaded into the assigned aircraft. So, through the entire process no one knows the entire story. The drivers who picked up the loads know where they picked up the cargo, but not what the cargo is or its quantity.

"At the aircraft loading area, they know what and how much of it was picked up, but not from where. The only people that would know the 'where,' 'what,' 'when,' and 'how many' with respect to the cargo would be Col. Adams, his operations officer, myself, and someone who had access to the information supplied by the Chinese agents who was there at the pickup location, who saw the planes being loaded and the Chinese spy within the Taiwan military who could match the tail numbers, including the total number of the items received at Chin Chau Kang AFB. I spoke with Col. Adams and his operations officer just five minutes ago while I was waiting for you. No one has questioned them with regard to the shipment. In conclusion, the comments that were made a short time ago by my boss leaves little doubt that *she* is the Chinese mole you have been searching for."

Lee's staff car couldn't have broken down at a worst time! He was getting impatient while waiting for his replacement vehicle. "When' is the other car arriving?" Lee asked the driver. "Is there any way you can patch it together so we could get going?" The driver responded, "I just drive them, sir! I can't fix them!" General Lee had not heard from any of his other agents in the Taiwanese military with regard to verifying the shipment of hypersonic cruise missiles and nukes. His government had been so sure the Yanks would never equip Taiwan with missiles and nukes that the group that had drawn the overall plans had never run any "gaming" or crunched any numbers for that scenario. So, based on current information, he had asked them to do just that.

Finally he received the call he had been dreading the most: confirmation from a high-level source regarding the shipment and the existence of a new operations order with the ominous title of "Operation Game Changer." Just as he was about to send an email informing Xi of Taiwan's newly acquired firepower, the replacement vehicle pulled up.

Without further ado, Lee jumped in and told the driver, "This is an emergency, so step on it!"

CHAPTER 11

PAYBACK FOR THE BETRAYAL

Xi was getting briefed on the status of PRC units, when the phone dedicated to North Korea, rang. The line had been set up at Kim's request; it had special features that he had insisted upon. Xi's aide picked up the line and said, "It's Kim Jong Un, sir." The look on Xi's face indicated that this call was an unwelcomed interruption. Xi asked his aide to ask Kim if he could speak with him later, but Kim's answer was a resounding "No!" So, Xi got on the line, saying, "Hello comrade!" It was the usual greeting exchanged between the two… but not this time! Kim launched into a raging outburst. His forces were getting slaughtered, and frontline units had run out of supplies in all critical categories. With no cover from the air, his forces were retreating faster than they had invaded. "Hell, they almost got my car as I moved from the palace to the bunker complex," yelled the dictator. "I received a message from the President of South Korea that if I order my troops to surrender and lay down their arms, I would be given safe passage to a country of my choice, providing that country is willing to accept me. If I turned that offer down, they ensured me that they have a nuke that will vaporize—yes, that's the term they used—the entire bunker complex! So they are coming for me and I told them that once the PLA joins forces, we will turn this around."

Kim's voice was now markedly getting tense as he said, "Do you know what they said? Do you care to make a guess? They sent me an email that showed a folder that your secret delegation team had presented to the Americans. Then it became clear to me that you had always intended to sell me out for your own gains, you lying bastard! Even though the Americans have not agree to your scheme, now I understand why the supplies have not been forthcoming. Because you'll need them for your war with Taiwan! You've lied to me time and again, but this time you have gone too far. You are a ruthless, self-serving son-of-a-bitch, and I was right to plan for such a deception, you coward, you—"

"Listen to me you little fat man," Xi shouted. "You couldn't fight your way out of a paper bag. Your country has suffered mightily at the hands of your regime. Your family have been a thorn in our side for almost seventy-five years, and the world and your country will be better off once the Yanks drop that bomb with your name on it. No one will miss you and I will still be alive to spit on your grave, you pathetic little man! Ha! I can hear the bombs and artillery getting closer."

"Yes," Kim replied. "My time is short, but you will not have the luxury of spitting on my grave. I hope you have enjoyed the steady stream of flowers I have sent to keep that beautiful vase of yours full. You may remember the big purple vase that I had sent to your personal suite in the bunker complex. You know the one…what did it say on the side of the vase? Ah, yes, 'Victorious Together.' It's beautiful isn't it?"

Xi was getting impatient and retorted, "What the hell do I care about a vase?"

"Can you see it from where you are sitting?"

"Yes, I can, but not for much longer…the vase will disappear along with you," Xi answered.

"You are more right than you may realize!" Kim responded. Xi's voice was becoming more strained as he said, "Why would I want to keep a gaudy flower vase to remind me of you? You no longer matter!" Impatient with the conversation, he was about to hang up after that comment. "I may no longer matter, but neither do you and I will see you in hell!" retorted Kim. "I hope you know that my gift of flowers and the beautiful vase is a permanent going-away gift…along with the two kilos of 'Semtex.'"

With those words, Xi paused and pushed his chair back from the desk and slowly stood up. He turned to face the vase. Right at that time a series of high-pitched sound bursts came from the NK phone line filled the room, followed by what sounded like the tone one hears when two fax machines are trying to establish a connection. Xi could hear Kim say, "So long, you motherless bastard!" in Mandarin and then the phone went quiet. Leong, who was sitting at the end of the table, could see the fear in Xi's eyes as he pointed at the vase and started saying, "Get that out of here…"

The resulting explosion from the two kilos of Semtex hidden in the base of the vase proved to be more than sufficient payback for Xi's treachery.

The blast was followed by an enormous shock wave. The outside walls of the bunker complex were meant to withstand a nuclear hit. In most places, the walls were in excess of eight feet thick and meant to keep the massive shock wave from a nuclear detonation from getting to the occupants of the bunker. But thick walls also acted to keep the shock wave from getting out and dissipating. The resultant shock wave ricocheted up and down and back and forth until all of its energy was absorbed. In the milliseconds after the blast, the floors between the levels—though they were made of one-meter-thick reinforced concrete—collapsed like a house of cards. The collapsing floors ripped open gas lines that ignited into a huge rolling fireball, until all of the available oxygen was used up. By the time the shock wave was finished, the six levels containing working cubicles, sleeping quarters, cafeteria, and people lay at the bottom of a cavernous concrete-lined six-story pit. The debris at the bottom was essentially pulverized by the reoccurring shock wave as it bounced back and forth, yielding a mixture of dust, blood, concrete, machinery, and body parts. Those that were fortunate to be outside experienced what they first thought was an earthquake, but when the big steel doors at the entrance bowed out by several inches, they just stared in disbelief.

In no more than a few seconds the leadership structure of China had been upended.

Some of the personnel on the surface wondered if the Americans had used a new secret weapon that was so "stealthy" that it had not been detected before the explosion. But a quick review by some of the senior officers who soon arrived on the scene dismissed that idea. No one was sure what had happened or how; they were all in a state of shock. Just then, General Lee's car pulled up in front of the complex. The firetrucks were on scene along with ambulances, rescue equipment, and military police. General Lee walked up to the huge steel doors and saw rescue personnel doing what they could to pull the doors open. But Lee knew that if the explosion could do that to the doors, there was no one left to rescue; they might as well just fill in the hole with dirt and let it be. Now Lee had a much bigger problem to solve. He was now convinced that Taiwan was in receipt of and currently deploying the hypersonic cruise missiles along with the mini-nuke warheads. General Lee concluded that with Xi now gone, the whole operation was in jeopardy. If China were to attack Taiwan, America and its allies would most likely respond with a massive counter-attack; that, combined with the new weapon systems now in Taiwan's arsenal, would lead to a disaster of epic proportions.

The hours were counting down, as Lee jumped back into his car and ordered his driver to take him to the nearest military air base. Lee thought he would have a better grasp on troop activities if he was closer to the embarkation points along the coast. He ordered a staff jet to transport him to Luocheng Air Base. From there he would set up the communications center for Acting President Han to address all of the operational field commanders.

Meanwhile, the Joint Chiefs were just emerging from a meeting in the White House. They were, at the President's direction, going to DEFCON-2 and prepare to go to DEFCON-1 to deliver a massive strike on the Chinese mainland if Taiwan was attacked, based upon the fact that Taiwan now had at the new weapon systems at its disposal. The Pentagon was busy checking its inventory to find where the missiles and nukes had come from. At that point, a call came in from the Air Force's Chief of Staff's office, stating that they could not find where this rogue shipment had been shipped from. They were ordered to find "What the hell happened, given the administration's public stance with regard to not sending nukes to Taiwan?"

North was being detained prior to his removal to the Brig at Quantico. Agent Cole stopped by to visit him before he was to be transferred. "You know I think you tried to do what you thought might stop a bloody mess, but it looks like it's going to happen anyway," he said. North looked up and replied, "No it's not...there's no reason for anything to happen. China is not going to attack Taiwan!"

"Well, I overheard the Director being told that a large-scale response is being prepared," remarked Cole.

North jumped up. "No, no, no, no...that's the wrong response! If China gets a whiff of us getting ready to attack them, they may respond first! Then we will strike and it will only escalate from there."

"But Steve, China will not know that we are setting up for a strike," Cole pointed out.

"Have they arrested my boss yet?"

"No, I am not sure the Director bought your whole story."

"Then China will know, because she will tell them."

"Steve, how are you so sure they are not going to attack Taiwan?

To me it sure sounds they will!" Cole repeated.

"I don't have time to explain," North replied in an urgent tone. "You need to get me out of here and get me a chance to talk with the Vice President...this does not have to end this way!"

"I'm not sure if I can get you out, but I will talk to the Director and see what he is willing to do," said Cole.

"Please do!" replied North. "I've got to speak with someone who has the power to stop this before things go any further!"

General Lee had finally convinced most of the field commanders to attend a video conference. In the available time prior to the conference, he posted information about what had happened at the national bunker complex. Although still preliminary, expert sources ruled out any foreign connection to the destruction that had occurred at the bunker complex. Acting President Han was safe, had assumed leadership, and would address the armed forces during the video conference.

Lee had repeatedly impressed upon Han the importance of revealing the secret that had been kept from virtually everyone, except a handful of senior CCP members. There was still a problem: A few of the Generals told Lee that they suspected foul play and that some element within the CCP had opposed the efforts to take Taiwan by force; essentially there had been a coup. Those Generals said they wanted to hear from Acting President Han. However, most of the Generals were still preparing to attack Taiwan and the US targets that their mission mandated. Time was running out and General Lee was starting to fear that this plan of Leong's would bring destruction down on the heads of the Chinese people.

Agent Cole came into the room where North was being held and said, "I don't believe it, but the Vice President is still here at Camp

David and she will be coming to see you in a few minutes. Steve, I hope you have a good story to tell her; I just heard the Secretary of Defense tell the PACFLEET Admiral to have the carriers launched and have aircrafts on station at 8:45 am." Just then, the door opened and in walked the Vice President escorted by two Secret Service bodyguards. The Vice President sat down across the table from North and said, "Okay, Major North, what do I need to know that I have not been told already?" North drew in a deep breath and said, "First, you need to call off the DEFCON 2 alert. For the last few months, I have seen President Xi's Chief Advisor Leong's plan emerge, I have asked myself 'What is something that I should see, but am not? What's the point to all of these complicated actions?' Mostly, I followed the simple logical path that Leong was 'shaping the battlefield,' so to speak. But then I started thinking Leong was never that obvious with respect to what he was actually thinking. He was a student of chess and his normal way of playing was to create opportunities for you to think that you are winning, allowing you to take his pieces off the board. But the whole time, he was not playing the board, but you! He wasn't looking at the board to determine the advantages or disadvantages it offered, but the strength or weakness *you* show through how you conduct the game itself. So he would be willing to concede one or two games and once he understood you…he never lost again."

"So he was a student of chess. Get on with it; what's your point?" the Vice President said impatiently. "My apologies Madame Vice President, the point is that all of the steps he took were based upon a strategy of knowing his opponent, building on the latter's mistakes, and, if possible, achieving victory without a fight. I did not fully see this until I saw the list of concessions China was willing to agree to if we would not interfere with their effort to take Taiwan. So with all due respect, Madame Vice President, he looked at this administration and concluded that the Chinese could effectively project their growing military might, appear threateningly aggressive, and couple it with other actions that would create multiple pressure points or distractions that would each present a complex set of choices—before providing the administration with an alternative, a way to save face. They used very advanced computer simulations, years of data and advanced psychological profiling to predict likely outcomes using numerous situations that predicted how political leaders would respond to various actions that might threaten their political future. He used the same technique to predict the responses of the general public. Using the psychological profiles of the administration personnel; they determined what type of internal and external crisis would pressure this administration to abandon Taiwan. Given the additional long term effects of socialist indoctrination in our schools, media tilting to the left and China's willingness to spend whatever it takes to set the conditions for China to expand and more importantly, preserve the CCP. Because of the perceived weakness demonstrated by this administration thus far, they felt confident they could eventually get Taiwan without a shot being fired.

"China knows that they cannot win a war with us. They really don't want a war with us, at least not yet. If you consider the option of invasion, then they would actually lose ground in their pursuit of international influence and status, much like Russia has with its invasion of Ukraine. There would be numerous sanctions imposed on China around the world. International trade would plummet and the economy would suffer greatly, no doubt causing the citizenry to question CCP's judgement. The average mainland citizen would see people that look just like them being killed and for what? What threat does Taiwan pose to the man or woman on the street? The trust they have tried to build in the world would evaporate with the killing of thousands of Taiwanese civilians."

The Vice President remarked, "Perhaps they want recognition and influence."

"No ma'am, they want to eliminate a neighboring threat and gain respect, and they will use hard-edged power and money to get it. They are not willing to wait and build it over time, the way the US has done. And that is their problem: time!"

"Time?" the Vice President repeated. "I'm not following you."

"More than anything, the communist power structure wants the CCP's continuation! They, meaning the leadership, realize that their model of society cannot function long term, unless they continue their dictatorship. That means eliminating the nearest alternative political model—the Republic of China, Taiwan—as quickly as possible. It poses a threat to the mainland—not a military threat, but an ideological and philosophical one.

"Taiwan demonstrates 24,000,000 ethnic Chinese doing just fine without the CCP telling them what to do and how to think. Beijing doesn't give a rip about making China whole. Consider this: They do not need the land or the people...they are afraid of Taiwan's long-term influence. If they really cared about the Chinese people, they would concede that after an invasion, the cost of rebuilding Taiwan would be prohibitive. Taiwan will put up a devastating defense with its highly trained and motivated armed forces. It's well-trained air force and anti-ship missiles would inflict massive damage on any invading forces. By my estimates, the PRC would suffer at least 150,000-250,000 casualties, and at best it would be a pyrrhic victory. There would no doubt be guerilla warfare for years. China is actually afraid of Taiwan, much in the same way that they feared the existence of Hong Kong. China has always needed an Emperor, a strong man to keep it together and that is the main role of the CCP.

"However, Taiwan threatens, over time, to erode that long-standing vision, much in the same way that Hong Kong had done so far. As a way to remove that threat, Leong came up with a strategy to produce disruptions in America, all the time disavowing any involvement and keeping their hands clean, especially following on the heels of the North Korean invasion of the South. From the Chinese's perspective, the timing could not have worked out more favorably. In a little more than two months we will have a major election that will consume the nation's attention. All of those actions were designed to put political pressure on the current administration and essentially bully it into making a hasty, irrational betrayal of a thriving democracy in order to solve the problems that China had so cleverly brought upon us.

"Russia's war in the Ukraine is another aspect that the US must consider when it looks at its commitments. Using North Korea's invasion and the loss of US lives was their opening gambit. Then follow with the disruptions in America; the threat of an attack on US forces and Hawaii and Guam was supposed to knock us off balance and question our long- and short-term goals. Their continued display of military power is meant to intimidate and bully us into over-estimating their military capabilities. Then there's Leong's brilliant move to pay off the cartels to promote, coerce, and otherwise drive millions of migrants to literally invade the US with the purpose of instilling social and fiscal distress and upheaval. In the end, the threat of war and its terrible consequences must be convincing enough to push the US into making a rash, self-serving decision to change its position on defending Taiwan. Then there's their list of concessions; all we have to do is say publicly that we will not defend Taiwan, even tolerate a military invasion, to give China a free hand to annex it while we look the other way, and then China will return the favor for us and our allies. For the US, the Chinese will give us the Korean Peninsula, unified under South Korean leadership, while we do the dirty work of getting rid of Kim. It appears they have already abandoned North Korea by failing to provide the continued support that the NK forces need to sustain their invasion. We would win the war, because China would pull the rug out from under Kim. He would be destroyed and we would be victorious and in this way, we get the other concessions.

"That would be a huge political benefit during the next election cycle. Over time, China has very insidiously worked to change the tone of American sentiment by effecting socialist indoctrination via our education systems, resulting in citizens who would find it acceptable to abandon a freely chosen democracy such as Taiwan and its capitalist system to the Chinese. Right now the people of Taiwan feel somewhat emboldened by the soft or muted position of the US assisting them in standing up to the mainland. The people of Taiwan are not fools; they saw China mislead the world when it promised, in the past, that Hong Kong's government would be respected. China also faces the reality where if they invade, it would mean the destruction of Taiwan as we know it.

"However, Taiwan is no military lightweight. It would likely make the mainland pay dearly for its efforts. With only ninety miles separating the countries, strikes on mainland facilities would be inevitable. What if the PLA, in an effort to intercept an incoming Taiwanese missile, knocked it off course and it hit the Wuhan labs? The results of that strike are almost too tragic to think about. Ultimately, China would be negatively impacted to a considerable extent. The reinvestment in its own military and domestic industry and the lives lost would burden the mainland for years. The required reinvestment to make the island of Taiwan productive would be astronomical. Some might think that the mainland would get the chip-making plants in Taiwan. But I have confirmation from reliable sources that those plants and their research labs will be destroyed by the Taiwanese themselves before they can fall into the mainland's hands. In addition, the outcome would likely result in the US becoming less dependent on overseas chip suppliers and build more plants domestically— which is also not in line with Chinese interest.

"But if the US cuts a deal, accepts the concession list, and abandons Taiwan, the Chinese win without a firing shot; they portray us as weak and untrustworthy, which would improve their stature in the world. Taiwan would realize they are in an untenable long-term position and the US selling out Taiwan would eventually lead to China winning the battle before it's even fought. You see, Sun Tzu approaches war as mostly a mental exercise to study your opponent and determine their weak points relative to the upcoming battle. That is just what Leong did. I'm sure you have heard the old adage about how the Chinese plan for the long term; the saying goes, 'If we plan for a day, they plan for a week; if we plan for a week, they plan for a month; if we plan for a month, they plan for a year; if we plan for a year, they plan for ten years; and if we plan for ten years, they plan for hundred years.' It actually is a well-designed and effective plan. They never intended to invade. It was all a big bluff! They are hoping for what I would refer to as a 'Hong Kong, *redux*.' They got Hong Kong without a shot. Then when they found it to their advantage, they broke their promises of honoring the Hong Kong government and proceeded to do exactly what they had always intended to do. And the World stood by and did not raise a finger to stop them. So, whatever concessions they say they are willing to make, aren't worth the paper that they are printed on. The only way they win is if we fall for their plan of deception, misdirection, and manipulation. We need to show the world what China attempted to do by way of their lethal Covid-19 variant, hiring criminals to murder our citizens, flooding the country with millions of illegals meant to trigger social disruption, shutting down our day-to-day utility and financial operations, and topping it all off by pushing and supporting North Korea to start a war which will cost thousands of lives—just to further their misguided effort to tighten political control over their own citizens via the Communist party. All of it done under the banner of reuniting Imperial China.

"We should lay all the cards on the table. And we need to rally the world to ensure that China does not get away without some form of rebuke or punishment for this travesty. So, Madame Vice President, we should not provide China with an excuse or reason to overreact, but we must make it very clear that we will not be bullied and we will defend Taiwan's right to exist as an independent nation!"

"Major North, your points are well made! But the mainland could still chose to invade; is that not true?"

"Not likely, given the way Leong would have planned it. I am sure he would think, 'Why take all that risk when the reward may not be worth it?' His experience would remind him that there are always unknown variables in every scenario. For instance, what if the invasion was not a clear-cut victory? His plan keeps China's vulnerabilities to a minimum. No doubt, if the PRC chose to invade, they would suffer from sanctions on trade, much like Russia. That would cause a massive slowdown in the economy, which China is very dependent on to keep its citizens accepting of the one party, communist rule by the CCP. You see, China's economy is like one of those 'spinning top' toys. As long as the top spins at a fast rate, the top stays up right, if it slows down significantly, it starts to wobble and ultimately falls over. If the economy falls, so might the CCP.

By the way, you should also know that Taiwan does not actually possess hypersonic cruise missiles or the mini-nukes; it was an exercise to fool the Chinese into realizing that if they did invade, it would cost them dearly."

As he paused, the Vice President leaned back in her chair and smiled. "So the Pentagon is 'chasing its tail' so to speak, looking for something they thought they had lost, but never did, right?"

"Yes ma'am. That is correct."

"So if I understand this correctly, we can choose not to take the bait as it were, and we will win the war with North Korea, the Korean Peninsula will be unified under South Korea's leadership, China will not invade, so, Taiwan will still operate as it does, at least for now, and China will most likely de-escalate? Fascinating! We will consider what you have just said. Thank you Major North, if we do choose to follow your advice…by the way you used the words 'this administration.' I infer that you did not vote for us?"

"No ma'am, I did not!"

The Vice President leaned forward and said in a low voice, "Yet, your actions and advice may just very well get us another four years in office." She glanced at him. "By that look on your face, that possible outcome doesn't sit well with you." North looked up and said to the Vice President...

"What I said, did, or advised was for the good of the country, ma'am, not one party or the other.

The Vice President leaned back and smiled, saying, "Of course, that is what we all want.

Now I must advise you, this conversation never took place. Oh, by the way, we're searching for your boss. She sold out her country! You will likely never see or hear of her again." At that point, a Secret Service agent came in and gave the Vice President a note. Her eyebrows rose up, and then she put the note in her pocket. She got up and started walking to the door, just before leaving, she turned around and said, "one last bit of information Major, President Xi and many of his General Staff have been killed in a major explosion in their command bunker complex; that news should make the evening interesting, heh? Good night Major North!"

General Lee was getting more concerned by the minute. The clock was nearing 9:00 am, and most of the Chinese units were in their staging areas or had already embarked on the equipment they had been assigned for the invasion. Aircraft were fully armed and the pilots were on standby. The PLA was waiting for the order to execute. Reports from the Taiwanese spies on the mainland conveyed that what had been predicted for a long time was going to finally unfold. The President of the Republic of China issued top-secret orders to arm and prepare to detonate explosives that would destroy much of the high-tech labs and factories that the Chinese might hope to acquire through the invasion. The tension that had been brewing between the two since 1949 was nearing an explosive culmination. General Lee was handed a message from the mole in America that a recommendation had been given to the President to go to DEFCON 2 and to prepare for a massive strike.

"This message is eight hours old and says that the President's highest-ranking advisors are recommending that action," General Lee remarked. "We must find out if the Americans have actually escalated things accordingly. Get ahold of her; we need an immediate update." After that, Lee was handed a message that a US Naval ARG (Amphibious Ready Group) with a Marine BLT (Battalion Landing Team) on board was heading out of the Subic Bay in the Philippines toward Korea, via the Strait of Taiwan, in the next few hours. What would happen if a PRC pilot made a mistake and attacked the US ARG? He reasoned that one wrong step could bring a massive military strike from the US. The communications operator responded, "General, we have repeatedly tried to connect with our agent in the US, but we haven't received any response." As the time for the video meeting grew closer, Lee was increasingly worried. Without Xi to explain that the secret plan was actually a "calculated bluff," some of the Generals might chose to attack.

When Lee had finally arranged to have all of the unit commanders attend the video conference, he was already hearing that a few units were ready to move forward and attack the American fleet that was supporting the fighting on the Korean Peninsula.

Just before the video conference was due to start, Acting President Han asked General Lee, "what might happen if things got out of hand and the military chose to mount a full scale invasion anyway." Lee looked at Han, "With the new fire power that Taiwan has recently received, it would result in a disaster and I think the CCP would be blamed, leading to a nationwide revolt and the end of the CCP."

General Lee came on screen first. What all the attendees were expecting was the latest information on the US troops' situational awareness, but what they heard was something very different.

The Secretary of Defense had just finished a video call with the President and the Vice President in the Oval Office. As he emerged from the session he directed his aide to arrange for a meeting with the Joint Chiefs. With the internal threats to the US mainland virtually nullified, he had them call the National Command Center and return the US to a status of DEFCON 3. He directed the Joint Chiefs to contribute their full support to the Korean conflict and to not do anything to provoke the Chinese. However, recon flights should resume normal operations through the Strait of Taiwan only when the RC and PRC forces stand down. The administration decided that the potential reduction in the possibility of war with China was worth the risk and kept more than enough firepower on standby, should the Chinese choose to attack.

CHAPTER 12

PLANS CHANGE

Acting President Han began the meeting with his advisors with an ominous announcement: "The death of President Xi, Leong, Senior Generals and all other staff had come about at the hands of the North Korean Premier Kim Jong Un. As far as we can tell, based on what was recorded and archived at a digital comm center located several miles from the bunker complex, Kim apparently suffered a nervous breakdown along with paranoid thoughts that Xi was planning to abandon his regime. If the President were alive and with us, he would inform you that you have played a part in a complicated plan that has evolved over the past twenty-five years. The plan, code named 'Bright Star,' has unfortunately not played out as we had hoped. Because of its complex nature and efforts to maintain absolute secrecy, the number of CCP members, including military leadership personnel, that were informed of the plan's details was very limited—less than twenty. The point being, the preparation for an invasion was critical, but an actual invasion was not the objective, nor part of the plan.

"Using deception by way of appearing to ramp up our military forces for a full-scale invasion of Taiwan as well as a major battle involving America and its allies was meant to force a decision—for the Americans to abandon their commitment to Taiwan. The main objective was to annex Taiwan peacefully and transform its government to our form of government on our timetable. Essentially, we aimed to have the United States, by their own choice, publicly declare that it would not defend Taiwan, but announce that they supported long-term reunification of the two countries. The PLA and all other units of our military have prepared superbly. Your continued growth will prove to be of foremost importance in our drive to see China take her place as the world leader. The CCP's central committee applauds your dedication and devotion to our people. You will likely never hear of the steps taken to ensure the plan's success, but we have more to do. The attack on Taiwan and the US and its allies will not occur, at least not now. We will employ additional means of pressure to have Taiwan join us in the future, but we have considered the options and an attack on Taiwan at this time does not deliver the benefits we had hoped for. Therefore, I'm giving you a direct order to stand down. However, if America or one of its allies, including Taiwan, does provoke or attack us, we will turn to our military for a quick and decisive counter-blow."

On hearing Acting President Han's speech, the response from the Generals was just as expected; they were full of disbelief along with anger. Several Generals maintained that it would be a quick victory, while others felt they should at least take advantage of the fact that the number of US warships was concentrated and would provide easy targets. Others asked for permission to at least test out their weapons system to see how effectively the Americans can defend against them.

"Such efforts and proposed actions only invite further escalation, especially if such a limited clash is misread as an opening salvo, rather than a mistake," responded Han. Then he frowned and said, "If any of you feel that you cannot comply with or carry out my directives, feel free to 'step down' from your current post and turn over your command to an officer who understands and can carry out my orders." Then General Lee started to call out names from the list of unit commanders and asked them whether they will comply with Acting President Han's orders. One by one, the Generals were called upon. Even though the Generals were in disagreement with the proposed plan, they pledged to follow Han's orders. General Shin did not say a word; he just switched off his monitor. Lee had known Shin for many years and suspected he might be a problem. His airborne units were the largest and best trained of all of the PLA's airborne units. General Lee was familiar with Shin's second-in-command Brigadier General Nu. Lee knew he could not blindly trust Shin, so he wanted to contact Nu immediately.

However, Lee was informed that Nu was out on the flight line and would be back shortly. "Have Brigadier Nu call me immediately upon his return!" Lee demanded. About ten minutes later, he got a call. "Nu here, can I speak with General Lee?" Lee's first question was, "Where is General Shin?" Nu remarked, "Strange you should ask. I was speaking with him five minutes before the unit departed and when I turned around he was gone. According to one of the ground crew, he climbed onboard the lead aircraft and left with his troops."

"The whole fleet of Y-20s has left?" General Lee asked in a horrified voice. "Yes, the whole fleet, 18 aircraft and 1600 paratroops."

"Did the General say anything to you about the mission getting scrapped by Acting President Han?" asked Lee desperately. "What did you say? The mission had been called off? Did I hear that correctly?" Nu blurted out. "Yes, the mission has been called off. There is to be no attack on Taiwan! I am giving you a direct order to call back the entire fleet of Y-20's, immediately!"

"Yes sir, I will try, but you should know I heard the General give an order to all aircraft to go silent, with no communications at all. I will try my best, and call back shortly."

Soon, Nu called Lee back. "Not good news, sir, none of the 18 aircraft responded to the calls." General Lee asked, "What is their flight path?"

"Sir, the flight path will run parallel to our coast until they reach Fuzhou, but on command, the fleet will pivot and turn southeast. At that point they will be approximately 90 miles northwest of Taiwan. The fleet is timed to hit that location at 9:00 am with the objective of capturing Taipei International Airport."

Immediately, General Lee called to advise Acting President Han. "We may have a problem with one of the airborne units refusing to follow your orders. General Shin has pre-emptively ordered his fleet of 18 troop transports into the air and to follow the planned attack route. When I ordered his second-in-command to contact the fleet, they did not respond. Unless we take immediate action, the fleet may be mistaken as a vanguard of a larger assault. I have just been handed a note that confirms that the Taiwanese coastal radar is tracking the fleet; also the US carrier named Ronald Raegan has locked onto them. It is now reported that the carrier has launched several of their F-35s and F-18s. In response, I have ordered PRC coastal defense command to launch one of their Shenyang J-11 flights. I suggest that we send our fighters to visually contact Shin's fleet and escort or force them to land at the nearest airfield."

Han responded, "That seems a bit dramatic, doesn't it?"

"Yes sir, it does, and that's just how I hope the Taiwanese and the Americans will see it!" Han took just a moment to think about it before saying, "Then do it!"

"Get me on the line with the CDC," Lee ordered the communications operator. "I want to speak with the Wing OIC (Officer-in-Charge) right away!" Soon he received a call.

"Wing OIC Chu here!"

"This is General Lee. Now listen carefully, this is what I need you to do…"

Twenty minutes later the flight of J-11s were pulling alongside Shin's Y-20 troop transports. The flight leader pulled alongside the lead troop transport aircraft. The pilots of the two aircraft could clearly see each other. The fighter pilot indicated the fleet should follow him to the nearest airfield. The transports did not respond and continued on their current course. The flight leader contacted his base and updated them on the transports' failure to follow his commands. The OIC instructed the flight leader to have them land at the Shantou Air Base, saying, "By any means necessary, put those aircrafts on the ground!"

The flight leader backed off and in full view of the rest of the fleet, fired several rounds from his nose-mounted 30 mm cannon into a non-critical section of the wing's fuselage of Shin's lead transport. After witnessing that demonstration, the rest of the troop transports broke formation and started to descend. But, the transport flight leader remained on the same heading. The flight leader again throttled his J-11 into firing position behind the General's aircraft. He tried one last time to warn the aircraft but received no response. Then he fired another short burst into the wing. This time, an errant shot hit one of the starboard engines. The plane lurched hard to the right, with black smoke coming from the starboard outside engine. The loss of the engine caused the fully loaded aircraft to rapidly lose altitude, falling from 12,000 feet to 5,000 feet in less than two minutes. With emergency lights blinking all across the control panel and alarms sounding, the plane finally settled out at 3100 feet. Once the aircraft had stabilized, more alarms started going off. With one engine gone, the aircraft lost altitude and airspeed. The reduction of airspeed afforded an opportunity for the troops to exit the crippled aircraft, which is just what they were doing, as fast as they could. With all four jump hatches open, the plane's wind resistance surged. With reduced airspeed and with all four jump doors fully opened, the pilots realized a kid with a slingshot could take them out. The two pilots looked at General Shin, as if asking permission to leave. He looked at them, nodded toward the rear of the aircraft, and in less than one minute, they had joined the rest of the troops, floating toward the ground. With the weight of the troops gone, the General was able to regain altitude and speed. The troop transport with the General piloting it was soon to reach the pivoting point in just a few minutes.

General Shin thought that if he could take his aircraft into Taiwanese airspace he might be able to create a situation where Taiwanese air defense would have to shoot him down. If that occurred, the General reasoned, the incident might trigger an escalation and lead to a much larger military exchange and the war he had so eagerly prepared for. The wing leader was ordered to finish the job and shoot the aircraft down. But the wing leader refused to do so. The General was highly respected and the pilot did not want to be known as the man who had killed the General. The other pilots also refused, choosing to head back to their base instead.

General Lee had been a fighter pilot, but due to a medical issue he had moved into the intelligence branch. Acting President Han ordered Lee to shoot Shin down—before he could violate Taiwanese defensive airspace. Lee realized he now stood between what had been seen as a well-outlined plan and actions that could escalate into a massive disaster. He had precious little time to act, let alone to think about it. General Lee and General Shin had been friends for many years. Lee knew there was zero chance of dissuading Shin once he made his mind up. What Acting President Han had ordered Lee to do set his stomach churning! Now in his flight suit, Lee raced out to the flight line to climb aboard an old friend, a Shenyang J-8. He knew he must not delay, so for the first time, there was no preflight check list. He opened up the throttle to max out his speed, but it soon became apparent he would not likely be able to intercept the General's aircraft before it entered the Taiwanese airspace. But he would try.

On the other end, the Taiwanese coastal radar had been tracking the fleet and noted that all but one aircraft broke away and landed at a nearby base. An anti-aircraft missile battery was put on alert. Clinton Tsi had arrived at the Defense Center about an hour ago and had witnessed the apparent efforts to turn that single aircraft around. Tsi was not sure how to interpret what he was seeing. The perspective of an experienced American who had apparently been aware of Leong's plan might help.

North was just drifting off to sleep when his phone woke him up. Tsi described what had transpired, then what he was currently seeing on radar. North asked, "Just one plane, you said?"

"Yes! Just one and it's a troop transport. I think once it enters our airspace we intend to shoot it down."

"No! No! Don't do that," North responded. "I believe that would be a huge mistake. You said that at one time your radar was monitoring a total of 18 aircrafts in that fleet. Then they were picked up by a fighter escort and all that was left was the lead aircraft, correct?"

"Yes, that is correct."

North continued, "I think what you may have witnessed was an effort to prevent an unplanned attack on Taiwan. I believe that is the most logical explanation based upon what you have told me."

"The radar screen now shows a single J-8 jet fighter approaching the transport at very high speed," Tsi said, raising his voice in surprise. "The transport has now turned on a course for Taiwan airspace directly in line with Taipei. The fighter jet has just launched a missile that is tracking the transport. The missile is starting to fade… it has exploded. From the screen it is hard to tell what damage may have been inflicted on the transport. Coastal radar requests permission to fire." Again, North said, "It is not a significant enough of a threat, show restraint."

"Coastal radar is again asking for permission to fire! One of the duty officers is asking what if they are trying to fool us. They may have a nuke on board."

"No, no…do not fire on the aircraft," North repeated before asking, "Clinton, who is in command there?"

Tsi looked to the command desk and replied, "General Lieu is the Operational Chief." North's voice was becoming more strained as he said, "Tsi, switch me over to the General's desk." Tsi tried to connect North to the General's location, but the system would not let him through! North thought for a second and then asked, "Can you put me on the intercom speaker?"

"I think so...there, you are now on the intercom."

"General Lieu, this is Major Stephen North, US Marine Corps, State Security Officer Tsi can vouch for me. I am aware that SSO Tsi has briefed the general staff about my uncovering of Leong's plans. If I am right, you are not seeing any other aircraft or troop movements. That is because the mainland has been bluffing all along; they had never planned to attack! I do not have time to further explain Leong's plan to you, but if you shoot down the incoming aircraft, that may trigger a response that will escalate, perhaps to a full-blown exchange."

There was a long pause before a weary voice replied, "this is General Lieu, Coastal Defense (CD), I am withdrawing permission to fire on the lone aircraft, even if it makes it into our defensive airspace. Capitol Defense Command, you do have permission to shoot down the lone aircraft if it violates your airspace perimeter. Major North, we shall see what happens next."

At the same time, PLA's Senior Generals Cho, Hui, and Chong eyes were fixed to a radar monitor on the other side of the Strait, watching and waiting to see how Taiwan's Coastal Defense would react. They had begrudgingly gone along with Acting President Han's directive to stand down and not to initiate any action, but now they were having second thoughts. General Cho turned to General Chong, smiled, and said, "Remember we can't initiate, but we can react!" They had witnessed General Lee's efforts to shoot down General Shin's Y-20, but they were not sure what damage may have been inflicted on the aircraft.

At CD, Tsi exclaimed, "Wait! The aircraft is losing altitude and speed. At the current rate of descent, it's plotted to crash into the swamp area by our most northwestern beaches. A coastal patrol boat has reported that the lone aircraft has an additional engine trailing smoke and another engine on fire."

The three PLA Generals moved closer to the radar screen, watching as the Y-20 started to fade and then disappear from the screen. The three men turned to the radar tech who reported that his equipment had confirmed that Taiwan's Coastal Defense had "negative" missile launches. The three Generals walked out of the bunker without another word.

On the other end, Tsi's voice lightened as he said, "Coastal radar now reports that the lone aircraft has disappeared from the radar screen. Wait, I have just been handed a message… they have confirmed that the aircraft has in fact crashed into the swamps. The patrol boat on scene says they think the water is deep enough for them to get to the aircraft, but not so deep that we have to worry about the plane completely sinking. They will check for survivors. Major North, it is now 9:25 am and everything is quiet. Our screens show negative radar contacts and no new reports of Chinese military movements. We will wait for our contacts on the mainland to confirm that the mainland Chinese forces are returning to their daily operational status before we initiate a stand down across our forces. I must go now; I'm told our President is calling a meeting of the Cabinet to review the actions and activity of the past several days and lay ground work for the future of our defense. So good bye and thank you again!"

CHAPTER 13

THE SMOKE CLEARS

After the call with Tsi, North leaned back into the sofa and closed his eyes to try to get some rest. He was awakened at seven the next morning by one of the FBI agents. He decided to text Kent and Howe to let them know the operation had worked out, the FBI was in route, and they were now free to go after the Chinese house on the South Riverfront. It was eight in the morning when two FBI agents came to escort North to the NSA headquarters. North knew he had stepped way over the limits of his authority. To top that off he was still guilty of hijacking military aircraft, threatening superiors, and using NSA funds to pay for part of the unauthorized Caracas operation, which included paying for prostitutes and expensive liquor. Oh yes, there was also the charge of damaging property at a bar in rural New Jersey and he was sure there was more, but he was too tired to give a shit.

An FBI agent put handcuffs on him and took him to the black sedan waiting by the front steps, for the ride back from Camp David to the NSA headquarters in Washington, DC. As they headed for the front gate, North could see that the Chinese delegation was loading up their luggage for transport to the airport and their flight back to China. North had overheard some of the US personnel mention how surprised they were when the chief Chinese delegate had abruptly walked into the US conference room last night and started to apologize. He stated that none of the delegates had been briefed or were permitted to see the contents of the folders before the meeting. He further stated that once he had finished reading from what the list, he had been shocked and had immediately called Beijing. Beijing had confirmed that all this had been a result of confusion and a massive mistake on the part of the CCP's central committee staff personnel. The folders they had presented earlier had been a major error on some clerk's part and the contents grossly misrepresented China's international position and intentions. Because of that error, all three delegations were being immediately recalled to Beijing.

During the drive back from Camp David, North stared out the window and said to himself, "what has taken place during the last few months and how many lives it affected, all the money, time and effort just to ensure continuation a one party communist dictatorship and the thousands of bureaucrats that feed off of it. It's just hard to imagine ...."

Upon arrival at NSA headquarters, North was taken to the waiting area in the Director's office. As he walked through the door, he had expected to see his boss, but then he remembered what the Vice President had said. There, behind the desk, sat her deputy stooge named Harris. North just rolled his eyes, thinking *this guy has always hated me and now he is really going to stick it to me*. Harris smiled and said, "Well, Major North, by the time you get out of prison I will be retired. And furthermore—" His speech was cut short by a phone call. He stopped talking and picked up the receiver. "Acting Director Harris speaking."

"This is the Attorney General. Let me speak with FBI Agent Bell!" Harris handed the phone to Agent Bell who listened for a while before saying, "Yes sir, yes, Sir, right away sir." With that, Bell set the phone onto the receiver, took some keys from his pocket, and proceeded to unlock and remove the handcuffs from North's wrists. The NSA Acting Director was confused. "What...what are you doing?" Harris stammered. Pointing at North, he said, "That man is a criminal and should be locked up!"

"Not according to the President of the United States," replied Agent Bell. Then he handed an envelope each to North and the Acting Director. Harris quickly opened his up, read it, and then fell back into his chair, speechless. The note which was signed by the President of the United States stated as follows:

Stephen V. North 1September

Major, US Marine Corps (Res)

I must admit that I am never surprised by the extraordinary level of dedication, risks, and sacrifice that Marines such as yourself are willing to exercise in the defense of our great nation. In this case, that sense of commitment also extended to a neighboring democracy, Taiwan. I received a personal call from Taiwan's President, expressing the nation's gratitude for your efforts to prevent a potential conflict with China. I have directed my staff to arrange a luncheon between us two on September 21. I will use this opportunity to both hear about and acknowledge your efforts and those of the people who assisted you in this extraordinary campaign. I look forward to meeting you in person! Please contact my staff at the number listed on the envelope to provide them with the names of others who had materially assisted you in this endeavor, so that they too can attend the luncheon and receive their due recognition.

Signed

President of the United States

After reading the letter, North smiled widely, turned around, and walked out of Harris' office. He thought to himself, I am going home and cracking open that bottle of Michter's 20-year-old bourbon I have been saving, pour myself a drink three-fingers deep, kick back, and sleep for a week.

On his way to the parking lot, FBI Agent Bell caught up with North, shouting, "Hey, North!"

North stopped and turned around. "I thought I would let you know: We finally located your old boss." North seemed a bit surprised as he replied, "I thought you would have her in a lock-up by now."

"Well, that won't be necessary. We got a tip that she was seen down by the Jefferson Memorial." North asked, "Well, then you arrested her?"

"No, you see the tip was accurate, almost…"

"What do you mean 'almost'?"

"She was by the Jefferson Memorial alright…in the tidal pool, face down. We fished her out and found one wound, a needle puncture, on the back of her neck. We're not sure if it was done by her Chinese handlers, to cover their tracks, or by one of our people. But it will save us the cost of a trial and the current administration a major embarrassment."

North said, "Thanks for the info. I'm out of here!"

As Bell and his fellow agent walked to their sedan, he yelled at North, "They will probably offer you a job in the White House!"

"No thanks, not interested!" North yelled back. Bell followed with, "Hey wasn't there a Marine named North who worked in the Reagan White House?" Bell shouted again. "Are you related to that guy, by any chance?" North just kept walking.

Bell said to his partner, "I guess he didn't hear me."

As North exited the parking lot in his old truck, Bell noticed the bumper sticker on the truck. Bell put on his glasses to see the words "Ollie for President" on the sticker.

Bell looked at his partner and said, "What the hell does that mean?"

His partner just shrugged his shoulders and said, "Let's go and get some lunch!"

The End